BODY
SLAM

BODY SLAM

A Touchstone Agency Mystery

REX BURNS

MYSTERIOUSPRESS.COM

OPEN ROAD
INTEGRATED MEDIA
NEW YORK

Cover design by Michel Vrana

ISBN: 978-1-4804-4570-3

Published in 2014 by MysteriousPress.com/Open Road Integrated Media, Inc.
345 Hudson Street
New York, NY 10014
www.mysteriouspress.com
www.openroadmedia.com

To the Three Remaining:
Christopher, Erik, and Kari—
Seize the day with both fists!

BODY
SLAM

I

A hooded fluorescent light over the elevated ring glared down on two beefy guys who lunged at each other. Hands slapped loudly as they parried grabs for an arm or neck. Suddenly, one of the men jabbed a hand under his opponent's jaw and dropped in one smooth move to scissor his legs and smack them into the thick calves of the other. Roaring in anger, the victim landed facedown, and hard. The crash filled the room like half a ton of washers dumped on sheet iron and made the following silence even deeper. Breaths rasping, they lay on the stained canvas, which still bounced gently. The odors of liniment, sweat, something like onion, and something else indefinable that may have been oily dirt mixed in the thick air. In the gloom beyond the ropes, a line of folding chairs was crammed between the platform and the yellow wall. Their backs caught the ring light like a row of bared teeth. One of the teeth was blacked out by a shirtless man who wore a towel draped over heavy, sloping shoulders.

"You feel that?" He wiped his face with the towel. "You feel that deck pop when you went down?"

One of the men in the ring stirred and grunted. The other muttered as he pulled his legs up and flopped over on his back, arms spread wide to cool.

"What? What you say?"

"I said it fucking knocked the wind out of me!"

"Maybe it'll knock some of the crap out of you, too—teach you what wrestling's all about. Do it again—hand signs: baby-face gives the stiff-arm, heel does the scissor kick and layout. Get the timing down—get the goddamn timing down!" He added, "And remember: we got kids in the audience. In the ring you watch your goddamn language or we'll lose the little bastards to the Christian Wrestling League!"

The two men hauled themselves to their feet wearily, thumbs hoisting the tops of their sweat-splotched tights, and began to circle each other again.

"Mr. Lidke?" the representative of the Touchstone Agency, Inc., stepped through the open door cut into the side of the steel building. "Otto Lidke?"

A telephone call had brought her from LoDo, gleaming with its shiny new high-rises and transportation hub, to this prefabricated box of the Rocky Ringside Gym. The building was similar to the other small manufactories, ranks of storage lockers, metalsmith shops, and salvage offices that lined the grimy spur of Denver's Umatilla Street hiding under elevated I-25.

Squinting toward the glare of the doorway, the man stood. But he didn't gain height so much as width. A barrel-shaped body pushed his arms out at the elbows, and slabs of hairy flesh formed his chest and belly. A bald head the size of a cannonball sat on the heave of trapezius muscles that served as a neck. "I'm him. What're you selling?"

"My name's Julie Campbell. You phoned our agency. You wanted to discuss some urgent business with us."

Eyes squeezed by high cheekbones blinked twice. "I wanted Jim Raiford. I asked him to come over."

"He's my dad. He's tied up on another job right now. Perhaps I can help you."

"Raiford's your old man?" Lidke studied the tall woman: somewhere in her mid-twenties maybe, attractive and healthy looking, light brownish blonde hair pulled back behind the collar of her tan business jacket. Jaw was a little too long, and that seemed to be the only thing in her face of the Jim Raiford he remembered. "You don't look like a PI." In fact, she looked like window dressing—what was it called? The self-confident "Colorado Look"?—for a corporate office.

Julie smiled politely. One of the things a private detective wanted to achieve was not looking like a private eye. "But I am."

"How long you been working for him?"

"With him. I've been his associate for over two years. If you prefer to talk to him, he'll be back this evening."

With him. One of those ballbusters. Raiford's kid despite her looks. "How late?"

"Six or seven. He may be able to come over in the morning. But you said you were an old acquaintance and you said it was urgent. So here I am."

Another loud crash shuddered the ring and Lidke shook his head. "Meatballs. Want to be wrestlers—don't know crap about the game. You know anything about wrestling?"

She'd had to do her share, but not the kind he was talking about. "Just what I see on television."

"That ain't wrestling! That's crap, what that is. Bunch of candy-assed . . ." He caught himself. "Bunch of steroid suckers know how to wiggle their butts around the ring but don't know nothing about wrestling." Lidke scrubbed the towel angrily over his face: lumps of brow shading pale gray eyes, jaw like the scoop of a steam shovel. His nose was broken and flat except for the button of pockmarked flesh that bulged at its tip. "They put on all these smoke and strobe lights and bare-assed Jell-O matches that belong in the X-rated joints and call it wrestling. Put it on television where kids can see that crap! I'm talking old-time professional stuff. Real wrestling—you ever see that?"

Julie had cheered at wrestling matches in high school and college. But that wasn't what Lidke wanted to hear. "I guess not. Just what kind of problem are you facing, Mr. Lidke?"

He glared up at the tall woman for a moment. Then the plates of muscle on chest and shoulders lifted and fell in a deep, almost defeated sigh. "Yeah—why would you know anything about it? Nobody else does either. Goddamn sport's being lost. Come on to the office, Raiford's kid."

He opened a door to a smaller and even stuffier room painted the same yellow color. Another crash from the ring caught his attention and he leaned out to call, "OK, OK—that's enough! Do some sit-outs—take turns being on top, and put some speed in the moves! Speed—speed—speed!" He added to Julie, "Wrestling's more speed than muscle, but you can't tell these meatheads that. They already know it all—they seen it on television, too."

The tiny office was filled by a desk and two more folding metal chairs, one behind the desk and one in front. The one behind sagged like a weary tongue depressor and dipped even farther when Lidke sat in it. The visitors' chair had a string of dried yellow paint dripped across its back, the careless flick of some overfull brush. Lidke tugged on a dark blue warm-up jacket but left it open halfway down his hairy chest. The musty smell of tangled odors permeated the plywood walls.

"I got enemies."

Julie nodded. Most of the people she knew had enemies. But that alone wasn't reason to call a private investigator. "You've been threatened?"

Lidke's almost hairless eyebrows lifted with surprise above their ledges of bone and scar tissue. "Yeah!" He took a piece of paper from one of the drawers and looked at it for a moment. "This came in the mail yesterday." He shoved it across the gray compound of the desktop. Here and there, the rubbery surface was sliced or pitted where sharp metal had dug in: the gouging tip of a ballpoint pen, the nervous worry of a paper clip, an idle blade of some kind.

The edge of the paper scraped up a ridge of dust as it came to rest. It was, Julie figured, a third- or fourth-hand desk, seldom used for paperwork. She turned the creased sheet to read it. A newspaper headline, "Bomb Kills Man," was followed by "Salvador Pomarico, 43, was killed last night when a bomb exploded in his car. The explosion occurred in front of the Neapolis Social Club on West 48th Avenue. Witnesses said Pomarico left the club at about eleven p.m. and walked to his car. Seconds later, the blast rocked the neighborhood."

The edges of the clipping were straight, trimmed precisely. A furred corner showed where it had been tugged gently to release the cut portion from the page. Three even lines of glue held the clipping, one at the top, one at the bottom, and one precisely across the middle.

"Do you have the envelope it came in?"

The large, shaved head shook no. "Threw it away. All it had on it was my name and the address here. I should've kept it?"

"Maybe for the postmark." Julie read the clipping again and studied the type. "This isn't from a Denver paper."

The eyebrows lifted in more surprise. "Yeah—come to think of it, I never saw it in the *Post*. But I read about it in *People, Newsweek*, one of them. It happened in New York."

"Did you know him?"

"Pomarico? Never heard of him. Ain't been to New York

in years." Lidke leaned thick forearms on the creaking metal desk. His elbow nudged a small photograph of a wife and two children. The woman looked short, as did the boy. The daughter, older and taller, had inherited her father's shape. "Then I got a phone call. Last night around nine. Voice—some guy—asks if I got the letter. I says 'yeah' and he says 'that's what happens when people start'—uh—'screwing around with us.'" He tilted his head once. "Them's not the exact words, but you get what I mean."

She knew. "Anything else?"

"No. Just hung up." Lidke gazed toward the small window where a rectangle of blue September sky was pinched between concrete pillars that braced the freeway overhead. "So I called your old man. I want to know what the hell to do and I need to know soon."

"Do you owe money?"

"Who don't? But it's legitimate, you know? Got a mortgage on my house and a bank loan on this place. Our corporation borrowed it: Rocky Ringside Wrestling, Incorporated."

"Whose toes might you have stepped on?"

"Yeah." Lidke nodded. "You figure that, too. It's got to be Sid Chertok and his people—the FWO. After all the other crap's been happening, that's the only people it could be."

"What's the FWO, who's Sid Chertok, and what's the other crap?"

"The Federated Wrestling Organization. Chertok's their regional rep. Promotes FWO live events in the Rocky Mountain region—Denver, Salt Lake City, Albuquerque, you name it. All the places, you know, where they can get big enough audiences." The heavy shoulders rose and fell again. "I figure they want to wipe me out before I get started. Scare me off so I don't compete with them. And if that don't work—which by God it won't—well . . ." A stream of angry air whistled through the scrambled cartilage of his nose. "That's why I wanted to talk to Jim. I heard he quit lawyering and went into the detective business. Figured maybe he could give me some ideas about what I should do. How to get my people in a ring and bring in some money so I don't go over there and kick the crap out of Chertok. Pull that little s.o.b.'s neck so hard he looks like a goddamn chicken!"

Julie nodded. Out of sight, behind the desk, a small recorder rested on her knee. Her dad had told her that one of the quickest ways to stifle the story offered by a client or a witness was to let them see you tape their words. "It would help if you start at the beginning, Mr. Lidke."

Like a lot of beginnings, this one started with a dream. "We—me and my partners, Rudy Towers and Joe Palombino—we wanted to bring back good professional wrestling. Take Greco-Roman, combine it with just enough high spots to put on a good show, and build a following. Make it regional based, that's why we call it 'Rocky Wrestling': the Front Range—Cheyenne down to Pueblo . . . Albuquerque, maybe. You know, the kind of wrestling they had before these big national promotions took over and crapped up the sport with goddamn cartoon characters and freaks and soap opera story lines that make a porn star blush."

Julie did not know, but she nodded anyway. "And you think Sid Chertok doesn't want you to?"

"I don't think it—I know it." A thick, calloused knuckle made two muffled thumps on the piece of paper with its clipping. "He's got a monopoly, you know? Don't want any competition at all in the mountain region. Sewed up the arenas so people like me—independents, local promoters—can't get a venue nowhere." A sigh lifted sprigs of curly hair peeping out of his open jacket. "Hell, FWO's tied in with cable. They use TV to fill arenas all over the country for their goddamn gigantic closed-circuit grudge matches. But hey—that's fine. I don't want to go national anyways. My whole idea is a regional federation. Put together a string of a couple dozen wrestlers who know what the sport's really about. Have weekly cards with some local wrestlers that fans can identify with. Bring in a few heels from outside to spice things up. Sure, some stunts and glitz, but give them legit wrestling that elevates the sport, you know? But when I try to get a venue—the Convention Center, the Coliseum—no deal. These guys tell me they got a exclusive contract with Chertok. His show or nobody's. So OK. I understand that: FWO's the big promoter around here. Closed-circuit stuff, three, four road shows a year. They fill maybe five, ten thousand seats every card. Not enough for the Pepsi Center—hell, that's almost twenty thousand—but a good deal for these guys. No way I'm going to compete there. So I go to the smaller places: Market Center, the Merchandise Mart, Temple Events Center, the Columbine Arena. Eight hundred seats, a thousand max, you know? They say yeah, fine, love to have my business." Lidke's tongue made a dry, spitting sound. "Twenty-four hours later they call back, say no deal. Can't do it. Already booked. Fine, I'll change the date. They're booked then, too. They're booked no matter what date I ask for. I even start looking around in, for God's sake, Brighton, Golden, Broomfield arena, suburbs close enough to Denver to draw a crowd. Same damn thing for three months, now, and Chertok knows I can't last much longer! Got twelve wrestlers ready to go—they're ready to wrestle, and he's trying to make it so I'll be lucky to get a goddamn American Legion smoker or a Hadassah stag night!"

Lidke wrapped one hand around his other fist. An angry popping of knuckles followed. "Sent Rudy over the edge," he said in a low voice. "Invested everything he owned in this place. Worked his . . . Worked real hard to teach meatheads like those two"—he stabbed a finger at the ring—"what wrestling's really about. Then when we're ready to go, we can't go. Chertok."

"Over the edge?"

The man's baggy eyes studied something stuck in the gummy compound of the desktop. "Shot himself. Put every penny he had in this gym and the equipment. It's only second-hand crap—enough to get by with for now—but it still took all he had. Rudy believed in what we're doing, you know? And then we try and try, and not even a chance to show what we can do!" Another angry breath. "He went over the edge."

"When did this happen?"

"Two weeks ago. Three, now. Seems like yesterday. Up in

Central City. He shouldn't've. We weren't at the end of our string then. And we ain't yet, but we're getting goddamn close. It ate on him, you know? We all figured that the business'd at least be breaking even by now. What with training fees and ticket sales, we'd have the equipment paid for and the loan payments covered. All we need is a venue, and we'd be there. But whoever we try, they just tell us no. And those goddamn moneylenders—those people break their butts to get you to take their money, but smell a little trouble, and they're first in line to suck your blood!"

A brief silence. Then Lidke swore and hammered his fist against the desktop. The loud bang sounded like a body slam in the ring next door. "Rudy put up everything he had for collateral. House, car, insurance policies. Then he went up to Central City to try his luck at blackjack. Thought he could get enough money that way to carry us another couple months. It was his game, he thought. A sure thing. Poor bastard never had a chance. And we're not getting a chance—Chertok!"

"You believe Chertok told the auditorium people to turn you down?"

"Who the hell else? Nobody says so—they give me this crap about conflicts and insurance problems and prior commitments. But who else wants to stop us if it ain't Chertok?" Another hiss of breath. "And then comes that letter and that phone call."

"But if everyone's already told you 'no,' why would he bother with a threat?"

"Because I'm not quitting! If I have to go as far as Cheyenne or Pueblo or goddamn Durango, I'm not going to quit! I'll find somebody who'll rent me space!" He added in a softer but no less intense voice, "Be harder than hell to fill even five hundred seats in places like that, but I owe that to Rudy—to his wife and kids." A thick, curved hand flapped toward the metal ceiling. "And I got to do it soon. This place, it's the only hope they got left. I mean, we don't owe Rudy's family nothing—not legally. I had his wife check with the gym's CPA to see if there was anything for her, but nothing—all the start-up money went into equipment and overhead, and we're going day-to-day on income."

"Who's the CPA?"

"Guy named Felsen. He don't think we're going to make it. He don't say so, but that's what he thinks. But we will!" He tapped the bulging sweat jacket. "I feel lousy about Rudy. He was part of this place—a partner. It's still part his dream and it can still work!"

Julie studied the hot eyes that glared at her. Their pale blue irises were tangled in a net of angry red veins. "What do you want us to do, Mr. Lidke?"

"That's why I called your old man. Tell you I know him from when I played professional football? No? He was a lawyer then. I hired him to help me get a fair deal on my player contract." The round head wagged. "That part didn't work out too good, but when I found out he was a PI now, I figured he can handle this." Another deep sigh. "I don't know what to do, except I'm goddamn sure I'm not going to be pushed out of the wrestling game!" Hunched over the desk, he stared at his thick hands. The scars and calluses of past damage made a history on the skin stretched over large knuckles and strong fingers. He looked up. "I got to do something—anything. I thought Raiford could maybe give me some ideas where to go from here. Investigate this Chertok, maybe—get him for, what, illegal monopoly, unfair competition, extortion—whatever. I mean it can't be legal for a guy to go around talking people into not doing business with people, can it?"

Fair trade laws existed, but there were a lot of loopholes in both the civil and the criminal codes about unfair practice. "How much do you want to spend on an investigation?"

"Yeah. That's another reason I called your old man. Our pockets ain't all that deep, that's for sure. I mean, we don't want no special favors, but I figured this time your old man would give me my money's worth." He added quickly, "Raiford and his associates, I mean." The pale eyebrows pinched together. "What kind of expenses we talking here?"

Julie told him the rates. The man's frown deepened, and she added, "If we're lucky, it might not add up to much. If we're unlucky, it could cost a lot and uncover only a little."

"No guarantees, you're saying."

It was Julie's turn to shrug. "That's what an investigation's for: to find out what, if anything, is there. It might be better to spend your money on an attorney, Mr. Lidke. Have him bring the arena owners into court to say under oath why they won't rent to you. If Chertok's behind it, you might get a cease and desist order, perhaps even some damages."

"I don't know . . . lawyers . . ." He shook his head doubt-fully. "They'd have to investigate Chertok anyway, right?"

"It's possible."

"So that way I not only add a two-hundred-dollar-an-hour middleman but it takes twice as long to get something done, right?" He started to say more when the doorway filled with a broad-brimmed hat and a body even wider than Lidke's. This man had a full beard bleached almost white except for the roots. His similarly bleached hair was gathered into a ponytail that dangled down the back of his thick neck. Like Lidke, a pattern of purple nicks and scars ran above his eyebrows, and he moved in a manner that emphasized the bulk of his muscles. Julie stood to be introduced and had the sensation of watching a massive draft horse wearing a cowboy hat. Lidke waved him in. "My partner, Joe Palombino, the Palermo Palo-mino."

The Palermo Palomino touched his hat politely as his eyes traveled from Julie's breasts down to her legs and back to her face. Heavy lips lifted to show stubby and wide-spaced teeth in what she thought was meant to be a beguiling smile. His thick fingers pressed with surprising gentleness on her hand. "Pleased, I'm sure, Miss Campbell. Really pleased." His voice sounded like gravel rattling down a sheet of tin.

Lidke explained why Julie was there.

"You're a detective?" He stared and wagged his head once.

"She's Jim Raiford's daughter—the guy I told you about."

The gravel rattled again as the man settled on a complain-ing chair. "Oh. Well, Chertok's a scumbag, for sure." Julie wondered if the Palomino had suffered too many choke holds. "You don't need no investigation to find out he's a scumbag."

"Yeah, Joe. Everybody knows that. But that's about all we do know. What I want to find out—what we want to find out—is what we can do about it fast. So Miss Campbell here's telling me what we do and how much it's going to cost."

"Oh, yeah." His face settled into dull attention. "So tell."

Julie repeated the figures and the room was quiet for a few moments. From the ring came another thundering crash followed by a grunt and a gasp. "Jesus, Albert, you're supposed to break my fall, not my goddamn back!" The pulsing wail of a siren streaked along the concrete sky above them.

"What do you think, Joe?"

Palombino looked at Lidke and frowned. "I guess we could quit, like Chertok wants us to. Or we could fight him. Every time I think of Rudy, I want to kill the sumbitch." He dug his fingers into the black roots of his beard. "What do you think, Otto?"

The cannonball nodded. "I figure we fight, Joe. But I want it OK with you. You heard what Miss Campbell here says: it might cost."

The Palomino snorted and Julie half expected to see him paw the floor with a foot. "Can't cost me no more'n I got, and it's all in this place anyway. You want to fight that scumbag, it's all right with me, Otto. You know that."

Lidke turned to Julie. "OK—your old man's in this, right? I mean you and him, you two'll be doing this, right? And you'll do it quick, right?"

"It will be priority, and he and I will handle it." Julie gave both men tips on basic security techniques—don't open suspicious packages, vary routes and routines, be alert for anyone hanging around home or office. Call immediately if anything suspicious happens. Then she opened her briefcase and took out a standard contract, filling in the blanks while Lidke watched. Palombino scratched somewhere under an arm. In the hot room, their breaths made long, faint whistles through mashed noses.

"Do you want your names on the contract, or is your corporation the responsible party?"

"Rocky Ringside Wrestling, Incorporated," said Lidke.

"The name was my idea." The Palomino grinned with pride. "You know, the three R's."

Z

When she reached the office, Julie telephoned Bernie Riester. An ex–newspaper reporter, since the *Rocky Mountain News* folded, Bernie was one of the best paper hunters in the business. She knew which databases contained what facts, what records the various government functions held or hid, and, most important, who to ask for what in little-known offices that fed information to regulatory and tax agencies. "A little schmoozing, a good bottle of scotch at Christmas, and don't ask anything that seems too important or calls for any risk." She also had a rare feel for the connections between libraries, archives, and computer sources, which—she once told Julie—came from years of tracking down her ex-husbands and their hidden incomes to squeeze child support out of the deadbeats. She was so good at it that, more and more, her time was taken up with national speaking tours to news-gathering groups and public and private intelligence organizations. Julie felt lucky to find her in the office.

"Anything specific we're looking for?" The soft click of a computer keyboard came over the telephone's remote as Bernie took notes on the Federated Wrestling Organization, Chertok, and Mammoth Productions, his business.

"No. Just a general profile: corporate officers, major shareholders, profit-loss statements, liens—the usual. But if anything suspicious turns up about Mammoth's business practices, be sure to put it in." Julie added, "And of course we'll need it as soon as possible."

"Of course. If it's a public corporation, I can get back to you first thing in the morning. If it's private, it might take a couple of days—and cost accordingly."

"Do what you have to, Bernie. Thanks." Julie hoped her father would not scream at that "cost accordingly." But she was following office protocol, even if it hadn't been cleared by him.

Raiford came into his daughter's office as she finished transcribing her notes on Lidke from her voice recorder. Overhead, a series of *pock, pock, pock* sounds marked the path of high heels across the ceiling. Glancing up, Raiford shook his head. "I wonder how much force it takes to pound concrete that hard?" He set his catalog case on the floor and helped himself to coffee from the freshly brewed pot on the corner of

Julie's desk. Then he perched on the edge of the chair beside her desk with a small, satisfied smile.

Julie eyed him. "Well?"

His finger tapped the catalog case. "Contract. Lansdown wants us to screen Technitron's plant security."

"Wonderful! I thought that might be why he called you. But I didn't want to get my hopes up!" A large part of Technitron's business was for the Feds, and their policy required periodic security reviews by outside agencies to maintain the company's clearance rating. Her father had submitted their bid almost two weeks ago and they had been waiting to hear something. "Did he quibble over the price?"

"Nope, seemed to think it was fair. Wanted to know if I could do it tomorrow."

"Wow—need help?"

Raiford shook his head. "Not for the inspection. It should just be a routine walk-through. The plant's been gone over several times already."

"No new construction since the last time?"

"Nothing structural was mentioned in the job description. Quit salivating, Julie; it makes your chin wet."

"And you're dribbling coffee on your tie, Dad."

He looked down to study his tie.

"Their security's in-house?"

"No—out-house, I guess you'd call it. The Wampler Agency." He frowned. "I still don't see anything."

"Which is why you wear god-awful paisley." Wampler, founded by a team of FBI and Treasury Department retirees, was now national in scale, but had not yet competed with Raiford and Julie for a job. Mainly because Touchstone was too small. "I thought Wampler was primarily a personnel provider?"

"I thought so, too. But Lansdown said they installed his updated security devices three weeks ago, and that's why we have this job: Fed regs call for an inspection by an independent agent within thirty days." He added, "They might have subcontracted that installation. But if they did, I don't think it was with anyone local."

If the Florida firm was expanding into surveillance equipment and industrial counterespionage, it would mean major competition for local firms such as Touchstone. It crossed Julie's mind that she could readily understand Mr. Lidke's anger at being stepped on by a bigger outfit. "Suppose you do find a problem, will we compete with Wampler to rectify it?"

Raiford once more scanned his tie and then gave up. "That I don't know." Still talking, he rinsed his cup in the small sink before rustling around in the equipment closet. "My guess is that if a problem does turn up, Wampler has a guarantee on its work and will make the correction at no cost." He sorted electronic sensors, scanners, transmitters for tomorrow's job. Coming out of the locker with a handful of wires and charger units, he added, "But let's cross that bridge when we have to. And speaking of jobs, what was that message about Otto Lidke?"

Julie told him.

"Sounds just like Otto—bumping his head against the biggest thing he can find." Raiford gazed out the window past the new construction and toward the distant wall of mountains whose faces always grew darker as the sun moved west. "But I'm surprised he would call me for anything."

"Why?"

After a silence, Raiford shrugged. "His was the contract I screwed up—the reason why I left the practice."

Julie studied her father's frown. "But that wasn't really your fault!"

"Yeah. It was. It was my fault for taking a job when I shouldn't have."

"You were under a lot of stress, Dad. We both were."

"But I shouldn't have taken that job. No fault but mine."

It had been at the time of her mother's death, Julie knew, but she didn't understand all the details—just that her father had been too distraught to scrutinize the contract. Lidke, cut from the team and his severance package negated by an unnoticed clause, hired a new lawyer to sue her father's firm for malfeasance. The partners paid Lidke off to avoid bad publicity and then offered her father the choice between a public disbarment hearing and a quiet retirement from the practice of law.

"Why was Lidke cut from the team?"

"He was pretty good at blocking for the run; he just couldn't handle a pass rush. Too short. Linebackers used his face mask for a ladder. Besides, he had foot problems."

"Bone damage?"

"Tangle foot. When he pulled on a sweep, he'd trip over

his own feet. Or the quarterback's. A lot of times, it was the chalk line."

"Then he can't blame you for getting cut."

"He didn't. He blamed me for screwing up the severance clause in his contract. And he was right."

"I wondered why he said you would give him his money's worth this time."

"He said that?"

Julie nodded.

Raiford sighed. "Yeah. Your mother would think that I owe him, and I guess I do, too."

"How did he get into professional wrestling?"

"College—he was good at wrestling, had a college scholarship in California, I think. I heard he went on the pro circuit sometime after his football career ended. Being a college boy and a pro football player, he started off as a good guy, but he was too ugly to be a hero. So they made him a bad guy. I think his ring name was the Bulgarian Bruiser."

"His partner's the Palermo Palomino. He thinks he's a stud."

Raiford glanced up from the wiring. "The stud give you a chance to try out your karate?"

"No way." Julie pushed her notes across her desk toward him. "But Lidke wasn't happy to see me instead of you. I promised him we'd both work on his case."

He studied the notes and shook his head slowly. "I owe the man, Julie. But I don't like the way he seems to be playing on my guilt."

"I already gave him a contract."

He stared at her with that almost emotionless gaze she remembered from childhood when she had done something wrong: it was a look that stifled affection and replaced it with judgment. "You gave him a contract?"

"It was that or lose out. He wanted help now."

"You gave him a contract without checking with me?"

"We're partners, aren't we? If one partner brings in business, it helps the other one, right? It's about time I brought in some business."

Her father's mouth grew tight with a familiar—and irritating—flash of quick anger. "Next time, ask me first. "

Julie tried not to bristle like a reprimanded child. She busied herself with straightening something on her blotter and reached to turn off the desk lamp for the night. "The man asked for help. It was my judgment that I could give it. And I didn't know about your history with him."

Her father recognized the tautness of his daughter's lips and stifled his retort. Julie was right: she did not know the story and she was a partner. A junior partner, maybe, but partner nonetheless. And she had been the agent on scene. And he did owe Lidke.

He sensed the occurrence of one of those key moments between child and parent, but he wasn't quite clear on its dimensions or ramifications. That knowledge, he knew, would come in time; but for better or worse, some step of separation had happened, and he did not fully understand it. He turned abruptly and went to his adjoining office, pretending to give it a once-through before leaving. Locking the door, he met her in the hallway. In silence they headed for the building's underground garage and the after-work sparring session.

As he steered through the homeward-bound city traffic, Raiford finally broke the silence. "Otto acts like a dumb jock, but he's not. I think he behaves the way people think a guy who looks like that should behave."

And Julie accepted her father's oblique attempt to regain neutral ground. "Do you know much about pro wrestling?"

"Just what I've read here and there."

Which meant a surprising amount, Julie knew.

"Do you have anything on this Sid Chertok yet?" he asked.

"I gave his name to Bernie. She said she'd call with what she can find."

Raiford held himself back from commenting on Bernie's rates and stifled asking how much Julie got from Lidke as a retainer. She had, after all, done what he would have. And since it was her case, it was her responsibility. He pulled into the parking lot and they took their gym bags out of the rear. "Well, I'll be back from Technitron tomorrow afternoon. Then we can team up on it."

Julie wagged her rolled-up karate suit at him. "I'll flip you for his office."

"Oh, no—I get the office on this one!" Raiford shook his head. "We flipped for residence the last time, remember? You almost broke my collarbone!"

3

But Otto's case did not wait until morning. Julie's hand, awake in the dark while her brain still slept, groped for the cell phone beside her bed and she half heard her own voice mumble hello.

The other voice was a rasp. "Miss Julie Campbell? You told me to call this number right away if anything suspicious happened."

"Yes—of course. What's up, Mr. Lidke?"

"Somebody torched my car. That suspicious enough?"

". . . What's your address? I'll be right over."

Lidke told her. It was on the southeast side of the city, across the Denver line in neighboring Aurora. "Have you called the police?"

"Didn't have to. They came when the fire trucks did."

"All right. I'm on my way."

As she tugged on her clothes and tried to brush sleep out of her hair before quickly plaiting it into a braid, Julie thought about calling her father, but there was no sense interrupting his rest; he had Technitron early in the morning, and dealing with Lidke was her responsibility. Her case, her responsibility—that's what would be in his mind.

Speeding through the silent streets, she avoided the stretches of late-night construction work. In what was once a rural suburb of modest split-level homes, a tangle of curving, ill-lit lanes led to Lidke's street. But even in the dark, the address was easy to find. It was, in fact, hard to miss. A chartreuse pumper truck was angled halfway across the lane. Its frantic and erratic flashes of red and white glare carved out an urgent and crowded hollow in the night. In the flickering glow, Julie could see a pair of police cars, their bubble lights dark. The noses of the vehicles pointed at a frame of heat-twisted metal. There, bulky shapes of firemen poked with hooked poles to drag wads of seat cushion through puddles of water. The shapeless lumps steamed and hissed faintly as they were dipped and swabbed by the iron hooks. Up and down the block, glowing windows showed silhouetted heads. A small cluster of bathrobe-clad figures huddled on the sidewalk. They stared as Julie walked toward Lidke's house. An occasional voice from the fire truck's radio sounded sharp and metallic against the steady roar of its powerful, idling engine.

The man's wife, an older and stockier version of the woman in the photograph, answered Julie's knock. The faded trim of her robe brushed both sides of the doorway. Bags under her eyes were heavy with worry. When she heard Julie's name, she silently led the PI across the small living room to a larger family room where Lidke stood looking up at two policemen taking notes. The paneled walls held rows of framed photographs: a much younger Lidke wearing a football uniform bearing the initials SDSU; Lidke's face, leaner, clamped in a glossy football helmet; Lidke in wrestling tights and pose; Lidke and other wrestlers grinning into a strobe light as they kneeled in a pyramid. Those that weren't of Lidke were autographed "To Otto." A broad, ornately gleaming belt hung in a heavy frame over the gas fireplace, and flanking it were shelves holding polished trophies with gilded football players or wreathed footballs. The dates went back to high school.

"Miss Campbell—thanks for coming over. I was just telling these people how much I don't know." Lidke introduced Julie to the older patrolman, the one with the notebook. The chrome nametag pinned above his shirt pocket said M. PAYLOR. He sized up Julie with a gleam of admiration that, when he heard why she was there, faded into the distance most police have toward PIs. The other cop, busy with his radio, was answering a query from his dispatcher about how much longer they might be tied up.

"I understand you're supposed to be providing protection against somebody who threatened Mr. Lidke?" Paylor's eyes said he didn't believe that an amateur, especially a female amateur, could protect Lidke or anybody else.

"Our agency's been hired to investigate a threat to his life, yes."

"So what have you found out?"

"Nothing, yet."

Lidke leaned forward. "Hey, I just hired her this afternoon, Officer. She ain't had time to do nothing yet."

Paylor's pencil scribbled something in his notebook. "Phone number?"

Julie told him. "What happened to the car?"

"Fire alarm was called in at one-twenty-seven by a neighbor. By the time the pumper arrived, the gas tank was on fire. Mr. Lidke, here, says he didn't hear anything until the fire truck's siren woke him up."

"The bedrooms are up in back—we sleep away from the street noise. We didn't hear a sound."

"What about your children? They hear anything?"

Lidke shook his head, voice dropping. "Naw. In fact, they're still asleep—sleep through an earthquake, they would."

Paylor, eager to wrap up and get back on the street to serve and protect, closed his notebook and buttoned it into a vest pocket. Then he fished out an Aurora PD business card and filled in the blank lines. "If you got questions, Mr. Lidke, call this number here. This here's my name and this is the case number. Your insurance man'll want that." He added, "A detective or an arson investigator will probably be out to talk to you in the next couple days. If you think of anything more, write it down so you can tell him."

Lidke studied the card.

"And if you find out anything," Paylor handed Julie a second card, "be sure and call this number."

"May I have a copy of your report?"

"Mr. Lidke can call for one sometime tomorrow afternoon. If he wants you to have a copy, he'll give it to you."

Julie nodded.

Paylor paused at the door. "You know what obstruction of justice means, Miss—ah—?"

"Campbell. And yes, I know."

"Good. You be sure and call if you find out anything at all, hear?"

Julie nodded again. The officers' leather belts creaked with the weight of attached equipment, of torsos thickened by body armor, of authority. Lidke followed the two men out. When the squat, bald man came back, he told Julie, "The cop said he's got no evidence of arson yet. Got to wait for an arson investigator to go over the car, he said."

"Do you or your wife smoke?"

"No. You mean was that fire accidental? No. I know who it was. So do you."

"Is that what you told the police?"

The man's heavy shoulders rose and fell as he stared at the championship belt hung above the fireplace. "Naw. I just told them I'd received a threat and that I'd hired you and Jim to look into it. I didn't know if I should mention Chertok."

"Best you don't until we know a little more."

"You mean until we can prove what we already know."

Or disprove it. But Lidke didn't want to hear that. Julie had the man go over the events again—no explosion, just the sound of the fire truck waking them up, and then the phone rang and a neighbor told them their car was on fire.

"Do you usually park on the street?"

"Yeah. My wife's car goes in the garage. Winter, it keeps the snow off her car, and if she or Patty come home late, I don't like them walking across the lawn in the dark, you know?"

He thought a moment. "And that was before all this crap. Now maybe I don't even want them walking across the kitchen after dark."

"You don't park in the driveway?"

"No. Patty's in high school. She's always going in or out. We'd be moving the thing all the time."

"And you've had the car for a while?"

"Four, five years. You're asking how they knew it was my car? I drive it all the time—to work, wherever. I figure somebody's been watching me."

It seemed that way to Julie, too. In the silence of the house, they heard a heavy rumble as the fire truck gave a lurch, and the flicker of its emergency lights moved, and then stopped. The thump of a fist at the front was followed by a murmur of voices. A few moments later, Mrs. Lidke came hesitantly to the family room doorway and waited until Lidke beckoned her in. The pumper unit roared again, and the lights began moving away.

"The fireman said somebody would be by in the morning to look at it. He said everything was out, but if we noticed any more sparks or smoke we should call immediately."

"OK, honey. You go on to bed now. I want to talk a little more with Miss Campbell."

The woman's light brown eyes, worried and nervous, lingered on Julie's face as if looking for something to cling to. "Do you think . . . was it an attack, Miss Campbell?"

"We'll have to see what the evidence says, Mrs. Lidke. I wouldn't want to say either way, yet."

Her lips pressed into a fleshless line and she nodded. It seemed to be a familiar gesture of acceptance. Her lank hair swayed along her cheeks.

Lidke's thick hand awkwardly patted the woman's curved shoulder. "Don't worry, babe. It wasn't no attack. They were just trying to tell me something. Right, Miss Campbell?"

"Looks that way."

They watched the woman, dumpy in her worn robe and wilting slippers, pad up the stairs.

Lidke wanted more information about protecting his family and himself. Julie gave him advice and suggested that if the inspector found the fire to be arson, Lidke should notify the local police and ask them to increase patrols in the neighborhood. He also wanted to know what the Touchstone Agency was going to do about it. That was a good question. Neither Julie nor her father wanted to be tied up with personal protection work. And she guessed that Lidke could not afford it, either. "We'll start by asking questions, Mr. Lidke. Maybe that will be enough to make them back off."

"Yeah. Maybe." The man stood in the open front door, his width filling it. His eyes looked at the empty street that led away into a dimness made darker by the black of silhouetted trees. Now that the fire truck had gone, they seemed poised to move closer. His voice was low and angry. "Me, that's one thing. But they do anything to my family, my kids, I don't give a shit about evidence. I'm going after Chertok."

"First, give us a chance to see what we can find out."

"Yeah."

Exactly what that chance might be, and how she might begin to find out, was on Julie's mind all the way home.

4

The next morning while her father loaded the electronics into his favorite satchel, Julie sipped coffee and brought him up to date on Lidke. She could understand the wrestler's anger at anyone who would include his wife and children in threat and fire. Her father, his focus on his equipment, said little. But she knew the arson had caught his attention. Their shared contempt for those who preyed on the weak and bullied the helpless was a major reason they were in this line of work. But they never talked much about it. They didn't have to.

When she was through, he nodded. "The guy needs help, Julie. You were right to take the case." He did not add that the violence of the arson made him worry for her safety. They both understood that any nose stuck in somebody else's business was liable to be hit.

And she refrained from telling him that she knew she was right. Instead, she said, "I'm going to visit some local arenas— see what the managers say about renting space to Lidke."

"Sounds like a plan. I should be back around four—I'll call you."

"Good luck."

"You too."

It was nearing ten before Julie could clear the office paperwork and drive toward East Colfax Avenue. Her morning coffee boost had begun to fade, and she felt last night's lack of sleep pressing hot on her eyes. *We strive in weariness,* she thought, *so hurrah for caffeine. More seriously,* she mused, *we strive in darkness, too.* A hundred years hence, some historian might offer a glimmer of meaning to illuminate that darkness and perhaps even find purpose in the striving. But despite the contemporary ill-directed efforts and failures of humanity, a few basic things remained certain. One was the right to defend against violence. On that, she and her father— despite their tendency to flare over some other issues—had no argument whatsoever.

The Columbine Arena was a tan structure built when masons had time and incentive to decorate walls with geometric designs of dark brown brick. These patterned walls sprawled half a block along busy East Colfax in an area teetering between two zones: Collapsing Urban and Struggling Business. Built in the 1930s as the Araby Ballroom, the arena had seen service as an indoor market after World War II and now survived because of its "historic" architectural designation. In the hard sun of a September morning, it sat faded and old-fashioned with pointed doorways and crumbling Moorish finials that provided nesting sites for pigeons.

The part of the building that fronted Colfax had been converted into shops. The ground floor was lined with sun-faded awnings sheltering display windows that no pedestrian paused to look in. At the corner of High Street, a line of vending boxes held several free ad-rags local to the neighborhood, as well as *Westword* and the *Denver Post*. Their headlines focused on the latest scandal in Denver's police department. Julie wandered past the blue metal boxes and around the corner to find the entry to the arena. It was another arched doorway flanked by dusty display cases whose only objects were notices: the arena was ideal for high school proms, for weddings, meetings, or small expositions; every Saturday in summer, it held the neighborhood farmers' market and featured organic produce. But none of the space, apparently, could be used for wrestling.

"That's right, Miss Campbell. I had to tell that fella we couldn't help him." The leasing manager, John Hernandez, according to the plastic sign on his door, lifted his hands to show how helpless he was. "I suggested he try the Market Centre out on South University. They're about the same size we are."

"But when he first called, you told him the date was open."

Hernandez seemed to be in his late forties, but his short, curling hair held no trace of gray. A thin gold chain glittered through the open neck of a white shirt and held, she guessed, a Saint Christopher's medal. It emphasized his dark skin and reflected the glints of gold in the white smile that had welcomed her. "It was. Still is. Hey, I wish I could rent to him—especially since I see who he's got speaking for him now." Another wide smile. "That's what we're in business for, right?"

"So who told you not to?"

"Insurance. Wrestling's a violent sport. Somebody gets hurt, and Columbine could be liable."

"But the promoter's responsible for the insurance, just like all the other shows. The arena's waived from liability."

"For the wrestlers, sure. But what about the audience? Somebody in the audience gets excited, throws a chair, hits an old lady in the chops. Bam—Columbine's got a lawsuit." An arm swept the cramped office whose second-floor window looked out over the cars parked along the curbs of High Street. "What we got here is a Denver landmark—a piece of living history, you understand? It would be terrible to lose it just because somebody's grandma ate a folding chair."

"Mr. Lidke said his insurance is comprehensive."

"That what he said? That's good to hear, but I got to go by what my insurance guy tells me. And what he tells me is not to rent it for wrestling."

"May I have his name? Perhaps we can clear things up with him."

The man's smile drooped a bit. "He told me, I'm telling you: no."

"You also said the date's still open."

"Yeah, well, I got a nibble for it. I'm holding it for a guy."

"We can move the date."

Hernandez stopped smiling entirely. "Look, Miss Campbell, I been real polite to you, taking my busy time to answer your questions, just because it's my Mexican heritage to be polite, you know? But this is a private arena and we got the right to refuse anybody, especially if their insurance is no good."

"Who told you it was no good?"

"A call. I got a call, all right?"

"From whom?"

"A secretary—somebody—a woman. Tells me Lidke's insurance is limited, asks me would I like to buy a rider to cover eventualities involving members of the audience. I said no. I especially said no given the price she quoted! I got the right to refuse, and that's it."

Julie smiled warmly. "Of course you do, Mr. Hernandez. I'm only trying to find out what we can possibly do to change your mind."

"Now? Nothing. I don't want nothing to do with that outfit." He, too, stretched a wide smile. "Good day, Miss Campbell."

Through his office window moments later, Hernandez watched the long-legged blonde stand on the corner and look up at the building for a moment. Very nice looking and dressed like money, but a snotty Anglo all the same. Went to college, he bet. Now trying out the work world before getting married to some other rich Anglo and spending her time at the country club. People like her never had to do a day's real work in their lives. Never had to sweat, never had to make it in a world that asked why you were behind the desk instead of cleaning it.

The story was the same for the Market Centre, except the leasing agent made no pretense at being polite. The attractive woman assessed Julie's clothes and hair before she decided to answer. "Yes, I originally told Mr. Lidke the space was available. But when I notified Mr. Brundidge, the operations manager, he said he didn't want that kind of activity at Market Centre."

"Did he say why?"

Her office was one of a cluster of rooms in the Caldwell Professional Suites, a collection of half a dozen three-story glass boxes placed to follow a tree-shaded irrigation ditch and landscaped to look like a natural stream. Downstairs, the graying secretary-receptionist who served this office complex had nodded Julie toward the small elevator that led to the third floor and a door that read HORAN LEASING SERVICE. There, she found Mrs. Horan behind her cluttered desk. The brisk lady wasn't angry with Julie; she just didn't like losing a commission, and talking about it brought back the irritation. "Only that he had a bad report about Mr. Lidke's business but he didn't go into detail."

Julie asked for the manager's address. "Did Mr. Brundidge mention Sid Chertok?"

"Not to me, he didn't. He knows my feelings about that scumbag."

"Care to tell me what kind of trouble you've had with Chertok?"

"No trouble, Miss Campbell. Just minor irritation. He's dealt with sports figures too long—he thinks a signed contract is a negotiable document. I handed the issue to my lawyers and they handed him a court date. That took care of it." The woman's eyes gained a note of curiosity. "Why are you asking about him?"

"My client believes Mr. Chertok's trying to close all the local arenas to him."

"That's interesting." The long red fingernail of the woman's forefinger tapped on a yellow ballpoint pen that said LOWE TITLE AND MORTGAGE COMPANY in red letters. "His name never came up in this deal. . . . But Chertok does promote wrestling, among other things. . . ." She picked up the telephone and punched in a coded number. "Mr. Brundidge, please. Kathy Horan." *Tap tap.* "Larry, it's me. Did you pull out of the wrestling rental because Sid Chertok told you to?"

Julie watched the woman's expression, trying unsuccessfully to read something. She didn't know what kind of businesswoman Mrs. Horan was, but she'd make a fine poker player.

"No. There's a woman here asking about it. A private investigator." She looked again at Julie's business card. "The Touchstone Agency. . . . That's right. . . ." A snort. "It's your decision, Larry." Hanging up, she told Julie, "He said it wasn't Chertok. It was a woman insurance agent who wanted to sell him some very expensive extended coverage if he rented to Lidke. He didn't want to pay so he didn't want wrestling."

"Do you know of any leverage Chertok might have on Mr. Brundidge?"

"Larry occasionally does business with him, but nothing consistent, thank God. I've heard a few rumors about the people Chertok runs with, but nothing I'd care to offer as factual."

"I'm interested in rumors."

Her full lips smiled, but her eyes remained flat. "If I hear any more, Miss Campbell, I have your card."

The next step should have been an interview with Larry Brundidge, but his secretary made it clear that the man wasn't in—nor likely to be in whenever the Touchstone Agency called again. Back in her office, Julie pushed open a panel in the window to snag what breeze there was, but all she caught was the noisy snarl of midday traffic swirling around the many restaurants that marked Larimer Square. She was entering the morning's expenses in the Lidke file when Uncle Angus opened the door and limped in.

"Julie—you look as lovely as ever! Jeez, it's hot in here!" He fanned himself with a hat whose broad brim stopped just short of cowboy size and whose shade helped stave off the skin cancer so prevalent at Denver's high altitude. "Used to be I was able to stand weather like this. Loved it. Loosened me up, you know? Now . . ."

Uncle Angus—her father's half brother—was almost fourteen years senior to her father. Though the man could retire comfortably at any time from his real estate business, he continued working, though at a slower pace, and had shifted from home sales toward consulting on commercial investment. Uncle Angus's wife was happy that he was still working—it took him out of the house and her kitchen; Julie's father was less happy to have him consult for the Touchstone Agency whether his advice was needed or not.

"You should wear something cooler than a three-piece suit." She offered a paper cone of water from the bottle in the office refrigerator. "No one wears that anymore."

"Thanks." Uncle Angus's head tilted back to drain the cup, and Julie noted with a little pang of lost time how loose and gray the flesh looked under his jaw. "This suit? You know the first rule in dealing with money? You got to prove you don't need it. This suit tells investors I don't need it." He crushed the paper cup in a broad hand and lobbed it squarely into the trash basket beside her desk. "Trouble is, you're not supposed to sweat, either."

Julie laughed and nodded at the large office window. "We need to get drapes or curtains of some kind. I've talked to Dad about that."

"Yeah. West window like that, in summer you need less view and more shade. Tell you what: I can get you a deal from one of my contacts—some nice drapes wholesale, you know? Get something that makes the place look a little . . . softer— less businesslike. Make your clients feel more comfortable. People in trouble, they want to feel at ease talking to you, you know? What say we do that: surprise your dad with a little interior decor and staging—he'll like it!"

Julie could imagine her father's reaction if she asked Uncle Angus to stage the offices for psychological appeal. "What do you hear from Allan?" Questions about family always veered safely from her uncle's suggestions.

"So he wouldn't like it. All right—he always was stubborn. One of these days he might grow out of that. Maybe." He grunted and wagged his head. "Allan—he got that promotion—called me last week. He's now some kind of division head." There was more resignation than pride in the man's voice, and Julie understood. A promotion meant her cousin was even less interested in coming back with his wife and children to the Denver area.

"That's good!"

"Yeah. It is." Her uncle settled into her upholstered guest chair and used his cane to lever his arthritic hip out straight. She stood to offer him the firmer desk chair, but he shook his head. "Easier to sit like this. How's things going? Seems kind of quiet around here."

It was his way of asking whether she had changed her mind about quitting her father's business to move into his real estate firm.

"Things are quiet now—we go through cycles. But Dad's out on a job that could lead to something big. And I picked up a case yesterday."

It was Julie's way of answering that she had not changed her mind.

Which her uncle understood. "Good for you—not so good for me. I'm not only getting older, Julie, I'm getting tired. I need an office manager, somebody I can trust, to take over the crap that wears me out. Besides," he added, "I'd feel better knowing there's a Raiford still in the business. You know I always thought of it as a family firm, but Allan . . . I mean, with you there it would still be a family firm."

"Uncle Angus—"

"Hey, it's just an old man talking. Let him talk, OK? Besides, I'm not saying you'd be stuck doing office stuff. But you'd have to get your license, and you'd want to start out in the office before you handled any sales."

"Why in the office?"

"It's a good way to learn the business. Pick up the threads, learn what happens with the paperwork. And then in a couple years when I step out, you'd be ready to take over the whole operation." He added, "You'd have something a hell of a lot more stable than running off to Abu Dooboo or wherever the hell Jim went last time."

"Abu Dhabi. He said it was interesting."

"Damn dangerous, too—a young lady like you running around alone in places like that. I don't know what Jim's thinking about, I swear!"

"Uncle Angus, I've told you: Dad drills me in security as well as in self-defense. And I'm not much for office routine— not even when I worked for the paper."

"Yeah. Office crap drives me up the wall, too. But you're good at organizing things—you're like your mother at that. Jim's not. I mean, look how you run this business. You do your street work and then come in and take care of all the office stuff. Jim says he leaves it all up to you because you're so good at it."

"He said that?"

"Yeah." Her uncle's voice took on a slightly pious note. "He really admires your ability. Talks about it all the time—how good you are at it."

Julie caught the teasing twinkle in Uncle Angus's eye, but she resolved to ask her father about it nonetheless. "I'm in this racket because I like it."

"Sure. I understand. Same way I feel about mine." He was silent a moment, thinking about his brother's stubbornness in remaining in this line of work when there were so many better-paying jobs he could do. And—despite what his niece said—jobs that were safer for both of them.

"Well, maybe when you're ready to try settling down again . . ."

"I tried that."

He caught the warning in his niece's voice and nodded, stifling what he was going to say to gaze out the window toward the gently rolling landscape and more distant mountains that could be glimpsed between the new towers of offices and apartments.

Julie typed the final entries in the accounts folder of Lidke's file.

After a few minutes, her uncle said, "You know, when Jim started up this business, I never thought it would last this long or do so well. Not for any fault of his, I mean, but just the nature of this kind of work—it doesn't have a steady demand you can count on. And then when you left the newspaper to join him, well, sometimes family gets in the way in a business. You know, you can't just tell a family member what or how to do something like you can the hired help. Family feelings get in the way, you know what I mean?"

Julie did.

"But you guys seem to work it out pretty well. Maybe I'm just jealous because Allan doesn't want to move back to Denver."

"Maybe he's like you. He wants to do it on his own."

"Yeah. Maybe. And maybe I want my grandkids where I can see them grow up."

Julie understood that. And the worry briefly crossed her mind that her father, when he reached his brother's age, might begin to think the same way.

"Well," Uncle Angus said, "if you change your mind, commercial real estate's a good business. It can get pretty exciting, too, when you watch an investment take off—I mean, just look at all the construction cranes out there putting in more buildings. Hell, it even gets more exciting if a deal flops. You keep it in mind, OK?"

"I will, Uncle. Thank you."

He let out a long hissing breath. "Yeah. You're welcome." A wag of his head. "As stubborn as your old man. So tell me, what's this new case you got?"

Julie watched her uncle's face settle more heavily into the deep lines and creases carved by the years. "A professional wrestler. He believes he's being threatened."

"Yeah? Pro wrestling? I know a couple guys used to be pro wrestlers. God, what a way to make a living—worse than a career in double-A ball!" Uncle Angus had played baseball in college and in the minors before finally surrendering to the knowledge that he would never move up to the majors. He still loved the game, had Rockies season tickets for behind home plate, and was happy to keep up with friends who had quit playing to become managers and scouts and coaches.

"Do any of them live in Colorado?"

"Yeah. Dutch Schwartz. Started wrestling as Mountain Man Schwartz and Sulemein the Savage in Chief Littlewolf's Traveling Athletic Show."

"Who's what?"

"Chief Littlewolf. Traveling carnival—small-town circuit, set up a tent, put on a show, move out the next day."

"Schwartz used two names?"

"Used a mask. Wrestled one bout as Mountain Man, then put on the mask and wrestled the next as Sulemein. Sulemein was always the bad guy and Mountain Man was usually a good guy—here in Colorado, anyway. The promoters had a hell of a time giving the fans reasons why Mountain Man wouldn't wrestle Sulemein. Sulemein didn't do much to help, either. He'd scream that he wanted to meet Mountain Man in the ring. Called himself some terrible names."

"Perhaps I could talk with him."

The heaviness faded from her uncle's face at the thought of contributing something to Julie's work. "Sure—I can phone him. I mean if you really want me to. I haven't seen him in a while, but you know how that is—we touch bases whenever." He added, "He works for a supermarket chain now—ware-house manager of some kind."

"Can you call him? Ask if he'll talk to me?"

"I can do it right now!" Uncle Angus fished a small address book from inside his coat. "He's been out of the game for a long time," he warned. "He may not have as many contacts. . . ." He paused.

"If you can arrange a meeting, Uncle, I'd appreciate it."

Satisfied, he settled his glasses on his nose and tilted his head back to study the face of his cell phone. "Damned trifo-cals. Makes the lines jump all over." His broad finger poked deliberately at the telephone's cramped number pad. He asked for Mr. Schwartz and a few moments later was leaning back and grinning at the ceiling as he traded insults with the man on the other end of the line.

5

Dutch Schwartz said he would be happy to meet Angus's niece. How about Matilda's Outback around three thirty. "Don't mention the f-word," Uncle Angus warned Julie.

"The what?"

"The f-word: 'fake.' You want to get a pro wrestler steamed, tell him his business is fake."

Julie looked at her uncle. "You're telling me it's real? Backflips off the corner posts? Hyperimmobilizing Death Claw grips? All that's real?"

"Hey, that's the showbiz part. But Dutch says he's broken more bones than he can count—some of them twice. They do stunts, and stunt men get hurt."

She hadn't thought of it that way, and on the drive east of Denver, Julie had to admit she still wasn't convinced. But

Uncle Angus had warned her, and his knowledge was usually founded on what he'd seen or what he'd experienced, so it was worth paying attention to.

Matilda's Outback was a restaurant and watering hole in a small shopping center on the prairie in eastern Aurora. It could have been a hardware store or an insurance office, any of the dozen businesses that fit in the generic boxes making up the long façade of plate-glass windows. On one side was a dry cleaner's and on the other a unisex hair salon. Inside the glass doors was an authentic Australian motif: plaster kangaroos hiding in plastic palm trees, potted vines, QANTAS posters of Sydney's harbor, ads for Foster's Lager, a movie poster for *"Crocodile" Dundee*.

This long past the lunch hour, the tables were almost empty. A few hadn't yet been cleared of dishes and crumpled paper napkins; but even if the room had been crowded, Dutch Schwartz would have been easy to spot: he filled one whole side of a booth near the unused dartboard in the bar area.

When he saw Julie turn toward him, his shoulders heaved with an effort to stand. But the table clamped his thighs to the bench and he settled for a wave of his arm that made his flowered Hawaiian shirt billow like a small tent. Above the shirt's bright splotches of frangipani was a bullet-shaped head so wide that it made his eyes seem set close together. "You're Julie? Angus's niece? How's he doing?"

"He said to tell you hello—and he's sorry he can't make it. His arthritis has him pretty sore."

"Yeah. That's tough. I got some spots in my joints, too.

Hurt like hell!" Schwartz paused while the waitress said, "G'day, mates." She wore a khaki shirt and shorts and safari boots with knee-high socks and smiled while taking their drink orders. "So what're you after, Julie? Angus said something about you do investigations of wrestlers or some such?"

She told him what she did for a living and a few things about the new case. "Can you tell me something about pro wrestling? It will help to have an insider's view of it."

"I'm no insider no more. But this guy hired you—Lipke? Lidke?—he's right about FWO. They're one of the big ones now. Them, the World Wrestling Federation, World Championship Wrestling, World Wrestling Entertainment. Outfits like that got the game sewed up. Television. They find a cable channel that needs programming, you know? Tailor the matches for five minutes of wrestling, ten minutes of ads. Use it to hype live shows coming to town as well as closed-circuit broadcasts. Can fill thirty thousand seats for a live match, plus closed-circuit sales out of town. Then they rebroadcast it a week later on regular television for a good commission and spend the rest of the time counting their money."

The waitress brought two frosted schooners of beer. Schwartz lifted his glass to Julie and sucked at the collar of foam. Then he wiped the corners of his mouth with thumb and forefinger. His lips had been split in several places, and the glossy stitching had not been cosmetic. A scatter of short ridges—hard purple flesh—marked his forehead.

"Some of their people really can wrestle. You can tell they

got the moves. But a lot of them, even the workers . . ." His large head with its close-cropped gray hair and wrinkled, pendulous ears moved back and forth slowly.

"Workers?"

"The guys who know the game, know the moves, keep the action going. There used to be workers and talkers. But anymore, I swear they're all turning into talkers. All they are is big and noisy. If they tried to pick their nose, they'd stick their finger in their eye. But, Jesus, they get paid. If they're in a top promotion, they get real money. Even the people wrestling prelims."

"How much?"

"Like fifty thou' for starters. But somebody like, who?—Hulk Hogan. I hear that sucker used to gross between five and ten million a year. Advertising income, souvenirs, all that stuff added in." Another long drink and a disgusted belch. "We used to make fifty bucks a night if we were lucky. Ride the Greyhound from one Podunk to another, eat grease burgers, flip a coin to see who got to sleep on the floor." His damaged lips folded back in a laugh. "Loser got the bed."

"Was it"—Julie groped for a safe word—"choreographed as much as it seems on television?"

"Choreographed?" Schwartz's voice tightened and he leaned over his glass to stare hard at her. "You trying to say 'fake'?"

"Arranged as to who would win and who would lose."

Satisfied, the heavy man swayed back to take a swallow of his beer and twirl the schooner for a moment. "Yeah, gotta have some kayfabe—you know, make it look real but hype up the hurt. Always has been a show—promoters want to fill seats. Hell, sometimes we'd just flip a coin to see who won that night." He added, "Unless one of us was a local. The local always won. Too damned dangerous in some of those railroad towns if he didn't." He shook his head. "Ever hear of Gorgeous George? Nah—you're too young. But that guy was a genius. He put it all together in the fifties: the television, the hype, the fan clubs. Big money. These new promotions, WWF and so on, they tightened up what he started and then went national. That was the beginning of the end for carnival wrestling and regional circuits."

"How did they grow so big?"

"Went out and did it, that's how. Used to be, what, twenty, thirty promoters had the country carved up into regions. Put on matches in local arenas or even tents, had regular circuits, even used a little local TV. Gave the stations free films of last week's action to bring in the house. But then came cable and national syndication, and that really got it going. Some guy . . . Newhouse, I think, started with some regional syndicate out east, twenty-thirty years ago. Providence? Anyway, started on local cable, tailored the matches for a couple hours' airtime with a lot of breaks for sponsors and hype for next week's grudge matches. Started dressing his wrestlers up like comic book heroes—costumes, music, lights, smoke, the whole bit. Had interviews, fan magazines, posters, shopping mall shows. I'm talking major hype, you understand—MTV with muscle."

Julie nodded. Like everyone else, she'd seen some of it. She didn't pay much attention, but apparently a lot of other people did.

"Cost him a bundle, I guess, to get going. But where the cable went, Newhouse went. Nailed exclusive contracts—he was the only wrestling show on the eye. Cable expanded, he expanded, pretty soon he's buying out the other regional promotions. They squealed—Newhouse wasn't playing fair, didn't stay in his own territory, and so on—but it didn't do any good. Next he had people coming to local arenas to see live the wrestlers they saw on TV. They could even act like idiots on camera in audience shots—a real bonus, you know? Then Ted Turner came along—TNT cable. Offered better deals to some of Newhouse's star performers, and his promotion took off, too." Another long draught of beer. "Now it's like rock groups—fans watch every week, see them in town a couple times a year. Kids buy T-shirts and lunch boxes and those—what you call them?—action toys. Add some broads wearing two Band-Aids and a cork, and start some story lines about girlfriends and sex parties, and you got a wrestling soap opera. Used to be family entertainment, but that's changed, too. And man, the money rolls in. Wrestlers even been elected governor."

"Jesse Ventura."

"Yeah. Him." The scarred head wagged in disbelief. "You don't have to be dumb to be a wrestler, you only got to be smart enough to act dumb. And they still elected him!"

"My client says he's only interested in local wrestling. He

says his plan will supplement the FWO instead of compete with it."

"What he says don't mean much. It's what the FWO thinks about him that counts." The bulky shoulders bobbed. "Maybe it could work that way, but Sid Chertok's got to protect his territory. He knows what Newhouse and Turner did to get started, and he'll be worried about market saturation, too. My guess is any local promotion's going to have to jump in bed either with Chertok or with one of the other majors, and Chertok wouldn't like that kind of competition." Schwartz's voice said he wouldn't put money on Lidke's success going it alone. "There's just too much money invested to let some local wildcatter start cutting into his territory."

"Even if the wildcatter's not planning to tap the television market?"

"What's to keep him from changing his mind? There's a lot of cable channels now. More every day, right? I mean, all the promoters got started that way, so they got to think that way, right? Plus the local arena gate's good money, too. Why should Chertok and the FWO lose any of that?"

Schwartz made sense. An organization didn't spend years putting together a monopoly just to open its doors to everyone. Julie sipped at her now-warm beer and turned that thought over. "You say it's a lot of money. Any idea how much?"

"For Chertok? No. But I read what World Wrestling pulled in a couple years ago. All together, now—the pay-per-view, house shows, franchised toys and souvenirs, cable advertising, and so on—the whole pie added up to, you ready for this? One-point-seven-billion. That's with a B. Billion."

Julie blinked. It wasn't enough to retire the national debt or satisfy a congressman, but it sounded like a good month's pay to her. "How did they squeeze out their competition when they were getting started?"

"How?" He shrugged. "Locked the cable company to an exclusive agreement, nailed down the major advertisers. Same as Newhouse. Booked the big arenas with guaranteed seat sales. When the smaller guys started losing money, the big boys either bought them out or laughed while they went broke."

"Where'd they get their start-up money?"

Schwartz's thick shoulders lifted and fell. "Venture capital. Where do you find that much venture capital? I don't know Texas, maybe—that outfit, what, Enron. The ones that wrestled their books and took a fall." The lips folded back again. "People in Vegas, maybe. They got lots of money to invest." Another shrug. "Ask Angus—that's his business, right?"

Julie would. "Did they ever rough up anyone? Threaten them?"

"Not that I heard. That don't mean they might not have. I just never heard talk about it." He frowned a moment in thought. "But I don't know why they'd have to, see? They got what they wanted through sharp dealing."

But the motive for violence was there; protecting a billion or so dollars was a lot of motive. "Chertok's name never came up with anything dirty?"

"His name comes up in the paper all the time. Seems he's one of these guys who likes it there. But I never heard about him pushing anybody around." Schwartz drained his schooner and slid it back and forth across the table. Its wet bottom left a smear of water that quickly evaporated in Colorado's dry air. "But then that's not something many people talk about. If Lidke's got troubles, yeah, that's where I'd look first, too. But I can't swear you'll find anything. I'm too far out of the game now to know. Too old for it, too. Now I got a job where I don't have to break any more bones."

"Do you think Lidke's idea can succeed?"

"I'd like to think so. Used to be a little dignity to the sport, you know? People put on a good show, sure, but they could really wrestle, too. Now you got steroid freaks caring more for their costumes than for the sport. Weightlifters pumping for definition instead of strength. Naked women having a 'lingerie showdown.' It's all showbiz now." Schwartz slid to the end of the bench and heaved himself up, heavy flesh and bone, a hulking man almost three times Julie's size. "Muhammad Ali, he was showbiz, too, but that sucker could box! That's the way wrestling used to be." In the slanted light from the bar, his face was a sad map of slightly crooked lines and oddly placed lumps from old damage. "I got to get back to the warehouse. What's-his-name—Lidke—I hope he can pull it off. Be nice to see the real thing again."

6

Slowed by late-afternoon traffic, Julie reached the office after five. Her father was already there, wiping down and stowing his electronics gear.

"How'd it go at Technitron, Dad?"

"A walk-through, as I thought." Raiford settled a meter on its charger unit and shook his head. "But Mr. Stephens wasn't happy with what I had to tell him."

"What's that?"

"They did some remodeling since the last inspection—a heating and air-conditioning upgrade. Turns out, nobody secured the air duct accesses, and I had to point out they were big enough for somebody to crawl through."

"Somebody like you?"

"No—a small somebody, but a somebody who could plant

bugs everywhere from the corporate conference room to the executive toilet."

"You couldn't sweep the ducts?"

"I did what little I could. But they're hidden behind the ceiling panels and Stephens didn't have a diagram. To meet security, he'll have to have a visual and electronic survey of the whole system, install monitors at access points, and motion sensors along the grid."

"And he didn't want to hear that."

"No. He especially didn't want to hear that if a bug does turn up when the ducts are swept, all the secret government work they've done since they were installed is compromised."

"Oh, boy."

Raiford nodded. "They should have been made secure the day they were put in and routinely inspected since by his security agents."

"Did you tell him we could do it?" It would mean subcontracting a body that could fit into the ducts, but Julie had a name in mind.

"I gave him our full-service, gold-plated, silver-tongued sales pitch, partner. He said company policy was to bid all jobs."

"When?"

"My guess is they'll want to do it as soon as possible to maintain their security clearance. They have to forward my report to the Feds, and any problems—like those unsecured ducts—require an immediate lockdown of all sensitive work while a damage assessment is made. Then the problem has to be rectified and the work certified by a federal inspector."

"Who else might bid?"

"Well, Wampler will want to rectify their work for sure." He snapped shut an equipment case. "They have egg on their face for neglecting it in the first place. You can bet they'll try to repair the damage for no or minimal cost. Less than we could do it for, anyway. Our chance will be if the Feds insist on someone other than Wampler."

"We could get Rob Haney. He's small enough to crawl through ducts."

"The human swizzle stick? Drinks a glass of tomato juice and looks like a thermometer?" Raiford grinned. "Good idea. I'll see if he's available just in case. And speaking of freaks, where are you on Lidke?"

Julie told him about her interviews with Hernandez and Horan and her talk with Schwartz.

Raiford listened without interrupting as he watched the sun sink behind the mountains to make the thin strips of cloud that heralded a change in weather turn from bright red to cold gray. When Julie finished, he nodded. "Maybe Lidke's right about Chertok."

"We can begin finding out tomorrow."

"And you can begin being careful, right?"

"Oh, Dad!"

Raiford had claimed surveillance of Chertok's office, and a telephone call from a secretary at Mammoth Productions made it easy for him. Their headquarters was in one of the widely scattered high-rises that erupted along South Colorado

Boulevard. Local boosters called the area the "other down-town," but to Raiford's mind, it lacked the density and even the gritty feel of Denver's real downtown. In fact, just behind a board fence that marked the building's rear property line, a green canopy of trees sheltered the homes and backyards of a residential area that antedated the business develop-ment. The tall office tower stood starkly between one- and two-story commercial structures. In front of it, six busy lanes were banked by signs for fast-food restaurants, repair and ser-vice shops, electronics dealers, bars, pet stores—the lures that snagged cars from the river of traffic.

Raiford turned into the side street leading to the building's rear. Automobiles filled most numbered slots in the parking area but a few marked "visitors" were available. In the lobby's small entry, he scanned the directory for Mammoth Produc-tions, and took the elevator up to do what he—or any repre-sentative of the Touchstone Agency—had been requested to do: come by at his earliest convenience to discuss a matter of great importance with Mr. Chertok.

Not more than a mile away, Julie cruised in Touchstone's silver-colored Subaru Forester. She liked the model because it was so popular around Denver that it was almost invisible. Chertok's home was one of a dozen on a long block of quiet and gently curving streets. The lawns of the upscale neighbor-hood blended into one another and, unbroken by a sidewalk, stretched to the low molding of the street's asphalt curb. The development, an older one, was within the city limits, but the curving lanes and lack of streetlights and sidewalks made it seem rural. Heavy shrubbery and clusters of mature trees reinforced the country feel and took the place of fencing. Apparently, covenants restricted fences to rear yards to give an impression of spaciousness.

Julie found a spot of tree shade and parked to study Chertok's rambling, single-story home. Its white brick was cushioned by spreading evergreens and the dark red leaves of plum shrubs. Her clearest view was of the garage. Its white doors—a double and a single—were closed against the peaceful quiet of the neighborhood. The place looked empty, but at this time of midmorning, so did most of the other homes. Julie estimated the house at around $750,000, maybe more if they had amenities out back: swimming pool, tennis court, whatever. It was large and comfortable, had the cared-for look of a lawn service. Still, the home wasn't outrageously pretentious, not like some of the airplane hangars in Cherry Hills Village that had been targeted at dot-comers and bankers. Not the kind of residence to attract the envious attention of enemies or of the IRS. Julie could see Chertok having his neighbors over on warm summer evenings to dive into a pitcher of martinis and brag about their golf scores. Wives would talk about the college plans of their almost-grown kids. Or about grandchildren spawned by the ones whose wedding receptions neighbors had attended in the past. And it crossed Julie's mind that if she had remained married to Gavin, she would be involved in that life now. But the memory had nothing to do with Gavin and it wasn't a feeling of loss. It was simple curiosity: What type of Junior League matron would Mrs. Campbell have turned out to be? She smiled to herself. The very curiosity that made her wonder about an alternative life was one of the several reasons she had done what she did.

She started the Subaru and pulled slowly past, camera resting on her arm as she clicked a couple of shots just to feel like she'd accomplished something. There were easier homes to keep an eye on, should it be necessary. But this wouldn't be too bad, not at night, and with all those roadside trees and no streetlights. Might want to rent a more upscale car: Mercedes sedan or Cadillac. Something to better fit the environment. She had not seen any sign of a dog, thank God. If Chertok had one, it was probably a house pet that was only allowed to run in a fenced rear yard and was taken for a walk on its leash in the cool of the evening. A dog that could, like its masters, enjoy a placid and even-paced life in an upscale suburbia.

The secretary for Mammoth Productions had glossy black hair that fell straight down to her shoulders and eyes blue enough to be almost violet. Her skin was clear and features finely shaped, and, Raiford noted, she did not wear a wedding ring.

"Oh, yes. The Touchstone Agency." It was the cool voice he'd heard on his answering machine, and its self-possessed tone reinforced the woman's sculpted beauty. "Mr. Chertok is expecting you. May I tell him your name?" She offered Raiford his choice of the two molded chairs that guests could perch on, and she buzzed an intercom. The reception area was small and dedicated to function rather than visitors. Raiford figured that Chertok went to his clients' offices to cut deals or used neutral ground in some restaurant or bar. Nonetheless, either for the rare visitor or for Chertok's vanity, a series of photographs ran around the light tan walls: public relations shots of rock groups, stage scenes, sports figures, and faces as vaguely familiar as those on a television celebrity game show. The inscriptions inevitably mentioned "Sid" and said "Thanks" and sometimes even "Thanks for Everything." The handwriting on a number of the photographs looked remarkably similar. An entirely different photograph sat at the corner of the secretary's busy desk: two small girls whose coloring and symmetrical features matched the woman's. She was in the midst of a series of telephone calls to people who apparently expected to hear from her. She used first names and often laughed at whatever their comment was. She wrote something down as the unheard voice continued, and then said "Thanks," and dialed again. After a good twenty minutes, the intercom buzzed, and she paused in her calls to smile at Raiford. "You may go in now. I'm sorry about the wait."

"No problem. Lovely girls—your daughters?"

Her smile gained warmth. "Yes. That door, please."

It was down a short hallway past an alcove that held the copy machine and a coffeepot. A sign said PLEASE KNOCK. Raiford did. A voice barked, "Come in."

Chertok's office was a large corner room. One row of windows looked south over the sprawling city toward the plains and the blue hump of Pike's Peak rising some eighty miles away over the horizon. The other showed a picture-perfect view of the ragged Front Range twenty miles distant with its glinting patches of snow. The panorama dwarfed the room and even the broad desk. A slender man sat behind it, his brightly patterned shirt open at the collar. A thick gold chain nestled in curly black chest hair. Chertok tipped his head back against the leather of his throne and gazed at Raiford for a long moment. Then he nodded at the guest chair angled to the front of the desk. Its back was much lower than Chertok's, and its arms lacked the oak trim that, on Chertok's, looked like stripes on a uniform sleeve. Against one wall and facing the mountains, a wide leather couch showed the slowly relaxing indentations of recent use, as well as the folded pages of this week's *Variety*.

Chertok's dark eyes aimed down a large nose that hinted vaguely of a jungle rodent. "You're from that outfit that's been asking about me? Some kind of agency?"

"Touchstone."

"Why?"

"We're interested in the Federated Wrestling Organization. I understand you're its regional representative."

Chertok nodded. "Regional promotions rep. For FWO and other big-name accounts, too. What's your name?"

"Raiford."

"Raiford. You go around bothering my professional acquaintances and maybe you think I won't hear about it, right?" He showed capped teeth in a bright smile. "But they're my friends—business associates—people I work with. They call, they ask what's going on. I don't know what to tell them because you got no manners. You say you're interested in the FWO but you don't right off come to me and ask me what you want to know." The smile disappeared. "Now what the fuck's with you, Raiford? Just what are you after?"

"Have you heard of Rocky Ringside Wrestling?"

The man's dark eyebrows pulled together. "Rocky Ringside?" He shook his head. "No. Where the hell are they?"

"Here in Denver."

"Here?" Another shake. "Never heard of them."

"How about Otto Lidke?"

"Him? That's what this, what, Rocky Ringside Wrestling is? Otto Lidke?"

It was Raiford's turn to nod. "He's hired us to look into threats he's received. He believes someone's trying to keep him from producing local wrestling matches."

"Lidke?" Chertok's head slumped toward Raiford in disbelief. "Otto Lidke is trying to produce wrestling?"

Raiford repeated, "And he thinks someone is trying to prevent him from doing it."

"I'm supposed to be the someone?"

"That's what he wants me to find out."

"Well, for Christ's sake! Well, I'll be goddamned!" The slender man leaned back in his tall chair and shook his head at Raiford. "Otto Lidke thinks I give a shit what he does?" Then Chertok leaned forward again. "Why in hell didn't he just walk in here and ask me? I'd've told him he can do whatever the crap he wants—I don't care! Why didn't you come and ask? What, you're running up his bill asking other people—my friends and associates—about me? Look, Raiford, Lidke is nothing to me. Not him, not his goddamn Rocky whatever—nothing!"

"Someone threatened him and then torched his car. He says you and the FWO are the only ones who have any reason to worry about his wrestling plans."

The man's dark eyes studied Raiford for a long moment, then his shoulders eased out of their fighting hunch as he drew a deep breath. "Look, let's be reasonable here. You see that gal out front when you came in? Caitlin? A real looker—you can't miss her, right?"

"Very attractive."

"Attractive. You know what she is? Class. She's class. Look around: real leather upholstery—go on, feel it. Carpet? One hundred fifty a yard. View—got any idea what this corner goes for a month? Class, all of this. Because I can afford it, Raiford. And the reason I can afford it is because I got world-class accounts. World class, goddamn it! Accounts that I don't want you or any of your people fucking with and giving wrong impressions about me!" He didn't wait for Raiford to reply. "All the time while you were waiting, Caitlin was on the phone, right? You know what she was doing? She was getting gate receipts. Daily gate receipts on productions I got staged from here to the California line." His gaze dropped to the desktop and he paused a moment before looking up. "Mammoth Productions is too big to give a crap what a nobody like Otto Lidke does. I don't care what Otto Lidke does. I got no reason to threaten him or torch his car or whatever, because I don't give the tiniest squeaky fart what Otto Lidke does. You understand me?"

"I'll tell him you said that, Mr. Chertok."

"Do that, Raiford. Exactly how I said it. And tell him if he's got any questions, he can come see me anytime. My door is always open. He can ask me anything he wants, and he don't have to hire you people to sneak around behind my back. He walks in, we talk like gentlemen and settle this crap real quick, because whatever Otto Lidke does, is nothing. He is nothing!"

7

After Raiford and Julie returned to the office, Julie called Lidke and gave him a summary of what Chertok said to her father.

"You believe him? I sure as hell don't."

"He could be lying. But now we have his attention. Maybe that will make him back off."

"Yeah. Well, we'll see. I don't get a venue soon, it won't make no difference if he's lying or not."

Two nights later, Lidke's stuffy voice told Julie, "Chertok was lying. And your idea about the son of a bitch backing off didn't work."

"What do you mean, Mr. Lidke?"

"I mean Joe's dead. My partner, Joe Palombino. Son of a bitch killed him."

"Where?"

"The gym."

"Where are you? Are you all right?"

"Yeah, I'm here—the gym. Son of a bitch."

"I'll be right over."

When she called her father to tell him what had happened, he did not want her to go to the gym alone. It wasn't out of any sense of her being shocked by a homicide scene—he knew she could handle that. It was the fact that someone involved in Julie's case had died violently, and Raiford did not want his daughter getting in the path of a killer. Better that a person so careless of human life and self-centered enough to kill someone would look toward him as the possible threat.

"I can handle it, Dad."

"Julie, you haven't worked a case involving a murder."

"But I won't be trying to find the killer—that's the job of the police."

His voice was patient but insistent. "You know that and I know that. But the killer might not. Let's keep him confused, OK? We're a team, remember? I'll swing by and pick you up—I'm on my way."

They had to park half a block away. Police vehicles, unmarked cars bearing city license plates, and a television van cluttered the street. Yellow police tape cordoned off the metal building and its adjoining parking area. In the graveled square beside the building, officials in uniform and civilian clothes stood or kneeled to study the ground. A television crew's lights glared down on an empty patch of gravel. Apparently, the victim had already been removed by the private service that carried away the remains of accident and homicide victims for the City and County of Denver. Near the metal wall of the gymnasium, and lit brightly by the television lights as if on a stage, stood Otto Lidke. He talked to a man who wrote on a clipboard to fill in the blanks of a witness interview form. Raiford identified himself and Julie to a uniformed officer guarding the tape who nodded and disappeared into the building. A few minutes later, a figure, short but with shoulders that fit a much taller man, walked toward them. Raiford recognized the bantam strut. He was a homicide detective who did not like anyone except other cops, and, from what Raiford heard, not many of them. But he was supposed to be good at his job, and Raiford was content that his tax money went for expertise instead of brotherly love. "We have to stop meeting like this, Detective Wager."

The short man did not return Raiford's smile. Instead, he measured the taller man as if looking for a place to chop him down. "Mr. Lidke says the victim was one of your customers. I hope you got your money up front."

He should have remembered: Gabe Wager did not have a sense of humor; instead, he had a sense of sarcasm. "Mr. Lidke hired us to find out if anyone is trying to sabotage his business." Raiford nodded toward the lights glaring on the murder scene. "How was he killed?"

The other side of the small parking lot was a grime-streaked concrete wall that ended in a high mesh fence. Plastic strips laced the mesh and partially hid the heavy equipment stored beyond. A detective from the crime lab kneeled to stretch a measuring tape from something in the illuminated patch to a tiny flag that marked a reference point. His partner waited with his clipboard to note down the measurement. The uniformed cop who had stopped Julie and Raiford stood and watched; the fingers of his clasped hands tapped lightly behind his back. As the kneeling detective murmured the measurement to his partner, a man wearing a dark suit and followed by a cameraman made his way through the vehicles. Wager eyed the television reporter like a dog sniffing spoor, then turned back to Raiford. "Tell me more."

Raiford turned a shoulder to block his response from the TV team. "Mr. Lidke received a threat a few days ago and called us for help."

"What kind of threat? And when?"

"A newspaper clipping about a bombing in New York. Came in the mail Monday. That night he had a phone call saying that's what happened to people who caused problems. He hired us the next day. Tuesday."

"Did the threat mention Palombino?"

"No, neither the clipping nor the note with it." Raiford added as proof, "He gave them to Julie."

"Julie?" Wager glanced at her.

"My partner—and my daughter. She took the case."

Wager wrote something in his small notebook. Then his flat brown eyes went back to Raiford. "Do you know where the note and clipping are?"

"In our office safe."

"Bring them by homicide in the morning."

It wasn't a request. Raiford nodded.

"What have you found out about the threats?"

"Not much. As I said, it's Julie's case. You'll want to interview her. But Lidke's car burned three nights ago."

"Arson?"

"That's the guess." Raiford read from his copy of the case notes. "An Officer Paylor caught it. Here's the case number. The fire inspector was supposed to be out a couple days ago. His findings should be in by now."

Wager finished writing and looked up. "You people better stick to industrial security. You're not doing too good in the personal protection racket." That might have been a twitch at the corner of the detective's mouth. "Now tell me everything you've come up with."

Raiford and Julie told Wager of Lidke's theory about the FWO, of Julie's response to the burning of Lidke's car, and of Raiford's visit to Chertok. "The man swears he didn't threaten Lidke—he says Lidke's no challenge to his business."

"Chertok." Wager stared down at his notebook. A thumb rubbed a small scar beside his mouth. He glanced toward the reporter who had moved closer. "I've heard that name."

Raiford guessed what crossed Wager's mind: it was a name with connections all over Denver—acquaintances who owed favors, friends who could make discreet phone calls to city officials, to police commanders, judges. He knew Wager would not be intimidated by that—the homicide detective never seemed to care about anything or anyone except a little bit for the victim and a hell of a lot for the perpetrator. But no detective wanted his case tangled by political garbage.

"Officer Wager, can I ask you a few questions?" The television reporter, whose name Raiford could not quite recall, leaned toward them. His hair was swept back in sprayed and sparkling waves, and a light dusting of powder stifled any gleam from his forehead and cheeks. Beside him, the cameraman swung his lens from Wager to Raiford to Julie. Raiford stepped back, tugging Julie with him as the camera's spotlight glared.

"We're not prepared to issue a statement yet." Wager struggled to look pleasant.

Raiford figured the police department's public relations office had been talking to its minions.

The reporter angled to face the camera and hold the microphone closer to Wager. "Can you identify the victim for us?"

"No. We don't have a positive identification from the next of kin."

"Is this another gang-related killing?"

"We can't rule that out. But it doesn't look like it." Wager's good nature began to ebb.

"Do you have any suspects at all in this, the city's latest murder?"

"No."

"But I understand the victim had received death threats. Do you have any idea why someone would threaten him and then carry out that threat?"

"I can't comment on that."

The reporter stepped away from Wager and addressed the camera lens whose light followed him closely. "John, from what this reporter has learned through his own investigations is that the victim and his associates did receive death threats. What we do not yet know is why, and of course, who. But we do know that Denver has one more statistic in the rising tide of violence that is blowing across the metropolitan area." He paused to stare grimly into the lens. "This . . . is Garvey Henshon . . . reporting live from the thirteen hundred block of Umatilla Circle." The hot lights flicked off to a dying red glow, and Henshon handed the microphone to a soundwoman. "Wrap it and let's get the hell out of here."

They watched the crew follow the reporter's quick strides to their Channel Five Alive van and pull away down the street.

Wager puffed a disgusted sigh. There were a few people he liked, a great number of people he neither liked nor disliked, and then there was a third population that included reporters. "Maybe I should join you and Julie in the private sector."

Julie asked sweetly, "Are you qualified in industrial security?"

Raiford asked quickly, "Are you going to talk to Chertok?"

The homicide detective's eyes shifted from Julie to her father. "What's going to happen is the human meatball over there will make a statement about the threats, the car fire, and who he thinks is behind it. So, yeah, Chertok's name will be in the file and I'll have to go talk to him" A shrug. "I hope this case doesn't get ugly. I hate ugly."

Raiford agreed. "I'd appreciate knowing what the fire inspector found."

"Check with me tomorrow. And, Raiford, any more threats to your clients—yours or Miss Julie's, here—you call me immediately if not sooner, right?"

"You got it."

Raiford and Julie waited in the darkness beside their car until the uniformed officer finally escorted Lidke away from the crime scene. The barrel-shaped silhouette, elbows out in a muscle-bound stride, ducked under the yellow tape. Raiford spoke his name.

"Yeah? Who wants me?"

"Jim Raiford."

He squinted against the darkness and leaned forward to make out Raiford's face. "Been a long time."

"I'm sorry we have to meet like this."

"Yeah. Joe was a good man. Thanks for taking me on again. You and your daughter, here."

"We'll do what we can, Mr. Lidke," said Julie.

"Thanks." He gazed off into the night. "Joe didn't deserve this."

"Were you here when it happened?" asked Raiford.

"Just what that cop asked. I was and I wasn't—I went out to pick up a pizza. Joe stayed behind to start cleaning up. I was going to bring it back and we'd eat and then finish cleaning. I pull into the parking place over there and my headlights . . ." He rubbed a hand across the slabs of his face. "I didn't know what it was at first. I mean my eyes told me what it looked like, but my mind couldn't believe it. I must've sat there two, three minutes, just staring before I could get out of the car." He shook his head again. "I could see the blood—I could see who it was. I knew he was dead from just the way he looked, you know? But even then I said, 'Joe, what the hell you doing?'"

"Did you see anyone around? Hear anything?"

The shadow of large, round head wagged. "All I could see was Joe."

"How long were you gone?"

"Ten minutes. Fifteen at most. Just long enough to pick up the order and come back."

"They don't deliver?"

"Not at night. Not down here. I phone in the order and pick up a six-pack on the way." He added, "They don't deliver beer even when they do come."

"Was Joe threatened?"

"Not that I know of. I'm the only one. I figure they came looking for me and found Joe instead." The round shadow wagged once more. "They mistook Joe for me in the dark."

Raiford thought he might be able to find out more after Detective Wager pulled together the forensics reports: whether Palombino had put up a struggle, how many shots the victim received, probable weapon. Things like that could help clarify the man's last minutes of life. And the homicide detective would sift methodically through the rest of Palombino's life for any other possible motives for his death.

Julie asked, "Has his wife been notified?"

"I called. But I couldn't tell her he was dead. I didn't have the guts. I just told her he was shot . . . and it was serious . . . . And they were taking him to Denver Health."

Where the hospital staff would inform her. "Have you called home?"

The stock silhouette's head jerked up. "No—Jesus!" He turned and half-trotted toward the building, the uniformed policeman quickly coming up to him as he crossed the barrier into the light.

Raiford and Julie went as close to the building as they were allowed. Through the partly open door the wrestling ring looked dim in the ill-lit space. Through a brightly lit doorway that Julie knew was Lidke's office, the man's rasping voice could be heard. "I'm OK, pun'kin. Yeah—I know. It's terrible. No, she's probably at the hospital—Denver Health. Yeah— yeah, I think that's a good idea."

There were a few more murmured words, and then Lidke turned off the desk light and, followed by the policeman, came back into the shadows where Raiford and Julie waited. "She's OK," his silhouette said. "She's going down to Denver Health to be with Nancy."

"We think you should consider moving to a relative's home or a motel for a few days," said Julie.

"You think they might come back? To my house?"

Detective Wager had commented on Raiford's lack of success at the bodyguard business; he wasn't exactly blaming Raiford, but he easily could have—and maybe should have.

"Why take a chance, Otto? We'd feel more comfortable if you and your family changed routines for a while."

"My kids got to go to school. And I got to go to work."

"It shouldn't be too long, Mr. Lidke. And it might be best if the children missed a couple of days of school. Ask their teachers to give them homework to keep up." Julie added, "At least until we see what the police come up with."

"Yeah." He waited for a long moment, watching the police and detectives make one last sweep across the parking lot, watching the uniformed cop click shut the padlock on the gym's sliding door. "I guess that's the safe thing. And I ought to close the gym for a couple days anyway. Out of respect for Joe."

8

When Julie reached the office on Monday morning, she found a message from Lidke on her voice mail: "Me and the family moved first thing this morning. We didn't want to go to my sister-in-law's—too many kids in one house. It's cramped here, but there's a kitchen so we don't have to eat out all the time, and it ain't that far from the gym. I can walk so Joanna can have the car." When she returned Lidke's call, she found that "here" was a Residence Inn on Denver's west side, almost directly across the shallow valley of the South Platte River from Touchstone's LoDo office. Through her window that glimpsed the mountains brought close and bright by the morning sun, Julie could just about make out the bell tower that advertised the Spanish-style inn. "I don't advise walking to work, Mr. Lidke."

"Yeah. I understand that. But it'll be daylight. The gym's closed for two, three days—you know, because of Joe. But there's paperwork I got to keep up with, so I got to go down there." He added, "Anyway, I hope we won't be stuck here all that long."

"I hope not, too." She paused a moment. "Mr. Hernandez, the manager of Columbine Arena, told me he wouldn't rent to you because of insurance—that your insurance doesn't cover actions by your performers that might contribute to harm for a member of the audience."

"It would, if I bought it. And I'd buy it if I had a venue. That's just a cost of production." He added, "Sometimes the lessee pays, sometimes the lessor—depends on the contract, that's all."

"So Hernandez could have safely leased the arena to you?"

"Sure! Chertok told him not to, that's all. He's the one behind all this."

"Mr. Brundidge at Market Centre said the same thing. Both men told me a woman called to say that your insurance was limited and the caller cited an exorbitant price for all-inclusive coverage."

A pause. Then, "Could be Chertok told his secretary to call and scare them off. Easy for him to do, right?"

Julie made a note. "How's your family handling the move?"

"Joanna's trying to treat it like a vacation—there's a swimming pool and sauna and game room, that kind of stuff. But Patty's upset; she don't like missing school. All her friends, you know. John likes it—thinks he's gonna get out of schoolwork."

Julie told the man that she or Raiford would be by later in the day, then she asked for Palombino's address. "We'd like to interview the family. They might have noticed something."

If there was anything Julie hated worse than mean dogs, it was dealing with recently bereaved widows and orphans. But her father, not without some relief, reminded her that she had chosen "home" and he had "office"—and "home" included all the principals of a case. Besides, and she knew he was right on this, grieving widows often responded better when the questions came from another woman than from a man.

"I would do it for you, Julie—really. I know you don't like it. But you'll get more out of her. She'll talk to you easier than to me. Sisterhood, right?" He added kindly, "And you won't have to break the news to her, so that's something."

"Thanks. She'll probably have a dog."

"Besides, I have to meet with Detective Wager. He wants that threatening letter Lidke got, and I want what he has on the arson and Palombino investigations."

"A big, mean dog."

"Think of it this way: Wager's worse than any mean dog."

Julie steered to the curb in front of a split-level whose upper floor rested on a single-car garage. It was an anonymous house on an anonymous cul-de-sac where lawns and sidewalks held scattered tricycles and kids' toys. On the worn grass in front of the Palombino house lay a tattered foam football. That, the silence of the house, and the sense of sadness that seemed to radiate through its curtained windows, weighed on Julie's shoulders. If there was a dog, it was hidden in the house or backyard.

She took a couple of deep breaths, then thumped the scratched brass knocker. A minute later a thin, worn-looking brunette answered.

"Mrs. Palombino?"

She was, and Julie explained who she was and showed her ID card. It looked very impressive in its leather folder with a photograph and ornate seal and even a registration number. But all it meant was that she had the $38.50 to pay for it. Colorado didn't require private investigators to be licensed.

And it didn't impress the sharp-faced woman. "Yeah? Private investigator? I suppose you're gonna tell me the bastard died owing somebody else money! Well, tough shit, lady. I don't have a dime to give you." She started to close the door.

"Wait—no, ma'am! We're working for Mr. Lidke. I'd just like any information you can give me that might help our investigation."

"Information? Here's some information: if they shot Joe in the goddamn head, it wouldn't have hurt him. He's only a little bit dumber now he's dead than when he was alive!"

"May I ask just a few questions, Mrs. Palombino? I really need your help."

"Ah, crap—why not. I don't know what I can tell you, but come in."

Julie followed the woman into the cramped living room made smaller by the drawn curtains. From somewhere down a short flight of stairs came the mechanical laughter of a television program. It was a mindless noise that tried to combat the silence of the rest of the house, but it was swallowed.

"The kids are staying with friends. I just . . . ." A catch of breath ended in a pinched squeeze of Kleenex at her nose. "I just wanted to be by myself for a while. He was a dumb son of a bitch, but I'll miss him."

"I can understand, Mrs. Palombino."

"Oh, yeah? Well, understand this, too: there was plenty of times I wished that asshole dead!" She sighed. "Now I got my wish. What I should've wished for was a decent insurance policy, too. He left me with two kids and every goddamn penny we have tied up in that stupid gym. Him and Otto dumbshit. That's who you say you work for, right? Otto dumbshit?"

Julie nodded. "Perhaps what you tell me can at least help find Mr. Palombino's killer."

"Right. That cop said the same thing. Fat chance." She took another deep, shaky breath and gestured toward a large, worn easy chair. "Might as well sit. Get a goddamn crick in my neck looking up at you. You're tall as those goddam wrestlers." She glanced down. "Jesus, you wear heels, too."

Julie felt the cushions and springs give weakly beneath her and guessed it was Palombino's favorite chair. Like his wife, it had suffered under the man's weight for a long time. "Did you or your husband ever receive threats of any kind, Mrs. Palombino?"

Her dark hair, resting on her shoulders and curling about her sharp face, shook to say no. "He told me about Otto getting a threat in the mail and about Otto's car. That really got him upset: somebody torching Otto dumbshit's car."

"Perhaps he received a threat and didn't tell you? So you wouldn't worry?"

"You kidding? That's how he made his living, worrying me. Joe told me everything. He had to—I did his thinking for him. The last time he tried to think for himself, he went in on that goddamn gym."

"Did anyone have a grudge against him?"

"Besides me? Who knows? He was big and he looked mean, but he was like a overgrown, dumb dog, you know? All those muscles and somebody had to tell him all the time what to do with them. Then me and the kids go off to Sacramento to visit my mother, and when we get back, he's quit his job and set up with Otto dumbshit. I walk in the house and see that look on his face and I know he's done another stupid thing."

"What kind of job did he have?"

"Truck driver for a meatpacking plant. Had a paycheck, medical plan. Money came in each week, regular. But it wasn't good enough for him. No, he had to listen to the crap Otto and Rudy gave him about how rich they were all going to be. How great it was gonna be back in the wrestling game. With their own promotions. A goddamn gymnasium for wannabe wrestlers!"

"He had the money to invest?"

"No! We had almost fifteen thousand saved up for a rainy day. Joint account, stupid me. Man like that needs a twenty-four-hour keeper!" She looked disgusted. "My mother was sick, we went to visit her. When I come back . . ." Another sneer. "Rocky Ringside paid about half of what he was making as a truck driver. But Jesus, the big dreams! Big names, regional circuit, major venues, even national exposure and copyrighted action toys. Crap—all pure crap." She looked up from her twisted fingers to the beige wall of the small living room. "Good goddamn thing I got a job, we'd be out on our asses right now, me and the kids. Ask that goddamn CPA that Otto Dumbshit hired—almost every penny!"

"No hard feelings with his boss when he quit the trucking company?"

"Nah—dumb shit even said he could come back. Any time."

"Did he ever mention a Sid Chertok or the Federated Wrestling Organization?"

"The FWO? Sure. Otto dumbshit was always talking about them. How much money they made, how they got started from nothing, how they could maybe team up with them for local cards. Oh, yeah, I've heard of the FWO. This other guy, Sid whoever, no."

"Do you have any idea who might have done this, Mrs. Palombino?"

"The cop said it looked like an attempted robbery. Some kid, I guess. Some damn kid with a gun, and Joe probably didn't even understand what he wanted. Didn't get his hands up because he was too goddamn dumb to know what the kid wanted."

Julie asked a few more questions and was allowed to look through the sketchy notes and papers that her husband had collected on Rocky Ringside Wrestling and kept in a shoebox. It was, as Mrs. Palombino said, evidence that her husband should never have thought of himself as a businessman. As Julie left, she promised that they would do their best to help find her husband's killer. The woman only shook her head once more as she closed the door. "Man that dumb's better off dead. And I'm better off without him." Her voice faltered only a little. "I keep telling myself that, anyway." The door shut firmly.

Raiford paused by the large concrete fountain that some architect thought would mask the sterility of the Denver Police's central administration building. But the entry with its windowless first floor was designed more for defense against the citizenry than for welcoming them. Though the fountain probably looked nice in the architectural drawings—graceful arcs of spray contrasting with the hard geometric concrete of the patio's walls—it was another large barrier to anyone who might want a straight line of fire or a vehicular assault on the doorway. The afternoon sun cast long shadows from neighboring high-rises, and the breeze between the concrete tower of the admin building and the adjoining county sheriff's tower stirred dust and litter and heat and carried the exhaust of downtown traffic. In the echoing lobby, a uniformed officer behind the duty desk ignored Raiford until he cleared his throat.

The sergeant looked up from whatever was out of sight behind the chest-high service shelf. His dark eyes were flat with boredom, official power, and dislike of the civilians he was sworn to serve and protect. "Help you?"

"Detective Wager's expecting me."

The sergeant deliberately finished what he was writing, the pen scratching faintly. Then he picked up a phone. "Name?"

Raiford told him.

"Man down here waiting to see you, Detective. Name of Raiford." The officer listened for a moment. "Right." He handed Raiford a clip-on visitor pass. "Elevator to the third floor. Turn right down the hall to Crimes Against Persons."

A lock buzzed Raiford through the low wooden gate in the partition guarding the elevators, and he followed the desk sergeant's directions. The third-floor hallway led to a glass-faced suite and another desk where a middle-aged woman with short hair surveyed visitors. "You're here to see . . . ?"

"Detective Wager."

"Have a seat. It'll be just a moment." She pushed a buzzer.

In the movies, the private eye never had to wait. Raiford sat on one of the short wooden benches that flanked the doorway and hoped he'd put enough quarters in the parking meter. Movie PIs always found free parking, too. Behind the receptionist, gauzy curtains muted the outside glare of the hot September sun and helped the building's air-conditioning. Down hallways to both sides, telephones rang and voices murmured steadily. After a few minutes, Wager appeared in the hall on the right.

"Thanks for coming by." The homicide detective was a little more relaxed this morning. Some time and distance away from a corpse seemed to do that for him. "Let's go back to my desk." Then again, it may have been because the detective felt more at home.

Wager's desk was in a large room at the end of the hallway. Half a dozen gray metal desks were generally empty of people and full of paper. An occasional muted transmission from a radio pack resting in its charger unit brought the life of the street into the room. The detective settled behind his desk and swung a chair from a neighboring desk around for Raiford. "That the note to Lidke?" He took the plastic baggie holding the news clipping and its threat. "No envelope?"

"Lidke threw it away."

Wager grunted and studied the clipping. "Doesn't look like a local story—no dateline."

"I think it's from the *New York Times*. West Coast edition. It looks like their font."

Wager grunted again and made a note. "Lidke know anybody in New York?"

"He told Julie that he hasn't been there in years. The newspaper was probably bought here. The *Times* has vending boxes all over town."

"Yeah. But I wish we had that envelope. You look up what day the story ran?"

"Haven't yet." He waited until Wager made yet another note, then tried calling in the debt. "Any prelims on Palombino?"

"Death apparently by gunshot wound to the heart. Single

entrance wound points to a medium-sized round, possibly a .38. No exit wound, so we'll know for sure when we find the slug." He shrugged. "Full autopsy'll take another couple days, but I don't think Baird's going to give us much more."

"Any self-defense wounds?"

"That'll be in the path report."

True. But it was something Wager would have noticed when he and the coroner made the initial examination of the corpse. Something Wager could share with Raiford if he wanted to. "Any evidence from the crime scene?"

The detective leaned back in his chair, increasing the distance between them. "Nothing worth telling you about." He smiled. "The lab people were out there this morning, going over the scene in daylight. Maybe they'll come up with that fatal clue, just like on television."

Raiford shook his head. "Usually they don't. Then the private eye visits the scene, notices what they missed, and solves the case by himself."

"Bullshit!"

"Hey, Wager, I can't help it if that's the way it is. Usually the police are very cooperative with the private eye, too. They help him all they can."

"That's because they don't have to worry about compromising any evidence. And because they know the PI's going to deliver the perp before the last commercial."

"My plan exactly! Have you talked with Chertok yet?"

He winced. "No. I got an appointment with him in a couple hours." Wager sucked at a coffee cup that said WORLD'S

GREATEST DICK. Probably a gift from his associates. "You come up with anything more there?"

"Just what I've already given you. How about you—any new leads?"

"If I had any, I couldn't tell you. But I don't, so I guess I can tell you: no." That was an exit line Raiford could recognize, and Wager stood to make it even clearer. "If you come up with anything, best let me know as soon as possible, OK?" He added, "You or your daughter. How's she working out, by the way?"

Raiford stood, too. "Fine. I'll tell her you asked." But he didn't leave yet. "What about the report on the car fire? Was it arson?" Raiford did not want to leave empty-handed; an information exchange was supposed to go both ways. Which Wager might have considered, because after a moment he shrugged. "Yeah, it was. Accelerant used on the seats, front and back. Probably gasoline. But we haven't found anybody in the neighborhood who saw or heard anything that night." As he escorted Raiford down the hall to the elevator, he added, "That's for your ears only. And don't say I never did anything for you."

9

Julie rode with the windows down. The late September sun was still hot, but the air was cool and blew away the lingering mood of her interview with Mrs. Palombino. Either the woman had an airtight alibi, or in her anger it never crossed her mind that she might have to deny killing her husband. But despite the woman's explosive tangle of emotions, Julie did not think she'd done it. She had seen the hurt that Mrs. Palombino tried to deny, and it wasn't just Julie's professional dedication that made her tell Mrs. P. that Touchstone would do its best to help nail her husband's killer. Like the bumper stickers said, shit happened—but you didn't have to eat it with a grin. Still, any attorney in town would have warned the woman against some of the statements she had blurted out.

Julie glanced down at the names and addresses in the open

notebook on the adjoining seat. It was a sketchy list of Rocky Ringside trainees from Palombino's notes. Only one had an address. She and her father hadn't talked about interviewing the stable of wrestlers, but it should be done and the address was nearby.

She swung off elevated I-70 and coasted down the Swansea exit into the narrow streets of the old blue-collar neighborhood in north Denver. The main arteries had long ago been turned over to commerce in the city's search for tax revenue. But residential blocks still managed to survive on a number of secondary streets. Small brick bungalows that had been built for the swarms of Bohemian smelter workers a century ago had been sold and resold to succeeding waves of immigrants. Now, signs and advertisements said the neighborhood was predominantly Spanish, and the crooked, heaving curbs were lined with cars that had no place else to park. They were mostly aging family sedans and pickup trucks; newer models and the occasional SUV were rare and tended to be parked in driveways close to the house for security. The address Julie looked for was on a corner. A small porch had stubby brick columns topped by square wooden uprights that braced its roof. The brick might have been red or dark brown originally. Now it was covered with a gritty black film that over the years had drifted down from the elevated freeways. Once white, the paint on the uprights had flaked away to show the sun rot of gray, cracked wood. A rusty mailbox was nailed beside the front door. It rattled emptily when Julie's knuckles rapped the doorframe.

She waited. Somewhere in the neighborhood a dog barked the mindless, ceaseless yap of a penned and abandoned animal. The boards of the porch creaked beneath her shifting weight. Finally, as she was about to knock again, a latch chattered and an elderly man peered through the rusty door screen from beneath shaggy white eyebrows. "Last door-to-door salesman to come this way got shot. Didn't look as good as you, though. What'd you say you're peddling?"

"I'm not peddling—I'm looking. Does a Herman Theil live here?"

"Yeah, he does. What you want with him?"

"I want to talk with him."

"Hope you like it." Forehead pressing against the dusty screen, the man stood silently and stared back.

Julie shifted. "Well?"

"Well what? You said you'd like to talk to Herman Theil. You're talking to him. I said I hope you like it. So if that's all you want, I guess we're done talking."

"Oh, wait—" Julie spoke through the closing door. "I mean a younger man. The Herman Theil who wants to be a wrestler. Does he live here?"

"You mean Little Herm, then. Ought to say who you mean. Wait a minute—I'll see if he wants to talk to you." The door finished closing and Julie heard the faint thump of stiff legs move away. A couple of moments later, it opened again and a young man, taller than Julie, stared out.

"Help you?"

Julie introduced herself and got a little more mileage out

of her official-looking ID. "I wondered if there was anything at all you could tell me about what happened Saturday night at the gym."

"Just what I already told some police officer. It really ain't much."

"I'd like to hear it. May I come in?"

"Yeah, sure."

He backed away from the door, and Julie let herself into the shadowy living room. The overstuffed couch, the throw rug, the little tables at each end of the couch were all worn. The old man looked up from an equally well-used armchair set in front of a large television screen. The screen showed a ruggedly handsome man with an eye patch staring into the wide blue eyes of a blonde whose shiny lips were parted. They gazed at each other without saying anything while a violin slowly warmed up on the soundtrack. "Three Herman Theils."

"What?"

"Three Herman Theils. Me, my son, my grandson. I'm Herman Senior. My son was Junior. My grandson's Little Herm. You got to say which one you mean."

"I'll remember that, Mr. Theil."

Little Herm gestured. "Come on this way." Then to his grandfather, speaking a bit louder, "We'll go in the kitchen, Grampa. So we don't disturb your program."

"Go where you want to—don't make no difference to me. Ain't my program, neither."

Julie followed through a doorway. In contrast to the dark and cramped living room that felt like a closed fist, the kitchen was sunny and large and open. Sometime in the past, it had been expanded with a back porch addition whose bank of casement windows looked into a small backyard with a miniature windmill, now rusty, and a concrete fishpond overlooked by a plaster Madonna who seemed surprised that the fish and water were gone. The counters were tidy; a short stack of plates and silverware sat drying on a folded dishcloth. Theil waved a hand at a dinette set, a plastic-topped table with tubular chrome legs and chairs to match. "We'll talk here. Grampa wouldn't want to miss his soap operas."

"You live here with him?" Julie felt as if she'd stepped onto the set of a '50s sit-com.

"Yeah. There's just the two of us now that Gramma's dead. My dad was killed in Desert Storm and I didn't get along with my mom, so I moved here. He's my family."

"And now you want to be a wrestler."

Little Herm's heavy, curving shoulders rose and fell. Despite his height, he wasn't overly big—more on the rangy side. But in time he should fill out, especially if he kept at the weights and ate well. "Always wanted to be one. Professional sports is the only chance a guy like me has to make real money, you know? I could go to college—my old man's GI bill would pay for a lot of it. But school bores the hell out of me, and there's no jobs anyway. I mean, I can work at McDonald's with or without a college degree, right?"

"That's what you do now? Work at McDonald's?"

"Naw. I used to. Now I'm a part-time security guard. Up at Flatirons Crossing—minimum wage and no fringes. Grampa calls it scut work; he wants me to get a real job, some kind of union work in industry or manufacturing or construction. But there ain't no real industry around here no more, and Colorado's not a union state. And construction comes and goes—mostly goes, lately. I tell you, there's nothing better out there. I looked. I even thought about going into the army, but Grampa didn't like that idea—giving one son to the oil companies is charity enough, he says."

"So you're going to get rich as a professional wrestler?"

"It's maybe worth a try! Those guys make a lot of money, man, and none of them's any smarter than me. If I had the five thousand, I'd hire me a WWE trainer or an FWO one and get into the game that way. But I don't so I can't. That's why Otto's gym sounded so good—it's a way to learn some stuff, and I can pay by the week. He's been talking about starting his own local promotion, too, and about how much you can learn on a local circuit so you're not just another stiff when you move up."

"What do you mean, 'hire a trainer'?"

"That's how you have to do it. I talked to some guys that wrestle for the FWO. They told me all about it. Just to get a shot at it, you got to hire one of the FWO-approved trainers and get certified. Then, if they like you, you can start as a stiff in the prelim matches out in the boonies—you know, little towns out east or down south and all. They match you with a worker who helps you learn stuff—holds, falls, timing. If you do OK there, you can move up to the bigger venues. Then it just depends on how far you can develop your audience and what your manager and the producers can do for you." He added, somewhat defensively, "It ain't so easy, neither. You not only got to learn wrestling and build up your body, but you got to be a, you know, good actor, too."

"Who did you talk with?"

"A couple guys with the FWO. They're real nice when you get to know them. And if they think you're really serious about being a wrestler."

"Where did you find these guys?"

"The Tap Out Lounge. Over on Federal Boulevard. That's where a lot of them hang out when they're in town."

"You don't have to have any wrestling experience to get started?"

"Not to get started, I guess. Not as much as Otto wants us to know, anyway. Just a few basic moves. They teach you the rest. That's one of the things the trainer is for—to show you. That, and how to get contacts with the pro circuits and their scouts."

"They guarantee jobs?"

"Well, no. Guy was up front about that—said it was a gamble and if I didn't catch on with the fans, there'd be no matches, irregardless of who your trainer or manager is. That's what I like about Otto starting his own circuit: I can get in on the ground floor, get experience in front of crowds and some local exposure to build up a following. That, and the fact Otto don't charge no five thousand up front." Little Herm gazed for a moment into a bright future. "If I do all right with Rocky Ringside, I can maybe jump to the WWE or the FWO later. You know"—he shrugged—"if enough local people like me and I get a following."

Julie noted the names of some of the wrestlers Little Herm had spoken with at the Tap Out. Then she asked the young man what happened Saturday.

"It wasn't no different from always: me and Ray worked out, and Joe and Otto told us what to do. Then I showered and left. First I heard about the shooting was on TV this morning. It's really too bad, you know? Joe was a really good guy." He added, "I don't know what this means for the gym, now. I ain't talked to Otto yet."

"Did Joe seem worried when you saw him?"

The young man thought a moment. "No. But they both seemed kind of different—neither one of them was really into it. Usually, they act mad and yell a lot. Stir us up for the last round, you know? A lot of times Otto gets in the ring and shows us stuff. He's real quick and in good shape, and if he thinks you're not listening to what he's telling you, he'll knock the cr— the fire out of you. But not Saturday. I mean, they made noise, but it was like they were thinking of something else." He glanced at Julie. "The police officer I talked to didn't ask nothing about that."

"What did he ask?"

"Just what time I left."

"Which was?"

"Nine thirty, maybe a little after." He explained, "I get off work at seven thirty most days and then put in a couple hours at the gym."

"And when you went home, that left just Otto and Joe at the gym?"

"Ray was there, but he was leaving right behind me." He thought of something. "Hey, we didn't know what was going to happen, you know! We didn't know we should've hung around!"

Julie assured him she understood that; she was just trying to get a clear picture of that evening's events. "Was anyone else around the gym when you left? Anyone who seemed to be waiting for you to go?"

The youth thought back and slowly shook his head. "That time of night, the only people down there are the wrestlers. I didn't notice anything different."

"Otto and Joe usually clean up after everybody's gone?"

"Usually, everybody on the night shift helps out; we get a little off the tuition for helping. I usually sweep, sometimes empty the garbage—that kind of thing." He explained, "It helps keep costs down, Joe said. That way they don't have to hire a cleaning crew."

"Who was supposed to wrestle that night?"

"There's four or five of us usually come in. Saturday night it was Todd and Jason—they like to work out together. And Eric was there. So was Pedro. And like I say, Ray."

Julie added to her notes. "How many wrestlers in the stable?"

"Ten? Twelve? I don't know for sure. Some work out in the mornings and some in the afternoons. And then the evening crew. I try to come in the afternoons when my schedule lets me—it's not so crowded then. But most of the guys come in after work at night or Saturdays. Some come every night, some every other night. Depends on how much they pay. I'm usually the last one in because I get off so late, so I'm the last to go, usually. But I don't know how many in all, day and night."

Little Herm couldn't tell Julie a lot more, not even the names of the wrestlers who worked out during the day. "We don't see that much of each other. Otto knows—you'll have to ask him." And he had no idea who might dislike Joe enough to kill him. "Nobody, man! I mean, he was a real decent dude, you know?"

"What about Otto? Suppose someone had been after Otto and got Joe instead?"

That idea was just as shocking. And he had never heard of anyone named Chertok.

10

Promptly after the lunch hour, Raiford's telephone rang. The cool female voice asked him to please hold for Mr. Chertok. As he waited, Raiford remembered a symmetrically lovely face and two striking dark blue eyes under raven hair. Then a not-so-nice voice came on.

"I thought we had an understanding, Raiford. I thought I made it damn clear to you that I don't give one small damn if Lidke or anybody else opens a goddamn local wrestling club or syndicate or whatever!"

"That's what I told my client, Mr. Chertok."

"But it ain't what you told the cops, is it? Cop's been over here half the morning asking all sorts of questions. Like maybe you told him I had something to do with killing what's-his-face."

"I told the officer what you told me: that you have no reason to be involved with my client."

"You shouldn't've even mentioned my fucking name!"

"I was asked about your name, Chertok. The officer asked me what I knew about you threatening Lidke. He wanted to know of any possible link between that threat and Palombino's murder."

"Jesus Christ . . . !" The telephone was silent for a long moment. Then Chertok's voice came back, at first talking to itself. "I don't need this. I really do not need this crap! In the first place, Raiford, I never threatened that bastard. And in the second place, I don't know a thing—not one damn thing—about anybody getting killed!"

"That's fine with me."

"Well, here's something else better be fine with you: you tell Lidke to stop talking about me or I'm going to be all over him like stink on shit. I mean that!"

"Is that a threat, Mr. Chertok?"

"No! It's a goddamn fact!" The line clicked into silence.

Julie was staring at the display on the computer when Raiford came into her office. "Are we in the black or the red, Julie?"

"Sort of gray, surprisingly enough." She keyed out of the program. "But it will be a lot blacker if Technitron comes through."

"Even if it doesn't, we'll be all right." He settled against the iron railing that protected the lower part of the window. "I not only have faith, but I know that God looks after the pure and innocent."

"Are we either?"

"Yeah—that is something to consider." But his focus was in a direction other than the state of their bank account and souls. "Wager's shy about giving information on Palombino. Maybe I should have bought him a bottle of scotch last Christmas. He sent his regards and he did say Lidke's car was torched—definite evidence of an accelerant."

"Cause of death?"

"He's pretty sure it was by gunshot, but the full autopsy'll take a few days. Wouldn't comment on defense wounds or much else. Other than that, he was his usual warm and outgoing self. How was your morning?"

She told her father about her visits to Mrs. Palombino and to Little Herm.

He nodded and said, "That's good thinking, partner." Then, "The kid didn't see anyone around when he left the gym?"

"That's what he says. Of course he wasn't looking for anyone, and that area's pretty dark. If someone didn't want to be seen, it wouldn't be hard to stay out of sight." The telephone rattled before she could test the idea that had formed on her drive back to the office.

It was Bernie Riester; she had finally reached the end of her paper search. "It took a lot of digging, Julie, but I thought you'd want me to go as far as I could."

That was Bernie's way of warning against the cost of the computer time and database vendors' fees, and it sounded as if Touchstone was diving back into the red. "That's right." Julie tried to sound happy as she flipped on the speaker so her father could listen. "Dad's on the line—go ahead."

"Hi, Jim. OK, here's what I came up with. Mammoth Productions is privately owned, so accessing tax records was a challenge, and I had to use several gateway companies to pull out what I needed."

"I heard you the first time, Bernie. Do what you have to."

"OK, Julie. I just don't want you to have a heart attack when the bill comes through. Sidney Chertok and his wife are listed as the sole owners, but the organization's start-up funding apparently was underwritten by at least two other companies. As much as eighty percent of Mammoth's profits are distributed back to them: Ace Holding Company and Miller Finance."

"Anything on them?"

"That's where it gets trickier. Both of those companies are private, too, and most of their listed principal officers don't have public records at all. No credit, birth, marriage records— none whatever." She paused for emphasis. "I have to tell you, it's a pattern I've seen before."

Raiford asked, "You're saying they're fronts for still another company?"

"It's not that simple. I think they're legitimate businesses on their own. But they're tied together financially in such a way that there's a lot of—ah—flexibility in what they report to the IRS. And here's something else: I've run across a couple of the names before. Ever hear of Champion Enterprises?"

Both father and daughter admitted ignorance.

"Private. Chartered in Illinois in 1995 for the usual 'all lawful business' purposes. But one of the principals was Willard Chambers. You never head of him, either?"

Right again. Touchstone didn't go back that far.

"OK. He was an Illinois state senator. Blue-blood family, son and grandson of big-time lawyers, preppie, Ivy League, the whole bit. In his third term, it turned out he'd been owned by the Cipetti gang for years. Him, you've heard of, right?"

"Yeah." A lot of people had. The Cipettis—father and son—were among the medium-sized fish churned up by the Kefauver crusades way back in the '50s. Not as big as Carmine Galante or the Bonannos or Tony Salerno. But big enough. Although the name wasn't often heard anymore, rumor had it that the son and now the grandson were still active. "Did you find any other links to the mob, Bernie?"

"Two more names. Edward Filippone, who's one of the partners in Champion, is also a principal in Ace Holding. No police record, but you can't forget a name like that. I knew I had run across it somewhere, so I ran a wider search. Turns out his old man is Eugene Filippone, who was pretty well up in the Balistieri gang in Milwaukee before he disappeared. Eddie's a CPA in Chicago. The second name's also a principal in Ace: Robert Wade. That's an easy name to forget and he has no police record, either, except I ran across him in the Filippone search. The Milwaukee paper identified him as an attorney for local crime figures."

"What about a Salvador Pomarico?" Julie asked. "Did that name show up anywhere?"

The line was silent and she could imagine Bernie's pencil jotting the name. "Who's he?"

"Some mob guy killed in New York a couple weeks ago. Car bomb."

"Can't remember seeing it. I can go back and look."

Julie hesitated. "What's the tab now?"

Bernie told them.

Raiford gave a little whistle. "Let's wait on that one," he said. "See how much our client wants to spend."

"No problem." Bernie added, "I saved the best for last: the Chertok name is not unknown in Chicago. Philip Chertok—a.k.a. 'Dirty Shirt'—is doing time in Lewisburg on contempt charges. He refused to testify in a federal racketeering case."

"Oh, boy!" said Julie. "Now tell us this stand-up guy's Sidney's father."

"Nope. His uncle. Sidney's father was killed in an automobile accident about thirty years ago. Apparently got drunk and parked his car on an unguarded railway crossing. Didn't hear the whistle."

"No suspicion of foul play?"

"All sorts of suspicion. No proof. Papa Chertok's record wasn't anything special—a couple of falls for burglary early on, and that's about it. The suspicion was that he seldom drank and that he was a gang war victim. It was after Carmine Galante was shot. A lot of maneuvering went on in both the

New York and Chicago organizations, and cops were picking up dead soldiers all over the place."

The information gave new dimension to the phrase "all in the family." Julie said, "Thanks, Bernie. Send us your bill."

"My pleasure."

Raiford's large fingers thoughtfully pinched one of his earlobes. "So Sid Chertok could be one of the boys."

"And Mammoth Productions, even if it's legitimate, could be backed by the family. Could even be a conduit for laundering money."

"Denver's been pretty clean of organized crime." There had been some over the years, Raiford knew. But it had been localized, historically centered around one well-known family whose usual hustles had been gambling and fencing stolen goods. Of late, criminal gangs, usually Hispanic and black, had been imported from L.A. But they were active mostly in the drug trade and in fights over territory. Periodically the police ran a sting that brought some familiar faces to the front pages, but on the whole, Denver's biggest crooks tended to be elected by the people. "But maybe times are a-changing."

Julie summed up what they had both been thinking. "And that throws a different light on Mr. Chertok."

"Don't it though. And it calls for even more."

She didn't answer right away. "We might want to think this over first, Dad."

Her father stopped tugging at his ear. "What's to think? We have a client, Julie—this is where his case leads."

"Chertok swears he didn't have anything to do with hassling Lidke."

"And now that you know his uncle's a wiseguy, you're convinced he's telling the truth?"

Julie sighed. There had been a time or two in the past when they'd reminded each other that Touchstone didn't drop out of a case just because things got sticky or a client got cold feet. Still, successful agencies were known for discretion more than for valor. "Chertok seems to be doing all he can to distance himself from Lidke and there's no evidence tying the two. Let's just go slow until we know what we're facing, OK?"

Raiford studied the expression on his daughter's face. Both the faint worry lines between her eyebrows and the reflexive caution reminded him of Heather and of the number of times when one of his decisions or actions had struck his wife as being too impetuous. "All right, Julie. But I bet you told Palombino's widow that we'd do what we can to find her husband's killer. Am I right?" He smiled. "Am I?"

Another sigh. "You're right. So—you have a plan?"

In the absence of a flash of genius, Raiford suggested that Julie ask Detective Wager to lunch and bring up the organized crime angle. "He might be more willing to trade information with a lovely blonde than an ugly brunette like me."

"That's what all the gentlemen prefer, Dad. But don't count on it with Detective Wager. A, he's all cop; and B, he's very close with a city council woman." She took a deep breath—now was the time: "But as you're willing to throw me to the wolf, let me tell you my idea for you. . . ."

*   *   *

The Tap Out Lounge was on South Federal Boulevard in a strip of businesses that looked huddled and grimy in the hard afternoon sunlight. In the middle of a block where four lanes of heat-shimmering cars surged between traffic lights, the bar was flanked by storefronts touting discount carpets, check cashing, auto parts, unpainted furniture, and something called "Wear 'Em Again Sam." The latter advertised Recycled Apparel for *Caballeros y Damas*. The open door to the Tap Out had windows on each side that started at shoulder height and went up to the eaves; a dusty sign in one said PLENTY PARKING AROUND BACK underlined by an arrow pointing left. Raiford turned right at the next corner and saw a similar arrow pointing down an alley fenced by sagging wire and sun-warped boards. He drove past rusty trash barrels and garage doors whose paint seemed to be varying shades of the same basic mud color. A third arrow marked a dusty recess of gravel holding a half-dozen cars and pickups. Here, half a block from busy Federal Avenue, the residential section of the Barnum neighborhood started. Rows of single-story apartments were interrupted by occasional three- and four-story apartment blocks. Farther away from Federal, the apartments gave way to small brick bungalows that tended to have motorcycles, pickup trucks, and vans parked in the driveways and along the curbs.

He parked and stood a few moments beside his car, wondering if Julie was right: that he did not look too old to do this. In fact, she had said, he looked so young that some of her acquaintances had mistaken him for her boyfriend. A sugar-daddy boyfriend, perhaps, but not impossibly old for a professional wrestler. And, he modestly admitted to himself, he was in good shape. Those evening sessions in the gym and sparring with Julie had kept him that way. So it just might work, and she was right: it was worth trying.

The rear entrance led down a narrow hall paneled with dark-stained plywood and past the restrooms—Pointers and Setters—to three currently empty pool tables. Beyond a waist-high partition was a dim cavern filled with heavy wooden tables and sturdy wooden chairs. Against one wall ran the bar, backed by rows of bottles and a full mirror. Above the bar in a corner, the television held a picture with the sound turned down and script running across the screen's bottom. From a speaker somewhere else, a steel guitar and an equally twangy voice lamented the bad luck of losing, in ascending importance, a woman, a pickup truck, and a dog. There weren't many people in the larger dining area, but the three who were sitting at a corner table took up a lot of space.

Raiford lowered one hip to a barstool whose brass seat was shaped like a saddle. The woman behind the shelf dried her hands as she left a sink of dirty glasses. "Afternoon—what'll you have?" A flick of her wrist, and a small fiber coaster advertising Coors settled expectantly on the dark wood in front of him.

"Draw." He nodded at the row of keg pulls. "Buffalo Gold. And a round for those guys—whatever they're drinking."

She nodded, long black hair spiraling down the front of

a very full red-and-white gingham shirt. Raiford watched as she carried a loaded tray to the table where the three sat with that spraddle-legged heaviness of bulky men. The one with his back to the bar looked over his shoulder to study Raiford and then shrugged and nodded thanks. Raiford lifted his beer in reply, left a bill on the bar, and strolled over. The men sized him up as he approached.

"Can I join you for a few minutes?"

Under the table, someone's foot pushed back the empty chair, and the largest of the three lifted his glass and drawled, "In haste we turn, on hospitable thoughts intent."

"That means yes?"

The man grunted. "It means you bought. Sit down." His black beard was woven into dreadlocks held at the ends by small, brightly colored beads. On his left sat a man with a stiffly erect, blond crew cut. The hair of the third man was trimmed to look like an upside-down bowl above his shaved temples and nape.

Raiford nodded to him. "Oromond the Ogre—I saw you wrestle last month at the Coliseum." He hadn't seen the wrestler; he'd only read about it in one of the wrestling magazines he'd been leafing through as research. But he didn't want to tell the Ogre that he'd missed the wrestler's big break. "You put on a good show."

"Thanks." There was an awkward silence while everyone drank. Oromond finally said, "You thinking about being a wrestler?"

"It's crossed my mind."

The crew cut snorted a laugh and nudged the beaded beard. "What I tell you, Donald? Everybody's got the dream."

Donald's teeth flashed white. "Each age is a dream that is dying or one that is coming to birth. You do look a bit old for starting the game, but you've got the size. How much do you weigh, my man?"

"About two-fifty."

"That's the size."

The crew cut nodded. "Sure is. Hell, I bet a big boy like him could get right up there on the national circuit in no time at all. Get him some franchise spin-offs—nothing to it!"

Raiford kept his voice pleasant and his eyes on the Ogre. "How'd you get started?"

The Ogre shrugged; it was a familiar question and he rattled off the facts. "Wrestled NCAA heavyweight. Penn State. Agent saw me and said he could get me a tryout with the National Wrestling Alliance. Paid a hell of a lot better than coaching middle-school sports."

"How'd you get to the FWO?"

"New manager—one with contacts. Changed my style, too. I started out the good guy. Handsome Henry, the Dutch Destroyer. That's my real name, Henry. Henry Van Dam. But the Dutch Destroyer didn't fill seats so I changed to the Ogre, and," he said, tired of telling a familiar story, "here I am." He asked Raiford, "You got any experience?"

"A little."

"Oh, man!" The crew cut sounded awed. "A little experience, too! I bet we got us another Randy Savage here. Couple months, you'll be with WWE and doing goddamn Viagra commercials."

Raiford looked past the crew cut to the beard. "How about you? How'd you get in the game?"

The biggest man kept his voice neutral, neither siding with the crew cut nor against him. "About like you're trying to do—hung around, asked some questions, found out who to go see." A shrug. "But I was a lot younger than you. I had the time to spend a few years on the tank circuit. First year, I made all of two hundred dollars for a six-night week. And around here, it's even harder to get started. What you have to remember is to 'render therefore to all their dues; tribute to whom tribute is due.' " He leaned back to drink. His large black thumb and fingers almost touched around the beer mug. "You know what I mean?"

Raiford smiled and gestured for another round.

Crew cut shoved his empty beer mug across the table to get Raiford's attention. "You want to know how I got started, too? It sure as hell wasn't by wimping around buying drinks and sucking ass, old man!"

Raiford studied the man's half-closed blue eyes and the challenging sneer. The two other wrestlers studied Raiford. It was bound to come sooner or later, but he didn't think it would be this fast. "Anything I want to know about you, I can read on the shithouse wall." It wasn't great wit, but it fit the audience.

"Well, goddamn you—"

"Settle down, Billy."

"Settle down my ass! I'm not letting no son of a bitch come in here and—"

"Gentlemen!" The woman's voice carried sharply from the bar. "Not in here, you ain't. You know the rules: outside and out back!"

The crew cut, eyes now stretched wide and suddenly bloodshot, half stood to lean over the table. "Come on, fuckhead! Come on out back, goddamn you—I'll rip your goddamned head off!"

Raiford, too, stood. "That's just where I was going."

Crew cut stepped back eagerly, clattering his heavy chair over onto the wooden floor. The beard rose more slowly, growing taller and taller until even Raiford had to tilt his head to look up at a man who was close to seven feet tall. "You don't have to do this, my man. Billy's drunk, that's all. And half your age. You come back in a couple days—I'll tell you all about the game."

Raiford didn't answer. Billy's shoulder slammed against the doorframe of the poolroom as he rushed toward the exit. The back door thudded open and he spun around in the hot glare of the graveled lot. Tugging his shirt free of his belt, he rolled his shoulders to loosen his muscles and began sidling toward Raiford, hands ready to grapple. "Come on, shithead!" He crouched, arms working in slow circles, and glided to his right.

Raiford took a deep breath and forced it out to clear his lungs and mind and to concentrate on the figure moving obliquely toward him. Then he settled into the open-legged stance.

"Well, come on, big mouth! Show us what you can do!"

The first move was basic. It was as much to loosen up and feel Billy out as to make contact: a quick step into the *gyaku-zuki*. Raiford's fist leaped forward and back like a snake's tongue as Billy blinked with surprise and tried to grab the flashing wrist. Then a quick half-step to the *mae-geri-keage*, a front kick that snapped hard against Billy's chest to make the man grunt and stumble back. Followed by a *mawashi-geri* that swung Raiford's leg in a wide arc to thud the point of his shoe against Billy's ribs.

The man gasped, eyes and mouth rounding with hurt as he sagged back. Then the alcohol was seared away by pain and anger. He roared—meaty fists pummeling the air—and swung for Raiford's head.

Billy may have been a good wrestler, but any training he had was lost in mindless rage. Still, he was young and in shape; he was strong; he was big enough to fight through a heavy hit. And he was fast. A wild fist glanced off Raiford's shoulder and numbed it as the man lunged forward. Raiford knocked away the second fist with his forearm and stepped forward to dig the tips of his fingers deep under the man's lowest rib. Reflexively, Raiford glided into a familiar rhythm of moves— thrust, kick, thrust, chop, swinging kick, and straight punch. For a long moment during the flow of kicks and punches, he did not even see Billy—his focus was on the air in front of his own body, striking through the imaginary spot and feeling the contact with Billy's flesh only as a momentary slowing of his hand or foot. In his ears was the controlled pace of his own breathing and the crisp, level voice of the sensei counting off the series again and again in the repeated forty-second drills. After the last *gayaku-zuki*, the blurry shadow that was Billy dropped out of his vision and Raiford stepped back, ready to block and to re-center himself for another series. But Billy, facedown on hands and knees with his head swinging loosely, gasped something unclear and then vomited.

"Jesus Christ!" Oromond the Ogre still had his hand in the air where he'd lifted it in a gesture to ask Billy to take it easy.

The bearded man looked down at the clenched, sickly heaving man and then at Raiford. " 'Who is this happy warrior? Who is he that every man in arms should wish to be?' You're black belt, aren't you?" There was mild accusation in his voice. "This is the way you get your jollies? Fight a drunk who doesn't even know karate? Is that why you wanted to come out back?"

Raiford cleared the tension from his chest and back with another long, deep breath before he answered. "No." He nodded at his SUV. "My car's here. I wanted to leave before things got ugly."

The man studied first Raiford and then the vehicle and finally made up his mind. Then he held out a hand almost the size of a tennis racket. "Well, my name's Donald Bausley. My ring name's Doctor Witch. My man, if you are serious—really serious, I mean—about being a wrestler, and if you can afford the fees, maybe I can help you out."

11

Wager had been out of the office when Julie telephoned and left a message. When her own phone rang, she thought it was the homicide detective returning her call, but a secretary for Wampler Agency asked briskly if she would hold for an important communication from Mr. Edwin M. Welch. The line clicked before Julie could ask "Who?" After a few seconds, a man's voice said, "Um—Edwin M. Welch here." The voice took time to caress each syllable of its name. "I am the regional representative for the Wampler Security Agency. Whom am I addressing, please?"

"Julie Campbell—Touchstone Agency."

"Ah—yes. I understand we are submitting, um, competitive bids for a project involving the Technitron Corporation."

"We're bidding on work there, yes."

"Yes. And I assume that you do not know that Technitron is an old and, um, highly valued client of our agency."

"Why do you assume that, Mr. Welch?"

"It is our usual custom, Miss Campbell, not to infringe upon the proprietary activities of local security agencies. We've come to expect the same courtesy. Especially by those smaller agencies such as yourself that might be, um, struggling to establish themselves." He added, "Wampler Agency feels that a variety of security options best serves the public interest." He paused but Julie said nothing. "We also are protective of those areas we rightly feel to be ours by virtue of established practice and or superior expertise and range of service." He paused again. This time she did say something.

"We were invited to bid, Mr. Welch. And we did."

"Yes. Of course. Nonetheless, you must realize that since Wampler Agency feels it must maintain relations with a customer as old and valued as Technitron Corporation, our bid will necessarily be considerably lower than yours."

"That's your decision."

"I mean, miss, that Wampler Agency is willing to bid at a palpable loss in order to maintain our account with Technitron."

"And if we withdraw our bid, you won't have to lose money?"

"We do have some smaller accounts we might be willing to, um, relinquish. Accounts that you might find more suitable to an agency of your more limited range of services." He continued, "I won't press you for an answer now. I'm sure you need to confer with your employer. . . . It's a Mr. Raiford, isn't it? But I will be calling again soon, miss. I do hope we can find a mutual accommodation that will be profitable for us both." He hung up without waiting for Julie to reply.

She set the receiver down and stared at it as if her gaze could carry its heat all the way to the other end of the line. Then she brought up the Technitron home page on Google and began to study the print. She had thought she understood Lidke's anger at being squeezed out by the FWO, but Mr. Welch had just made that abstract understanding far more concrete. In fact, she might be able to bring Touchstone's own bid down a little more—trim a profit margin here, double up on equipment there. Even if Touchstone didn't get the job, she damn well intended to submit the lowest numbers she could find.

She was recomputing hourly costs when the telephone rang again. This time it was Detective Wager returning her call. "What can I do for you, Miss Campbell."

"Just a couple of questions, Detective." She added, "And I have some information for you in return."

"I caught a certain homicide Saturday night and I've wasted all morning in court. I hope your questions are good."

"Have you turned up any links between the Pomarico killing in New York and Palombino?"

He was silent a moment, then, "Report I got is, it was a local turf war. Pomarico tried to push some Haitian dope dealers out of what he called his territory and they pushed back. Why do you want to know?"

She told him what they had discovered about Chertok's connections. There was a long silence.

"How reliable is that?"

"Bernie Riester." That was all she had to say. "You've never heard any rumors about Chertok? No ties to organizations?"

"No. He's been in Denver only a few years, though. No local police record. He got bonded with no trouble—promoters have to be bonded—but that's the only paper I found on him."

"It adds a new wrinkle to Palombino's killing and the threats to Lidke."

"Uh-huh." Then. "I'll check with vice, see what they've heard. I'll give you a call later."

"I'd be happy to buy you lunch," she said sweetly.

By the time Raiford made it back to the office in midafternoon, Julie was gone. A note said she was at the gym. He figured he'd had his daily workout and dialed a number from his cell-phone memory. The now-familiar voice answered and Raiford told her who it was. "I'd appreciate a few minutes of your time after work. I wouldn't ask if it wasn't extremely important."

She hesitated.

"We can meet wherever it's convenient for you," Raiford urged. "If you feel more comfortable talking to another woman, you can meet with my partner."

"No—I just . . . I pick up my children after work."

"It's very important or I wouldn't be so insistent. You say where and when, and I'll meet you there."

"When" was forty-five minutes before her official quitting time so she wouldn't be late for her children—Chertok apparently was out of the office for the afternoon—and "where" was a restaurant and bar on the corner of Fillmore and Second Avenue in the Cherry Creek area. The neighborhood was an upscale district for shopping, sampling restaurants, and the enjoyment of gracious living. Segments of streets had been blocked off to become short pedestrian malls sprinkled with name boutiques, kiosks, and festive with trees, fountains, and hanging baskets of flowers. Restaurants took advantage of the autumn warmth to claim sidewalk space with bright umbrellas and metal tables for al fresco dining. Even with the crowds of pedestrians and automobiles jammed into one-way lanes, the sense of people with time and money to spend gave a relaxed feel. Raiford, early for the appointment, paused a moment to enjoy the display of bright yellow and red chrysanthemums surrounding a flower vendor.

"Flowers for your lady? Buy some flowers for your lady?" The man, mentally handicapped in some way, smiled and held out a rose.

He glanced at his watch and then nodded; a single rose wouldn't seem too calculating. The man studied the bill a moment and then awkwardly, his lips forming the numbers, counted out Kirk's change. "Thank you, sir," he said with a wide smile. His crooked and ill-cared-for teeth said he was too poor to afford dentistry. He had probably been among those cut from state health care when the Congress shifted funds from poor people who needed help to rich people who wanted to pay less tax.

Raiford waved his change away. "Have a nice day."

"You too!"

Carrying the rose into the restaurant's lounge, Raiford chose a table where he could see the entry and lowered himself into a chair. It was one of those places that tried to make unescorted females feel comfortable. Even this early, women, in pairs or clustered in larger groups, sat scattered at tables talking and laughing. Their clothes marked them as business or professional. The barstools held mostly men, a few of whom sat with their backs to the mirrored shelves of bottles, and, while pretending to look for friends, casually studied the room. Here and there, a woman's eyes caught at Raiford, sizing him up and saying that he was interesting. But women weren't openly hustled, even those looking for action, and the two waitresses in slacks and long-sleeved white shirts with black string ties moved briskly between tables to take orders.

He saw Chertok's secretary hurry past the large window and then appear in the entryway to gaze over the room. She seemed close to Julie's age, no more than five years older, anyway, and drew lingering glances from the male watchers at the bar. Several seated women, too, studied her long black hair and sculpted face, her lithe figure, her clothes, carriage, and makeup.

Raiford stood to be seen, and she smiled with cautious relief when she saw him. As he held her chair, her name, he found out, was Caitlin Morgan.

"Traffic slowed me up—it seems worse every year."

"Just got here myself," Raiford lied. "And I've enjoyed people-watching."

She looked around. "I haven't been here often. But it's the only place I could think of when you called."

A waitress took their orders—Chardonnay for her, another beer for Raiford—and he handed her the rose. "I appreciate you taking the time to see me."

She hesitated, then accepted the flower with a simple "thank you." After toying with it for a moment, she said, "It's very pretty. But I don't understand why you insisted on this meeting. What's so extremely important?"

"May I begin by asking a couple of questions about Mr. Chertok?" He quickly added, "Of course you don't have to answer. In fact, if anything I ask makes you feel uncomfortable, please say so."

"I feel uncomfortable being here, Mr. Raiford. It seems . . . in a way . . . disloyal."

"I don't want you to feel either uncomfortable or disloyal. Here's why I need to ask questions: my client believes Mr. Chertok's denying him an opportunity to start his own wrestling promotion. Mr. Chertok swears that's not the case, and I believe him—I do. But maybe some of Mr. Chertok's business associates have in some way caused my client to feel intimidated. Mr. Chertok may not even be aware of it. That's what I need more information about: his business associates, the people he works with, anyone who might have—without Mr. Chertok knowing and maybe without intending it—caused some very serious harm to my client."

"Who is your client and what kind of harm?"

"Otto Lidke. Have you ever heard the name mentioned? Or heard about a new local wrestling promotion?"

"No."

"I'm certain Mr. Chertok knows nothing of this," he said again. "But someone has convinced local arenas not to rent space to him. Then my client received a threat—that's when he hired me. Then the threat was carried out."

"Carried out?"

He told her.

"Murdered?" The violet eyes widened. "His partner was murdered?"

"Perhaps you heard about it on the news." Raiford twisted his beer glass. His eyes were on the circle of cold water at its base seeping into the coaster, but his attention was on the woman across the table. "He was thirty-four years old. He had a wife and two young children." Raiford looked up into those deep eyes, trying to read the edge of worry he saw there. "That's what's so important, Mrs. Morgan. A man has been killed."

Her reply was slow in coming. "And you do suspect him, don't you? Mr. Chertok?"

It wasn't a reply Raiford expected, and he felt that little tingle of conviction: she was guarding something, something he wanted to know. The waitresses were moving faster now as the tables began to fill with more of the thirsty after-work crowd, and the shrill noise of competing female voices closed around them. "Chertok told me he has no reason to interfere with Lidke's plans. I have no reason to doubt the man, Mrs. Morgan. But," he smiled, "and maybe here is where you can help me, I do have the feeling Mr. Chertok hasn't been entirely forthright." He waited for objection but none came. "I don't mean he has any direct involvement with Lidke, but maybe he suspects that one of his business associates might have been more . . . defensive."

It was her turn to study the swirl in her glass, worry bringing a small frown. "I don't know much about any partners or associates, Mr. Raiford. As far as I know, he runs and owns the agency himself."

"But he does share the profits with someone else, isn't that right?"

A slow nod. "He has me make quarterly reports to someone. But who they go to, I'm not sure. He mails them himself. And he handles the budget himself."

"Perhaps mailed to Chicago?"

The sudden paleness of her cheeks heightened the deep color of her eyes as she stared at him. "You know something about him you're not telling me."

"I'm only guessing at a few things, Mrs. Morgan." He smiled again. "I think Sherlock Holmes calls it 'deduction.' I also deduce that you're not entirely comfortable working for him."

"Why?"

He leaned across the table and spoke more seriously. "Because my line of questioning brings up worries you've already had."

The color came back into her face accompanied by a wry expression. "Am I that transparent?"

"You're not a practiced liar, Caitlin. May I call you Caitlin? Perhaps if you tell me what worries you, I can set your mind at ease. Or even help." Another smile. "My first name's Jim."

Her slender shoulders rose and fell slightly. "I don't know that it has anything to do with your client. It's just . . . what you've told me—the man who was killed—it just reminded me of something that happened right after I began working for Mr. Chertok."

"Please tell me."

She looked down at her glass again, straight black hair swinging against her slender neck. "It was a few days after I was hired. He gave me a sealed envelope to put in my desk and told me it held two names. He said that in a week or two I'd read in the newspapers about two unsolved murders—I was to see if the names of the victims were the same as those in the envelope."

"He had some business with those people?"

"He didn't say so. I'm not sure he even knew them. I think he wanted me to understand that he was acquainted with people who did. He's that way—he likes to impress people. To give the impression that he knows much more than he'll tell. That he's arranged deals for important people, and that important people will do him favors if he asks."

"What happened?"

"The bodies were found somewhere in Kansas. In a field. Apparently, a gang execution, the newspapers said."

"And the names were the same?"

"Yes. The article said they had been dead for three days."
The violet eyes, openly worried now, lifted to Raiford's.
"When I read it, I seriously thought of quitting. But . . ." She
shrugged. "I managed to push it away. Not forgotten—I just
managed to ignore it." Her voice dropped. "I guess I didn't
want to think of it because I need to keep this job."

"Has Chertok done anything like that again?"

"No. He seemed satisfied he'd made his point. And I've
kept from thinking about it until now."

"Are there other things about the office that disturb you?"

She considered for a long moment. "He—Mr. Chertok—is
not an easy person to work for. He's a very . . . vain man. He
thinks he's very attractive to women."

"Especially women he hires?"

A curt nod. "None of which is anything new to the world,
is it? Fortunately"—again that wry smile—"we've managed to
reach an understanding."

"He doesn't bother you, and you don't tell your husband?"

"No. He doesn't bother me and I don't quit." She said fac-
tually, "I'm a very good office manager. Perhaps the best he's
had. And, as I've found out, he's had a large turnover of office
help in the past, which hasn't done his business any good.
It took me a long time to get his books and procedures into
some kind of order."

"But with your skills, you should be able to find another
position. Why do you stay?"

"He pays very well, Mr. Raiford. Better than any other

work I could get. My last job was as a waitress, which is where I met Mr. Chertok. When he offered this job and told me the salary, I couldn't believe my luck."

"What does your husband think of it?"

"I'm divorced."

"Ah."

"Unlike waitressing, this job leaves my evenings free to be with my children." That thought brought a glance at her wristwatch. "I'm not totally naïve, Mr. Raiford. I realize I'm fairly attractive and that sometimes he takes me to lunch to show me off to his clients. Occasionally, we drop in on a production so he can show his clients off to me." She added, "And I have to admit, it is exciting to go backstage and meet name performers."

"Mrs. Chertok doesn't mind?"

"I suspect she's made her accommodation to him over the years. Besides, I am his secretary, we do transact business, and—aside from a few unsubtle hints now and then—he does behave himself."

Raiford had his own ideas about how long that behavior would last. "Can you tell me the names of any people who visit the office frequently?"

She thought a moment. "Ron Hensleigh drops in a lot. He's a regional booking agent for a music promoter in Los Angeles. And Paul Procopio. I'm not certain what he does. Something in public relations or advertising, I believe. Vic Schmanski—he produces the local wrestling shows."

"Do the wrestlers come to the office?"

"Oh, no! They're not allowed there. They only talk to Mr. Chertok at the arena. Actually, he doesn't have much to do with any of the performers—only with their booking agents and managers."

"Any other names you can think of?"

She shook her head. "There are a few others, but I don't know their last names. They don't come by often. Most of the work's done by phone. But Mr. Chertok has a lot of people he sees at lunch or dinner. He likes that—being seen in good restaurants."

"And being seen with his attractive secretary."

"That, too," she said a little bit stiffly.

"Caitlin, any man would be pleased to be seen with you. You've helped me a lot, and I'm very grateful. In fact, I owe you. If you ever need anything from me, here's my card—anytime."

She took the small pasteboard and read each printed word. "Do you really believe Mr. Chertok has nothing to do with that man's death?"

Raiford's eyes traced the smooth line of her face from the high cheekbones down the soft curve of flesh, to a delicate jaw that held the slightest hint of a cleft. She was a lovely woman. She had that accented beauty found in chiaroscuro photographs, combined with a dangerous fragility.

"I'd like to be able to say I believe that absolutely, Caitlin. I'm sure he had nothing to do with it directly. But whether he knows who might be involved, I can't say."

"I feel a bit frightened."

"Then don't tell him you've spoken with me. If you have any reason to suspect anything, quit the job. The Touchstone Agency can find something else for you."

"I do look after myself, Mr. Raiford."

"I don't doubt it. You've shown that already. My doubt is about Chertok. The moment we know anything at all, my partner or I will get in touch with you. Is it all right if we call you at work? Or would you rather we used your home number?"

She paused before saying the work number was all right. But Raiford took her home number just in case.

12

Raiford reached his office early the next morning, but he didn't get much work done. Instead, he swiveled his chair away from the littered desk to gaze out his arc of window. Over the flat roof of the old warehouse across the street, past the thick fringe of trees lining the South Platte River, he could see, between the high-rises, the trees that shaded the homes west of Denver in Highland, Edgewater, and the more distant Lakewood neighborhoods. Low rises of earth stepped away in waves of fuzzy green and tiny rooftops. Then, miles beyond the suburbs, the earth finally tilted upward in the shallow slopes that led to the two mesas hiding the town of Golden. Next came the steeper mountains of the Front Range where, on their flanks, morning sun sharpened the contrast between ragged shadows of pine forests and tawny fields of dry grass and brush. Finally, above tree line and etched crisply against cloudless blue, was splintered rock with, here and there, snowfields shading from pale gray to glimmering white.

More distant through the valleys between those high peaks, even higher humps and spires could be glimpsed where the Divide was marked by Fourteeners: Bierstadt, Evans, Gray's Peak. To the north were the lower, thirteen-thousand-foot heights of the Indian Peaks: jagged ridges building to the towering, flat-topped massif of Long's Peak almost sixty miles away in Rocky Mountain National Park. Another twenty miles beyond that, was the snowy wink of the Never Summer Range.

The view of that landscape brought its essence to mind—the peaceful emptiness of wind and chasm, the faint fragrance of sun-warmed pine and tundra that he, Heather, and baby Julie had enjoyed so much during breaks between semesters and the occasional long weekend. Thinking back, those summers had gone by so very quickly: the two before law school when he carried Julie on his back before she was able to try her own legs. It had not been long before she surprised and pleased her parents with her determination to do without help as she explored the flowering meadows and shaded glades of the high country.

After Heather's death, their trips to the mountains became fewer. And in high school, Julie had her own friends to go skiing and mountaineering with. Raiford, trying to rebuild a career, focused more on his work, with only occasional escapes from the threats and demands that defined the lives of the people who hired him. And then, seemingly overnight,

Julie was in and out of college and charting her own life in the newspaper and with Gavin. What mountain trips Raiford had time to take became solitary. Which was fine—a couple of nights alone among the peaks were enough to bring perspective on the occasional insanity he dealt with. Still, on September days like this when the peaks were at their best, he could feel their tug and their memories. And feel, too, a wish to share their beauty and peace with someone who, like Heather, would feel about them the way he did.

And that thought led him to consider again what it was that made one person stand out from a thousand others to become the focus of thought and value, as he and Heather had for each other. Well, for one thing, she had been scary smart and very attractive. And there had been a kind of emotional fit that, even when they were angry with each other, tilted them into a mutual perception of their own absurdity: a constant flickering of wit, jest, empathy, and concern that they wrapped around each other and the daughter they tried to prepare for a world that could never love her the way they did.

And what had brought these morose thoughts on such a promising September morning? Perhaps it was the way the distant mountains looked. But something else had stirred in him, too, and roiled old feelings that he thought had gone. Violet eyes. The woman's determination not to give in to her fears. Perhaps it was simply Ms. Morgan's need for help. Which—Raiford smiled wryly—revealed less about her and more about him: that he was a sucker for a woman he thought he could help, and a fool who did not recognize his own age.

"Hey, Dad, are you in there?"

Startled, Raiford swung his chair around. Julie leaned over the desk to stare at him, puzzled.

"I walk in talking about Lidke's bill and you don't even hear me. If I'd been one of Chertok's hit men, you'd be dead and never know it!" She settled on a corner of the desk, a frown showing concern. "What's with you, partner?"

For a long moment, Raiford studied Julie's face with its traces of her mother: eyes whose gray color was warm and bright with intelligence, the line from high cheekbones to a jaw that was just a bit too prominent—his contribution; full lips that seemed always on the verge of a smile, her long hair like her mother's somewhere between light brown and blond and framing a high forehead. "Oh, just thinking."

"Well, it doesn't happen often, so enjoy."

He smiled and pushed himself away from the fading image of Heather and back to the day's business. But the thought of Chertok introducing Caitlin to his friends with the implication that she was his latest conquest still rankled.

"What's the matter?"

"What?"

"You look like you just bit into a lemon."

"Still thinking."

"If it's going to give you gas, perhaps you'd better quit." Julie suddenly became serious. "Is it something you want to talk about?"

"No." Raiford glanced at the clock, surprised at how much time had passed—both minutes and years. "Let's talk about

Lidke—I've got to be at the Denver Fitness Center in forty-five minutes."

"Why?"

"That's one of the things we need to talk about. I went over to the Tap Out Lounge and was lucky—I think I was lucky. Anyway, some FWO wrestlers were in town between gigs and we, ah, talked. This one guy said I could come by this morning and he'd work out with me, see if I had a chance to cut it as a wrestler."

"Really? He didn't think you were too old?"

"Well, young lady, I'm not that old. Besides, he says there are a lot of wrestlers in the game who are in their fifties and some even in their sixties. They keep in shape and know all the moves. A good wrestler can have a long career, he said."

"What's his name?"

"Doctor Witch."

"Who?'

"No, Witch. Doctor Who's the other guy—on TV."

"What?"

"Never heard of him."

Julie looked at her father but he seemed serious. "All right, you've been listening to Abbott and Costello again."

"No. Doctor Witch is a wrestler. He said he'd give me a tryout, see if I really want to be a wrestler." Raiford wagged his head. "He's OK, but there was this other guy. . . . I thought sounding stupid was just part of their act. But, Julie, this other guy practiced truth in advertising."

"Did any of them say anything about Lidke?"

He shook his head. "I didn't want to push that too soon—just make contact, like we talked about." He went on, "I did take Chertok's secretary out for a drink after work."

"You took her out? What happens when Chertok hears about that?"

"She won't say anything."

"But suppose you were seen, Dad? She could land in deep trouble."

"It was a place of her choosing. And she's had misgivings about him in the past. I think that was the real reason she was willing to meet me. And I told her that if she was fired, we'd find her another job."

It wasn't the woman's merely being fired that Julie had in mind, but she only nodded. "What kind of misgivings?"

Raiford told her Caitlin's story of the shootings.

She thought that over. "That sounds as if Chertok's more a wannabe than a player, or he wouldn't brag to her. But she's right to have misgivings. We should, too."

"True. But it also tells me Chertok's busy doing more than he wants us to know. And that make me want to know. I don't yet see any tie to Lidke, but something's there, Julie. Have you had a chance to call Wager?"

Julie told him the detective had learned that the New York shooting was a local turf war and seemed to have no connection to Denver. "But he was interested to hear of Chertok's link to organized crime. He checked the files for a jacket on him, but there wasn't one. And the complete autopsy on Palombino won't be available for another week or so."

"I'm glad you got something out of Wager."

She shrugged. "My superior interpersonal skills. We also heard from Edwin M. Welch."

"Who?"

"Don't start that again!" She repeated the Wampler Agency's offer. "I've gone over our bid and cut out a bit more."

"If we take it down much further, we might win the thing. Wampler's big enough to eat a loss—we're not."

"But I like the idea of that pompous ass sweating a bit."

"And I like your idea of fun, but don't offer what we can't deliver."

"Speaking of deliver, we're getting close to the end of Lidke's advance."

"Find out how much further he wants us to go. And I'd better deliver myself to the fitness center just in case. Wish me luck."

"Break a leg."

"Thanks. I think."

Some vague time after her father's heavy tread disappeared down the loft's metal stairway, Julie was pulled from her computer accounts by the telephone. As usual, Wager got right to the point. "I just had a phone call. Guy said I should cease and desist bothering Mr. Chertok."

"What guy?"

"A member of the Colorado House of Representatives, no less. The Honorable Robert A. Morrow."

"He threatened you?"

"Couldn't say it was that. Just a friendly call to let me know that Mr. Chertok found my interest in him to be embarrassing and potentially damaging to his reputation as an honest businessman. And that as far as he, Morrow, and his very good friend the mayor of Denver are concerned, if there are no bona fide grounds for suspicion of wrongdoing by Mr. Chertok, it would be better all around if my interest was curtailed. To avoid another embarrassing example of unwarranted police intrusion."

Julie caught the detective's real anger in the Spanish lilt that had entered his words. "What's the tie between Morrow and Chertok?"

"He didn't tell me and I didn't ask. Could be drinking buddies." He added a little more quietly, "And I don't intend to know any more than that. Right now, anyway."

Julie couldn't blame the man for thinking of his career. But she let her silence draw out a bit as comment. "So you wouldn't be interested in the names of some frequent visitors to Chertok's office?"

"They have anything to do with Palombino's murder?"

"Not that I know of," she said innocently.

This time the silence at the other end of the line was longer. "All right, yeah, give me the damn names. I'll run them through the computer, anyway."

She told Wager the three names. "Do any of them mean anything to you?"

"No."

"Could you let me know if the computer turns up anything on them?"

"For what reason?"

"Just call me nosy."

"Julie, I got a lot more to do in this job than take crap from a state congressman and do legwork for you!"

"Don't get sore, Gabe. They're names you didn't have before, and they might be important for our client."

"And you're tying them to a homicide investigation that you and your old man will not stick your noses into!"

"Of course not—never crossed our minds!"

"That's the way it better be! Good-bye."

So much for her interpersonal skills. But Wager would run the names, she knew. The man was sore at the Honorable Robert A. Morrow, so he'd ask. It would take a few days and be done circumspectly, but Wager—spurred by the insulting arrogance of a self-important politician—would definitely run searches of those names. Whether or not he would share what he found was another question.

She finished her bookkeeping and dialed Lidke's number at the gym. On the fourth ring she got the stuffy sound of his broken-nosed voice. "Julie Campbell here, Mr. Lidke. I wanted to bring you up to date on our costs so far." She summarized their time and the dollars per minute of Bernie's searches. "We've just about used up the retainer."

"Jesus—I didn't think it would go that fast."

"Most of the cost is in the computer searches. But it's information we need. The question now is how much more to do you want to spend?"

"Yeah." His breath hissed as he considered. "I got to put a limit on it somewhere."

"It's your call, Mr. Lidke." A lot of cases ended like this—the client didn't quickly get what he paid for, and neither Julie nor Raiford could in good conscience offer anything to justify further expense. "We can dig a little more or stop now. It's your decision."

"So where else you gonna dig? I mean, Chertok's the guy—no question. What else is there to find out?"

"Not a thing, if you're satisfied with what we've done so far."

"You make it sound like I shouldn't be. That what you're trying to tell me?"

"No. What I'm trying to tell you is that we have no real evidence tying Chertok to your booking problems. In fact, everything we've discovered points to no connection at all. Moreover, Mr. Palombino's murder has made things more difficult—the police frown on civilians involving themselves in any way with a homicide investigation." She went on, "But now the police will be much more inclined to provide protection for you, which will save you paying us for the service."

"Yeah. But for how long? And what good's a drive-by a couple times a day?" He thought a moment. "OK—just for the sake of argument, say it's not Chertok. Who else could it be?"

"That's a good question." She told him about Chertok's clients and questionable acquaintances. "Right now, we're looking into Chertok's involvement with professional wrestling. But none of it points clearly toward the attacks on Mr. Palombino or on you."

"It is Chertok. I know it's him. You just told me he's got

the contacts for it, right? That's what you just said, right? And those calls to the arenas—who made them?"

"But he doesn't have the motive, Mr. Lidke. Unless there are things you haven't told us about your relationship with Chertok—something other than the wrestling—no motive has surfaced for such a very serious and very dangerous act as murder. We have no proof so far that he's the one who prevented you from staging any matches. Nothing we've found tells us that he feels you to be any threat to his business."

"Joe got prevented, all right. Motive or not, he got prevented from living!"

"The police are working on that, Mr. Lidke. That's what your taxes are for."

"Police!" A snort of hot, tangled breath. "I'm not going to bull—uh—throw you, Miss Campbell. I'm hard up for money just now. So if you can't carry me for a little while, let's just drop the thing, OK? I mean I guess you and Jim talked this over, and he says to drop me, too, am I right?" Then in a more resigned voice, he went on, "Right. Well, you and him got to make a living, too. Tell him I said thanks a lot—I know he done his best."

Julie wasn't sure whether the last comment held sarcasm. "We'll get a written report to you, Mr. Lidke. And if anything new turns up, we'll let you know. Thank you for your business."

13

The Denver Fitness Center was a long way from the Rocky Ringside Wrestling gym, not only in distance but also in appearance and clientele. Located in a shopping center's refurbished supermarket, one pair of picture windows—frosted halfway up—showed the bobbing heads of women rhythmically challenging their cardiovascular systems in an array of Spandex colors. A third window gleamed with the chrome and black of machines designed for climbing, pedaling, or skiing without going anywhere. The last window bore a Day-Glo poster advertising a membership drive that promised the latest in bodybuilding technology, saunas, therapeutic pool and swimming lanes, indoor track, trained specialists in physical fitness, and child care staffed by pediatric physiologists. All, it said, dedicated to helping you reach your health goal. It was even more upscale and unisex than the fitness center Raiford and his daughter used, and it seemed a strange place for a professional wrestler to call home.

The entry to this palace of perspiration was guarded by a long wooden counter with a turnstile at one end. Behind it, a young woman wore a perky ponytail and a leotard like a thin coat of paint over a sculpted torso. She smiled cheerfully and glanced at Raiford's gym bag. "Hi! May I see your membership or guest card?"

"If I had one, you could see it." Raiford's answering smile was equally wide. "Don Bausley told me to meet him here."

The woman didn't stop smiling but her eyes looked puzzled. "Bausley?"

"His ring name's Doctor Witch."

"Oh, sure! One of our professional clients. Just a minute— I'll go tell him you're here. He can sign you in as a guest."

The lines where her bodysuit met her leggings did interesting things as she walked around a partition and disappeared. A couple of minutes later she came back, still smiling. "This way, please. Is this your first visit to our club?"

Raiford wedged his thighs through the turnstile, then followed her down the hall. "Yeah. I see you have a membership drive."

"We sure do! If you're interested, I can tell you about our rates and facilities." She paused at another small counter. It was flanked on each side by tiled doorways. One said MEN, the other WOMEN. From one of them came the sound of a running shower and the slam of a metal locker door. Reaching behind the shelf, she pulled out a rolled towel and a key with a numbered disk that she read. "Locker 81." A gesture at the men's side. "Go straight through past the showers and sauna and you'll find the weight training room. The Doctor"—her grin grew even perkier—"says he's in." She added, "And if you want information about membership, my name's Sandi—with an 'I'."

"I'll remember that Sandi-with-an-I." He could hear his daughter's warning: *Better not 'I' that Sandi.*

The only doors were on the lockers. A tile wall partitioned the dressing area from the toilets. Other tile walls separated the toilets from the showers, which, in turn, were partitioned from the sauna. Raiford peeked in there, seeing the scattered dim shapes hunched or sprawled on the top two benches where the air was hottest. The weight room was next and apparently reserved for the professional bodybuilders. Here, the equipment had less emphasis on design and more on sturdiness. It ranged from the simple—steel bars bending under iron disks—to the complex: wall-mounted systems of efficient-looking cables and pulleys that hauled bricks of metal up and down steel tracks and were aimed at specific muscles. The Doctor stood with his back to one, his arms outstretched. Slowly, he swung two rope handles together in front of a broad chest. His pectoral, deltoid, and trapezius muscles swelled with effort. As he spread his arms again, he inhaled with a long, steady rush of air. A curt nod to Raiford and his eyes again focused on a point somewhere in front of him in sweaty concentration. Finally, he expelled a burst of air like a rush of steam and eased the pulley ropes down to let the weights clank heavily. Shaking his arms and working his neck, he walked a time or two in a small circle. " 'Old age is the most unexpected of all the things that happen to a man.' I wondered if you'd show up."

Raiford shrugged. "Here I am. How old are you?"

"My official biography says I'm thirty-five." A dark eye winked. "But I look ten years younger than I really am, which is why I'm willing to consider you, my man."

The Doctor could have been five or ten years older—maybe even more. It was hard to tell. His dark skin was taut with muscle and healthy with sweat, and there was no gray on his head or in the sparse curly hair of his chest. Raiford looked around at the tiers of weights and benches that had the familiar utilitarian look of so many places he'd sweated in. "I'm surprised a club like this has a real weight room. I thought it'd be all chrome and pulse monitors."

"I advised them to put it in. Told them no pro would work out here unless they put it in."

"They pay you to use the place?"

"Some. My job is to bring people—like you—to the gym. They sign up so they can look like me. It's not much money, but, hey, the Good Book says that in every labor there is profit. And I say every little bit of profit eases every labor." He scrubbed the curly nap of his chest with a towel. It was dwarfed to hand-kerchief size by his fist and forearm. "And speaking of profit, there's no guarantee—and you've got to understand this—that you're going to make money in this game."

"But money can be made, right?"

"Aw, yeah! And more of it every year. But you will start at the bottom, and I mean the sub-sub-basement, my man. You able to invest a couple years in this endeavor? A year training and learning the moves and another one doing maybe six shows a week with a lot of traveling? Bad beds and worse food? All for a couple hundred a week if you're lucky?"

"I'm interested."

"And no guarantee that you'll make the main event?"

"Still interested."

The Doctor grunted. " 'A man's reach should exceed his grasp, or what's a heaven for?' " He gestured toward a thick mat in the center of the floor. "OK—get your suit on and come back. We'll see how you handle some basic moves." His smile had a wolfish look.

Raiford stretched to warm up, then they circled each other, thin-soled shoes sliding over the canvas-covered mat.

"None of that karate stuff, my man. Just straight wrestling. Remember, 'to be capable of honesty is the beginning of education.' "

Raiford nodded, eyeing the man who was larger than he was and wondering what it would take to bring down someone whose legs were that heavy with muscle. He had faced bigger men on the football field, and there the trick had been to get lower, to use speed and leverage, to make the heavier man's weight work against him. And even if football had different rules, the principle should be the same.

He feinted up and dropped to a knee, grappling an arm for

the Doctor's lower leg, intending to drive his shoulder against the man's knee and tumble him. But the Doctor was quick to spin and his muscles bulged to pry open Raiford's grip. An instant later, the man plummeted across his shoulder, full weight thudding Raiford into the mat and driving the air from his lungs. He felt large hands wrap around his wrists in an armlock and, fighting for breath, he instinctively kicked out, twisting and pulling to try and free himself from the grip. But the hands clamped tighter, shoving against his straining muscles and he heard the Doctor grunt with effort. Raiford slapped a hand across the man's broad back searching for a grip, trying to work his hand under the Doctor's arm to pull the man around to his front. The Doctor shrugged loose and shoved harder at Raiford's half-folded arm to increase the leverage on his shoulder. Raiford, face scraping across the rough canvas, fought to reach an ankle, a calf, anything to counter the weight that drove his arm up and twisted his spine.

"You call it, my man, ere 'painful pleasure turns to pleasing pain.' " The Doctor's voice pinched with his own effort. "When it hurts enough, you call it."

After a while he had to. It hurt too much. The Doctor heaved a relieved sigh and rolled off while Raiford doubled with the pain of stretched and twisted sinew that seemed to hurt even more after the sudden relaxation of effort.

" 'Only the strong shall thrive, and only the fit survive.' You're strong, all right. Not many people hold out that long in my hammerlock. Got pretty good speed, too."

Raiford tried to answer, but all he could do was grunt as another wave of pain flooded his shoulder when he tried to move it. He blinked to clear the blur of strain and sweat from his vision and saw the Doctor's wrestling shoes on the grimy expanse of mat in front of his face. One of the shoes disappeared, and an instant later Raiford felt a red flash of pain in his groin that convulsed him in a clench of shooting, throbbing agony. "God—" That was all he could get out before a heavy fist thudded against the back of his neck and stung his entire torso with a million fiery needles as the nerve ends flashed.

Fighting through the warring mix of numbness and pain, his anger, will, and reflexes pulled the scattered parts of his body together and, shakily, as quickly as he could, he rolled away from the high-top shoes that circled at the edge of vision. He clamped his mouth against the urge to howl as he pried himself to his knees. A swirl of hot red blanked his vision and behind it something moved, something that he wanted to get his hands on, something that he wanted to kill. Lunging, Raiford staggered up and waded through nausea and pain to establish a stance, even though his bowed legs gave him no tension. The thing moved again and he kicked at it, driving his leg through the sickening ache that spread from his groin to his stomach. Another kick, snapped quicker this time, more authority, feeling the slap of large hands trying to clasp his ankle. A whipping sweep with the blade of his hand followed by the grip of a thick arm that wrapped itself to bend his elbow backward while another rope of flesh tied itself around his neck in a tight band that threatened to pinch the flow of blood to his brain.

"Hold it now, my man. Hold on—I said none of that karate stuff."

"You god—"

"I just wanted to know if you could take the pain. A lot of people think there's no pain in this."

"I'll . . ."

"It's over now—I'm going to let you go now. Stay cool, now. I'm going to let you go . . ."

The arms slowly eased and Raiford felt the throbbing pulse of his rage begin to ebb. "All right—I'm all right." A large hand patted his shoulder and dropped away. Raiford wheeled, arms ready.

"That's it, my man. I have seen the glories I needed to see. You can take the pain. That's more important than how old you are. Your 'courage mounteth with the occasion.' " The Doctor added, "Most of the gentlemen in the game, they're all right. But there are some rogue players who like to hurt people, especially new wrestlers. You've got to understand"—a pointing finger emphasized his words—"there will be people coming after you, and you won't know them until after they get their hit in. You lay yourself open thinking he's going to pull his punch and he don't. You understand? You've got to be able to take it in order to get even, because if you don't get even, my man, you'll be dog meat. Unless they know you can take it and give them worse, they'll do what they can to you because it makes them look good to the crowd. And looking good to the crowd is the name of this game, my man."

Raiford let himself down gingerly onto the mat, bending to ease the sick, throbbing cramps in his stomach and testicles. He sensed, but didn't really feel, the pain in his shoulder and neck. Their turn would come later. "Like Billy?" he asked hoarsely.

"Well, no. There's worse than him. He's just hopped on steroids from trying to bulk up too fast. You got to watch for people like that, too—sometimes they just go off. 'R and R' we call it: ' 'Roid Rage.' " He shrugged "But that's nothing personal. Comes with the territory. The people you got to look out for are the really mean dudes who just like to hurt you and laugh while they do it."

Slowly flattening himself on the mat, Raiford began working and loosening the bruised and damaged flesh. After a while he was able to ask, "So now what?"

" 'The ever-haunting importunities of business.' I talk to my agent and see if he wants to handle a trainee. Which, if I say you will do, he will do." He paused to shake his head. "People in this game have short lives—suicide, heart failure, system collapse from steroids and painkillers of one kind or another. They're younger than you or me when they die." A shrug. " 'Early though the laurel grows, it withers quicker than the rose.' What happens next is I talk to you and explain what percentage of your take we get for sponsoring you, and for how long. And you talk to the front desk and enroll in our magnificent health club at the special professional rate."

He said it would take a few days to get an answer from his agent, a man named Salazar. If things went OK—and the Doctor didn't see any real problems there—they'd meet with Salazar to sign a contract. What Raiford also learned was that the wrestlers seldom saw Chertok; he was a booking agent, not a producer, and he worked with the FWO managers and agents like Salazar rather than the individual wrestlers. He also learned that the Doctor had never heard of Lidke or his organization, and, like Chertok, he didn't care whether or not Lidke developed a local promotion. "Something like that might even help build audiences or give somebody another venue to jump to if they don't make it in the FWO."

As Raiford dragged himself to his car and felt the stiffness of usually neglected muscles complain about turning the steering wheel and working the pedals, he wondered at the rising cost of information.

14

Julie heard her father before she saw him. A muted grunt of some kind sounded on the other side of the office door, then Raiford came in slightly bent and walking awkwardly.

"Are you all right?"

"Of course I am." He sank gingerly into her office's soft visitor's chair. "Why wouldn't I be?"

Julie studied the pale tautness of his face. "You look like you hurt somewhere."

He shrugged and tried to hide the wince. "A little muscle pull. I worked out with Doctor Witch—showed him a few moves."

"Well," she took a deep breath. "I hope you enjoyed it."

"Yeah—great fun."

"Good. Because that was your pay."

"Say what?"

"Lidke dropped the case."

Raiford stared at her.

"It was the right thing for him to do, Dad. Nothing we have puts us any closer to Chertok, and Lidke doesn't have the money to go beyond his retainer."

He nodded wearily. "Figures." Then, "Anything from Technitron?"

"Nothing."

Nothing. Raiford carefully rotated one shoulder, then the other before speaking again. "Let's consider this, Julie. One of Lidke's partners committed suicide, another was shot, and Lidke's car was torched. And despite what he says, Chertok is edgy as hell when we come around. Something stinks."

"You don't want to drop it yet?"

"Do you?"

Julie thought of Mrs. Palombino. "No." After a moment she added, "We have nothing else going."

"Let's find out if Lidke wants us to work on contingency. We do what we can and he doesn't have to pay unless he gets results."

"We have that money-up-front rule."

"Right. But I'm just plain nosy. Something is going on—you know it, I know it. Wouldn't you like to find out what it is?"

"Yeah!"

"That's my girl."

She sighed. "That's why we work for ourselves, I guess. Did you find out anything from Doctor Whom?"

"Witch—Doctor Whom's a pansy. I did learn a few things."
He told her some of the least painful. "It sounded to me like
none of the wrestlers had any cause to hinder Lidke. In fact,
Bausley thought a local promotion would be a good thing.
Said he'd like to see it."

"Doesn't that imply that a local promotion might make it
harder for Chertok to negotiate contracts with his wrestlers?"

"Only if Lidke could pay them enough to compete with
Chertok, which isn't likely. My guess is that the real competition's among the major promotions: WWE, WCW, Vince
McMahon's people, whatever. And wrestlers can always make
good money in Japan. A lot of mid-level guys go there, Bausley
tells me. The pay's a lot better than any tank-town circuit in
the States, and that would include Lidke's promotion."

"So what's next?"

It was Raiford's turn to sigh. "I'll be working with Bausley."

"Undercover? You made the connection?"

"I don't know if undercover's the term, but, yeah, he
believes I want to be a pro wrestler. He wants to get together
with his agent and develop a personality for me."

"A what?"

Her father looked slightly embarrassed. "That's what they
call it when you figure out your, ah, costume and all. It's for
marketing. You know: ring name, visuals, all that."

Julie grinned.

"Hey, now. This is part of my cover. And if you think wrestling's all fake, you get in the ring with Doctor Witch. He'd
turn you into a pretzel!"

Spreading her hands, Julie looked innocent. "I think this is a grand and wonderful thing you're doing, Dad. And when you make your debut, I'll be in the front row cheering!"

"Keep laughing. It's not going that far. This was your idea to start with, young lady. But if you have any better plan for getting closer to Chertok, let's hear it."

"I won't say a word. Discreet Silence is me. And if there's anything at all I can do to help out, just let me know." She looked serious. "You know, giving clients your autographed wrestling picture, answering fan letters, sewing your costume . . ."

Her father kept his lips squeezed tight as he heaved jerkily to his feet. "If you will excuse me, I have a couple of things to do." He exited with dignity in his limp.

Julie had a couple of things to do, too. One should have been to have Bernie dig deeper into Chertok's possible crime connections—court records, police files, a name collation. But that would take money, and right now Touchstone had more time than cash. So instead of Bernie's number, she pulled up her favorite online site for a people search. Their report would be poorly edited and incomplete, and there was always the risk that people being checked on had paid the fee to be notified when anyone asked about their public records. But at fifty dollars, it fit the budget and was the best she could do for now.

The resultant page on Chertok showed a lot of "not available" entries in the financial section. The criminal report listed a speeding ticket, the bankruptcy and liens section was clean, small claims and judgments listed only one entry. It was over ten years old and noted that the lien, filed by Douglas Construction, had been satisfied and removed six months from date of filing. His house value was listed—tens of thousands less than Julie had estimated, which indicated how old the records were. Neighbors were listed by name and address with a red connection that, for another fifty dollars, would search for that name's appearances in public records. In all, Chertok seemed to live a very private life despite the nature of his business, and he had done a surprisingly good job in staying out of public records. She printed what was worth keeping and tried not to feel overcharged for the meager result.

Then, with Nancy Palombino in mind, she searched the online Yellow Pages for a CPA named Felsen and called him. He was unwilling to discuss a client's business with anyone who wasn't a party to that business, was unwilling to talk to strangers about his own business, and was especially loath to impart information over the telephone. Julie could fix that.

The muffled and sterile entry of the low-rise office building gave air-conditioned relief from the early afternoon sun. On the third floor, the elevator doors opened to a hallway whose decor matched the entry. Near the end of the strip of carpet that silenced Julie's heels a carved plastic sign said JOHN G. FELSEN, CERTIFIED PUBLIC ACCOUNTANT. A much smaller sign on the door said PLEASE COME IN. Julie did.

The single, windowless room might at one time have been used for janitorial storage. A small worktable with fax, photocopier, printing calculator, and stacked CD file boxes filled half the cubicle. A large desk and tall filing cabinets took up the rest. A bony man with thinning hair and wearing a white shirt and dark vest punctuated by a pocket filled with pens of various colors looked up from the desk. Two computer screens anchored each of its sides. A series of electronic accessories were carefully arranged along the remainder of the oversized surface. He did not smile, and his voice was a funereal murmur scarcely louder than the breezy hum of his machines. "May I help you?"

"Mr. Felsen?"

"Yes." He sighed. "Please sit down—I'll be with you in a moment."

Julie sat on the straight-backed chair that provided a rigid perch in the narrow space fronting the wide desk. In the silence, computer keys rattled and the printer hummed and clicked. One wall held a blurry picture of a rainy street vaguely Paris-like. But the dim scene and soft colors only added more gloom. The facing wall held a large calendar with each daily square crossed precisely off. The printer gave a tiny chime and Mr. Felsen rattled a handful of papers into a tight stack and fed it into the automatic stapler before wrapping it in a green file. Then he turned to Julie, the tips of his fingers pressed together in front of his vest.

"Are you here about an account?"

"Yes." Julie introduced herself. "I believe Mrs. Palombino called you earlier about her husband's investment in Rocky Ringside Wrestling."

"She did. But I am very busy, Miss Campbell." He glanced at the calendar. "I really don't have time—"

"I will only take a few minutes, Mr. Felsen. As you know, Mrs. Palombino is recently widowed and desperately needs help. Any information you provide could assist in her efforts to support herself and her young children."

The man's long, pale finger tugged uncomfortably at the collar of his shirt. "I don't know what I can tell you. It was rather melancholy—a sad duty—to have to explain to Mrs. Palombino that very little remained of her husband's investment in the gymnasium."

"Wasn't there any value in the property?"

Felsen shrugged, his bony shoulders lifting his shirt like an uneasy ruffle of wings. "He pledged all his holdings against corporate debts—and the debts were there. It was a most unwise thing to do. Had I been consulted, I would have counseled against it." A long breath. "Never invest more than you can lose, that would have been my advice— safety first, then search for profit." He added glumly, "We have seen what ignoring that advice results in."

"Did you do much work for Mr. Palombino?"

"Not as an individual account, no. I was retained as the corporate accountant for Rocky Ringside Wrestling."

"So you wouldn't know about any other investments he may have had?"

"No. In fact, I can't recall ever meeting Mr. Palombino." He explained. "Most of my business takes place over the telephone or through the mails. Or the fax." He added with a tiny sigh, "Most of the time I don't even leave my office."

Behind his desk hung a state license. Around it, the cream-colored wall seemed to absorb light as well as sound. "But Rocky Ringside isn't bankrupt, is it?"

"No. Its profit margin has been very slender, but recent income has brightened the picture somewhat."

"What kind of income?"

"Profit above expenses."

He added nothing more. Julie asked, "Did you audit the company when Mr. Palombino died?"

"Of course. The death of a partner—a major investor. . . . Of course I had to do an audit following his death. His investment had earned a very small return."

"A small return?"

Another discreet shuffle of feathers. "I'm not at liberty to give you exact figures. Mrs. Palombino can, if she wishes to, disclose the sum."

"The income came before Mr. Palombino's death?"

"The account figures for August preceded his death, yes."

"Will the business do better in the future?"

"That I can't answer because I don't know, Miss Campbell. All I do is look at a corporation's past financial record. Developing growth projections is a separate field, and perhaps a happier one—if less precise." He smiled, a sad lift at the corners of his mouth that quickly dropped away. "I'm the one who has to fill in the bottom line—I think of myself as the Bearer of Final Truth."

"And the final truth was that Mrs. Palombino's share of the business was almost nothing."

"Sadly so, sadly so."

Julie thanked the man and closed the door softly on his silent office.

Raiford was to meet Bausley at the Tap Out Lounge, and from there go to his agent's office. Like Bausley, the agent spent a lot of time on the road hustling deals with clients, promoters, and other agents. Tonight was a good time to get him. The evening crowd at the Tap Out had that settled and comfortable feeling of a collection of regulars. Local residents stared in rapt silence at the large screen's play-off game; a few families with kids and plates of tacos and enchiladas crowded the square tables; long-haired construction workers lined the bar; and—a sprawl of heavy bodies—wrestlers claimed their corner of the large room. Except for an occasional glance from a newcomer or a bashful and wide-eyed kid asking for an autograph while grinning parents watched from a table, the other patrons gave the wrestlers their space. Raiford figured that was why they liked the place.

Bausley sat at a table with his back to the entry. As Raiford neared, the other wrestlers glanced up with wary or blank faces, guarding their privacy. Except for one, which flashed red with anger and embarrassment.

"Hello, Billy," said Raiford cheerfully. "Feeling any better?"

"What the hell you doing here?"

"Business, my friend. A little business with Doctor Witch."

Billy heaved to his feet. "I'm going to take a piss."

Bausley looked over his shoulder at the departing man. "I

think you made a friend for life, there, Mr. Raiford. But then, 'he makes no friend who never made a foe.' Let me introduce you to some of the greatest wrestlers of all time."

Following Dr. Witch's greeting, the atmosphere eased. As Raiford nodded around the table, he recognized one of the men by his ring name. The Cannibal was famous for his Chomp of Death and his costume decorated with cuts of raw meat that, when the camera was on him before a match, he liked to rip off and cram in his mouth while blood ran down his chin. Tonight he wore a billowing shirt decorated with smiley faces. "You the one kicked the shit out of Billy?"

"He wasn't too sober."

"That do happen. But I tell you what, he's even meaner sober than drunk. If you're planning on joining the band of brothers in the ring, watch out for your nuts or he'll have you singing soprano."

Bausley stood, a large dark shape that claimed all the nearby light. "True, Brother Russell. But I think Mr. Raiford has become aware of the pitfalls and pratfalls of the canvas stage. Excuse us, gentlemen. 'A man must make his opportunity as oft as find it.' " He explained to puzzled glances. "That means we have to decide if my man James, here, is going to be a heel or a babyface."

"Babyface," said the Cannibal. "Got to be a babyface while he can!" Laughter followed them as they headed toward the back door.

Raiford climbed into Bausley's oversized pickup truck. The rear seat had been removed to allow more legroom up front, and a lowered driver's seat allowed Bausley to see through the windshield without bending over. "What's a babyface?"

Bausley's chuckle was a low rumble. "That's what the Cannibal was laughing at: your face isn't busted up yet. Have to be a pretty boy to be a hero, and most in the game don't stay pretty for long." His chuckle rumbled again. "Think of it as a virgin visage."

The agent's office was a single room in a large brick home on Pennsylvania, a three-story, Denver Square design converted to business use—as many in the once residential neighborhood had been—and probably built in the 1930s. At one time the space served as either the living room or the parlor, and the black oak trimming of its bay window looked odd against the stark partitions dividing the area. A metal desk and filing cabinet made up the business part of the office; amenities were represented by two sagging chairs made of Naugahyde and chrome. Bausley told Raiford that his agent was into a little bit of everything—public relations, advertising, sports and entertainer promotions. In any game, money was his aim. And one of the man's chief claims to glory was promoting a recording to best sellerdom, an Easter song titled "Have Yourself a Merry Crucifixion."

"Anyone who could sell that I wanted working for me."

Sure enough, on one wall a large frame held a gold disc and an ornately wreathed nameplate with that title. Farther down the wall another impressive award had been won from the National Advertising Association for the Year's Best Slogan: "Euthanasia—Something to Die For."

Raiford shook hands with a stocky man in his late thirties. His hair sprouted in stiff black bristles on top. At the back a thin tail of hair hung down in a stringlike braid. He wore an open guayabera shirt under a tweed jacket with leather elbow patches. "Raoul Salazar," he said. "The Doctor tells me you're the next Randy Savage."

"If that's where the money is, why not?"

"Aw ri'! That's the attitude, bro'!" His glance measured Raiford's torso. "You on 'roids? You taking anything to bulk up?"

"I work out. I don't take anything."

Salazar gave him a look. "You really want to do good in this game, you'll probably have to go on a chemical program. You got a attitude about that?"

Raiford looked at Bausley. "You take anything?"

"I am neither 'a prisoner of addiction nor a prisoner of envy.' "

"He means no," said Salazar. "But the Doctor don't need to—he's big enough." He pointed to another picture, this one of a clean-shaven man with bleach-blond hair and bulging with heavy, flexed muscle that punched up his veins in wreaths beneath the skin. Behind the figure, a banner proclaimed World Bodybuilding Champion. "This guy was a nothing—your basic ninety-pound weakling. Signed with me, I developed him, directed his training program, marketed his image. Now look! And he's just one of my successes. I got major successes in all phases of the entertainment and sports businesses." The finger swung to a row of publicity photographs strung along the opposite wall: stiffly posed teams, faces with wide smiles, wrestlers in costume ready to grapple. "That's some of the people I handle. Big draws, big time: WWO, FWO, WCO, WWE—you name the syndicate, you'll find a Salazar wrestler. And you'll find them at the top. They got where they are because they do what I say. That's what you'll do, you want to be on that wall. Otherwise, don't waste my time."

"If I didn't want it, I wouldn't be here."

Salazar, catching something in Raiford's voice, stared hard at him. "You think I'm maybe one of these Mexican Americans, right? One of these Chicanos from the barrio don't know his anus from his elbow? That what you think?"

"I haven't thought about it."

"I'll tell you what I am—I'm one of the Boat People, man. *Cubano.* I come to this country with nothing—ten-year-old kid with no job, no training, no education, no nothing. Just the rags on my back and what I got here!" He thumped his fist over his heart. "Guts—maybe more guts than anybody you ever met before. I'm where I am because of me and nobody else! I know what I want and how to get it, and I can get it for you, too, you do what I tell you. You don't do what I tell you, you can disappear, man—I don't care. It's no skin off my teeth, you hear me?"

"I'm listening."

He stared again, weighing Raiford's sincerity. "OK—all right. You come to me at a good time. We got major developments opening up and if you listen what I tell you, you can be part of the Federated Wrestling Organization's development in this area. You don't, you're out of here. No apologies. . . . Let's talk contract."

The talk boiled down to an explanation of why Salazar would receive a very big bite of any money Raiford made for the whole of his professional wrestling life—"You wouldn't have it without me"—and what Raiford would have to do to get started in the game—"What I tell you." Finally, Raiford had a chance to ask a few questions.

"Chertok? Yeah, I know him—FWO's regional rep. Work with him all the time. Great guy—can't find a sweeter guy."

"Has he ever said anything about Rocky Ringside Wrestling?"

"Who?"

Raiford repeated it. "Or Joe Palombino?"

Salazar shook his head. "I don't remember. If he did, it wasn't anything to do with money. That, I'd remember."

"I heard Chertok wanted to close them down. I thought he might be starting his own venue."

"Chertok?" Salazar frowned and shook his head again. "No way—you heard wrong. Chertok's a real caballero and all, but he don't know shit about handling wrestlers. What he is, is a booking agent, not a personnel-type agent. Another thing, he's FWO. I mean, he's got to know what's going down with his own outfit."

"What's that mean?"

"What it means is FWO's already working on affiliation with a local promotion. That's what I meant when I told you you come at a good time: gives beginners like you a chance to build up a following in this region. You listen to me, you'll be on a local card in a month at most."

"Do you know who they're affiliating with?"

"Sure. It's my business to know, right? You think I don't know my business? American West." He pulled a manila folder out of his desk drawer. "Hey, great talking with you, but talk is time and time is money, right? Let's get the paperwork out of the way."

The contract was eight legal-sized pages giving Salazar rights to twenty-five percent of any and all of the signer's future income derived from any and every aspect of sports and/or promotions: direct earning, ancillary, subsidiary, licensed, indirect, special, residual, and any other sources "not herein named." A small clause extended his percentage to include any and all insurance payments if the signer was unable to continue his career because of injury in the ring. In return, Salazar would perform the usual and expected duties of an agent, though he was in no way responsible for any debts or obligations legal or otherwise that the signer was obligated for now or ever in the future. And he reserved the right to terminate the contract at any time free of any and every possible obligation or penalty if, in his sole judgment, the signer failed to perform as directed. Watched closely by the agent, Raiford signed.

"Aw ri'! Congratulations! You're in the Salazar stable—now I can start making you a star. But first I got to meditate. That's how I come up with personalities for my people—I meditate. I'll call you. It'll be sometime tomorrow."

In the truck, Raiford shook his head. "Tell me that Salazar scripts those television interviews with wrestlers."

" 'A man may boast while the garland's still fresh on his brow.' "

"What?"

"He talks big. But so far he's come through. Besides"—Bausley's laugh filled the cab—"I just earned a finder's fee."

"Is everything in this racket done for money?"

"As the good book says, 'Wine maketh merry, but money answereth all things.' " After a moment, Bausley said thoughtfully, "And speaking of answers and questions, you were asking me about Chertok, too."

"Like Salazar said, he's a big name in local wrestling."

"That may be true. And a 'disinterested intellectual curiosity is the lifeblood of real civilization.' I'm just not sure how disinterested your curiosity really is."

Raiford grinned. "I'm not sure how civilized, either."

15

Julie punched in the telephone number. A child's breathless voice answered the second ring with rehearsed politeness and a note of triumph. In the background, another piping voice wailed, "Mama—it was my turn!" When the woman came on, Julie introduced herself.

"What can I do for you, Miss Campbell?" Her voice sounded slightly puzzled.

"We haven't heard from you for over a week, and we wanted to be certain everything's all right."

Ms. Morgan tried to answer, but the wailing voice continued until a hand was placed over the receiver. Her voice came back. "I'm sorry, Miss Campbell—Sydney's upset because her sister went out of turn answering the phone."

"Please call me Julie—and may I speak with Sydney?"

The girl's small voice said with hesitant excitement, "Hello?"

"Hello, Sydney. Are you being a good girl?"

She answered yes, and Julie asked a few more questions: age, four; sister's name, Jessie. Did Jessie go to school? Yes, she was in the first grade and Sydney was in preschool. "You speak very nicely on the telephone, Sydney." When her mother came back, she complimented Julie on her skill with children.

"Sometimes it's easier when they're not one's own."

"Do you have children?"

"No—nor any plans for. Have you had any problems with Mr. Chertok? Any hints or questions from him about meeting with Mr. Raiford?"

"No. . . . Is there something I should know?"

"Nothing at this end. But I would like to ask you a few more questions. Would it be convenient if I dropped by this evening? After Sydney and Jessie are settled in bed, of course."

A pause. "What type of questions?"

"Mr. Chertok, his acquaintances. Visitors to the office in the last couple of weeks—that sort of thing."

"I don't know what I can tell you that's new."

"Perhaps something that doesn't seem important to you might tie in with something we've turned up." Julie added before the woman could object further, "Would you prefer to meet me away from your home? We can do that."

"No—babysitters are always a problem. Especially on short notice. And I don't often go out at night."

"Suppose I come by around nine. Will the girls be in bed by that time?"

"Yes."

"Fine—I'll see you then."

Nothing like bulldozing one's way in. Julie swung around a curving lane between clusters of town houses that, the small trees and uniformly clean-looking paint said, had recently come on the market. Caitlin Morgan's home, like the others, was a pod of four units that shared back walls and faced away from each other for privacy.

Large commons areas of grassy lawn spread between the clusters and were divided by curving concrete walks. The whole complex backed to a park that, in the distance of evening, showed lit tennis courts with a few players and a playground with no one. Streetlights glowed soft orange over distant intersections, and the gathering dusk made the shrubbery turn into shadows that led up to the homes like secret avenues.

Caitlin Morgan welcomed Julie into the quiet—and quietly decorated—home. Open walls and low dividers helped the living and dining areas seem larger than they were, and a staircase led up to the bedrooms on the second floor. Sliding glass doors showed small patios that extended from both the kitchen and the living room. Board fences around the patios gave privacy to the home's occupants and would do the same for anyone coming up the shrubbery to try those glass doors.

A tea set rested on the kitchen divider that formed a serving shelf. Julie answered that she would be very happy to have a cup. While Caitlin poured, Julie looked at the several photographs on the wall—most were of two young girls with backgrounds varying from mountains to seashore, a few of family groups with the girls front and center. A small bookcase held a shelf of children's slender volumes and another of larger books, several of which had library numbers. The television set was dark, but a scattering of dim food stains on the rug in front of it told of its popularity with the children.

"Has anything happened . . . Julie?" Caitlin put the pot on the low table in front of the couch.

She sat at one end, Julie at the other. "Little that we can make sense of. That's the reason I'm here—to look for anything that might make sense."

"Little seems to be going on. I really don't know what I can tell you."

"What about changes to his routine? Or any new people dealing with Mr. Chertok?"

She thought for a moment. "The only major change I remember is Mr. Procopio. He's called a number of times recently."

"Any idea why? Or what they might have talked about?"

"Not really. Once they met with a"—she glanced at a small appointment book—"Mr. Morrow. Mr. Procopio left a message on Monday that Mr. Morrow would be available for lunch on Wednesday, and asking if Mr. Chertok could join them."

"Morrow? Roger A. Morrow, the state representative?"

"I don't know. But it was important enough for Mr. Chertok to have me cancel another lunch meeting. And he was out of the office most of that afternoon."

Julie jotted the name in her own notebook and sipped the fragrant herb tea—mandarin orange spice from the Celestial Seasonings plant up near Boulder. She could have done with a little caffeine, but guessed from the room's quiet color scheme and snug carpets and drapes that Caitlin preferred calm. Understandable, with two young daughters. "Do you know if Chertok's ever been involved with professional gamblers?"

"You mean like Las Vegas?"

"Or local bookies. Has he ever bragged about being a big winner or losing a lot of money?"

She thought back, sipping at her cup. "He did mention once that he had money on the World Series. But I don't know if it was a large amount. Or even if he won. But I don't think he would be likely to say anything if he lost money." She added, "I can ask, if you want me to."

"No—don't do that. I don't want you to do anything that might make him suspicious."

A note of worry came into her voice. "Do you think he could be involved with that man's death? Mr. Palombino?"

"I can only say I don't know, Caitlin." Julie was hesitant to go any further, but the woman had put enough trust in Touchstone to jeopardize her job. "You might seriously consider looking for another position. An equivalent one, I mean—one that pays for your experience in office management. We can help you look, if you want us to."

"Mr. Raiford said that, too." She frowned at the little book that still rested in her lap. "Do you think working for Mr. Chertok could be dangerous?"

"We've found no evidence that he has anything to do with the Palombino murder, Caitlin. We did find out that he has relatives affiliated with organized crime in Chicago—family ties, so to speak."

The woman inhaled sharply. "I was afraid of that!"

"That doesn't mean he's one of the mob. His little trick of showing you those names makes us think he's more of a hanger-on, someone who wants to be thought of as made, but isn't."

" 'Made'?"

"Connected—an initiated member of the mob. Anyone in that situation doesn't have to brag about it. It might be dangerous if he did." Julie continued, "But there are fringe types who range from casual acquaintances to wannabes or even probationers. I put Chertok in that first category: he hears things from his relatives and feels knowledgeable, but he's not really on the inside."

"You seem to know a lot about it."

"Only what I've read and heard—I'm no expert." Julie explained, "Other than street gangs, there's not much organized crime in Denver, and its outlines are pretty well known to the police." She didn't add that organized crime, like any other organism, grew and adapted to its surroundings and moved toward new feeding grounds. If money was to be made and individuals such as Chertok could be an avenue toward profit, organized crime, like any other business, would be very interested.

Julie went through the remaining questions on her list, but Caitlin's answers were uniformly "I don't know" or "nothing like that has happened." At the door, the woman promised to call Julie or her father if she had any suspicions or fears at all.

"Please don't let my questions worry you, Caitlin. You've told me more than you know, and most of it points toward Chertok's innocence."

Her face smoothed with relief. "I'm glad to hear that."

"But as a caution, please remember: we're still investigating. Don't be worried, but do be alert."

Julie sat in her car for a long moment before pulling away from the curb. Be alert. But if their investigation of Chertok brought danger, alertness alone would not protect the woman and her two children. Not against someone who'd had no qualms about murdering a full-grown and physically strong man.

Be alert. She slowly pulled into the street. In the darkness of her rearview mirrors, a set of headlights appeared from somewhere down the block.

The curving residential lane fed into a divided and tree-lined parkway that was equally quiet this late at night. In the mirrors, the headlights formed points of glare. She drove slowly toward the traffic light that marked the juncture of the parkway with South Quebec Street, the main thoroughfare. As she waited in the left lane for the light to change, the headlights, on high beam, slowly drew close. Their glare blinded her to the vehicle, and she dropped the car's gear into reverse to throw a little more illumination behind. From what she could make out in the glow of the backup lights, the grille and headlights were of a late-model Ford, dark in color. But it had pulled too near for her to see the license plate, and her car sat too low for the backup lights to shine through its windshield.

She put the transmission back in drive and when the traffic signal changed, she turned south on Quebec toward the beltway that circled the metropolitan region. The dull orange glow of sodium lamps confirmed the type of car, but showed little else. Near the highway junction, the car fell back and turned into the parking lot of a shopping center whose stores seemed closed. Julie went on toward the ramp of C-470 East, an eye on her mirrors. But they remained dark. Perhaps a couple of shops had been open—a late-night convenience market, a liquor store. Perhaps.

Nonetheless, she eyed the road behind as she drove up the empty concrete ramp. A pair of lights rose in the black of her mirrors. It probably wasn't the same car—chances were against that. But she pressed on the accelerator anyway, swinging tight around the curving interchange that fed C-470 into I-25 North. The underpass lights were a blur of flickering glare as she shot past the concrete piers and into the nighttime traffic of the Interstate. This far south of town, the four lanes spread the traffic apart and she danced the car between shuddering semitrailers, SUVs, and sedans until she saw, up ahead, the silhouetted roof lights of a police car. Then she slowed to the speed limit and slid into the right lane, allowing a truck to come up on her bumper and block the view of anyone farther behind.

A handful of cars passed in the outer lanes, but none seemed to be looking at anything except the police cruiser that paced traffic a few vehicles ahead. The cruiser turned off at University Boulevard, headed for the District Three station, Julie guessed, and traffic immediately sped up. The semitrailer pulled around her as she angled into the exit lane for Downing Street. The lights of apartment complexes and shopping areas disappeared into the darkness of the South High sports fields, and I-25 dropped below grade level behind a steep embankment. She slowed on the exit ramp and as she reached the top made her right turn toward the mile-long darkness of Washington Park. Another set of headlights came up the ramp behind her.

The lights were too far away for Julie to tell if it was the same car. And no real reason to think so. But she went through a series of turns anyway: left for a block, then right for another block, then left again—turns that no one who knew the neighborhood would be likely to make. If Washington Park hadn't been closed to automobiles this late at night, she would have preferred those narrow black lanes winding past the ragged shadows of spruce and unlit meadow. Still, this would do—it wasn't enough to shake a tail, but it could reveal one.

She turned right again on Kentucky. The quiet bungalows that lined the street were almost all dark, and at the curbs parked cars sat silent and locked against the night. She was almost to the next intersection when headlights turned quickly onto Kentucky behind her. They slowed to follow her left turn; speeding when she turned right again, slowing abruptly when they caught her Subaru parked and waiting at the high stone of the old curbing in front of her house. Then the car accelerated gently—a dark Ford Taurus with tinted windows and a shape vaguely glimpsed hunched over the steering wheel. This time she did get the license plates: Colorado, 498 AVF.

Whoever it was knew he had been burned. Perhaps he wanted Julie to know she was followed. More worrisome, the driver had been waiting for her to leave Caitlin's home.

16

Caitlin's "hello" was hushed and apprehensive when she answered the telephone. But Julie was relieved to hear her voice. "It's Julie. I'm sorry to call this late."

"Is something wrong?"

"Someone followed me from your house. I suspect they were following me earlier, but I'm not sure. Be certain to check your windows and doors. Do you have dead bolts?"

"Yes."

"OK, that's good. I assume you have a cell phone."

"Yes."

"That's good, too. You can dial 911 from wherever you are. But be sure to give the operator your location. Sometimes cell calls are routed through a tower that's a long way from where you are.

"Is there danger?"

"These are just commonsense precautions, Caitlin. I don't think you and the girls are in any real danger—the person was more interested in me."

Caitlin completed Julie's line of thought. "Or he would have waited until you left and broken into my home, you mean."

That was something else Julie had not wanted to say, but she appreciated the woman's quick understanding of the possibility. "If you notice anything at all suspicious—anyone who seems to be hanging around the house, someone who might be following you, any puzzling telephone calls—let one of us know immediately. You have our twenty-four-hour number?"

"Mr. Raiford gave me one earlier." She read it to Julie.

"That's it—day or night. When you drive the girls to school tomorrow, take a little extra time. Make a few extra turns. Circle around a block, see if anyone follows. If you believe you are being followed, don't stop and don't panic. Just stay on main roads and drive straight to the nearest police station and report it. Do you know where one is?"

"I can look it up online."

"Good—do that. And look up the fire stations, too. Go to whichever is closer. Does a babysitter pick up the girls after school or do you?"

"My regular sitter does—Serena."

"Is she bonded?"

"No. She's just a high school girl. She lives down the

street." Caitlin added apologetically, "She's very reliable—and I can afford her."

"She sounds fine. Don't alarm her. Just tell her to get to school a bit early and park as close to the door as possible. She should meet the girls at the door and walk them straight to the car. Have her immediately lock the car doors on the way home and pull all the way into the driveway before getting out. If she has a cell phone, she should carry it with her. Tell her not to stop to speak with anyone on the way and never answer the door until you get home."

"And that won't alarm her? She's going to ask why, and I'm going to have to be honest with her."

"Tell her you read an article about child security. Those are steps any child-care person should follow."

"Are my girls in danger, Julie?"

"I honestly don't think so. But it's best to be alert."

"Do you have any idea who followed you?"

"No. But I did get a license number, and I'll check it out in the morning."

"Do you think it was Mr. Chertok?"

"I think it's someone who wants to know what I'm doing. Just go to work as if nothing's happened. If Chertok does accuse you of meeting with me, admit it. Most of what you can tell him is the truth: I came by your home to ask questions about your job, and you never met me before tonight. I asked about any unusual occurrences in the office routine and about visitors and callers to the office. You told me that nothing unusual happened and you refused to answer any questions about clients and visitors. Almost all of this is true. Remember, he doesn't know that you know who I am—that's the thing you'll have to keep from him. He'll just think I was trying to pump information out of you."

"You seem to have experience at this type of . . . dissimulation."

Julie heard the guarded note of sudden mistrust. "We deal in trouble, Caitlin—that's our business. But we make every effort to keep it away from our clients and from the people who help us. If Chertok doesn't say anything, don't volunteer anything. Just keep your ears open in case he lets something slip." She paused then said, "We don't know that it was him or an agent of his in that car. In fact, whoever it was might have no connection at all with Chertok or with you. We'll know more when the license plate's run, and I'll let you know what we find out then."

"All right . . . I think."

Julie spent another few minutes reassuring Caitlin and repeated the twenty-four-hour number. As Julie hung up, she knew that even if Lidke didn't pay another dime, there was no way Touchstone would drop this case now.

Julie arrived at the office earlier than her father and started with the telephone messages. That was the way they did it— whoever came in first handled the phones, while the later one took care of answering the mail, which normally arrived around ten and was usually less urgent. The message Julie answered first was from the Technitron Corporation. Ardis

Stephens would like to speak with Mr. Raiford or any other senior representative of the Touchstone Agency as soon as possible. She dialed his number and identified herself to a receptionist who said "Oh, yes" and put her through.

"Miss Campbell, is it? You're speaking for Mr. Raiford of the Touchstone Agency firm?"

"He will be in soon if you prefer to talk with him."

"No, no—I just need a little more information so we can make the best decision for our needs."

"I'm happy to provide what I can."

"Yes. Fine. Mr. Raiford uncovered a surprising and potentially embarrassing security lapse, which I won't detail over the telephone."

"He told me about it—in confidence, of course."

"Yes, well, I presume he also told you that we deal in government contracts of a sensitive nature?"

"Yes."

"Those contracts are very important to us, and you can understand our profound concern that any investigation should result in a compromise-neutral finding."

Compromise-neutral? Julie replied to what she thought the man meant. "Should we be awarded the contract, Mr. Stephens, we will guarantee that every surveillance possibility is investigated and that you will have a totally secure facility."

"Yes, of course. But what if your investigation reveals that security has already been breached?"

"If we find evidence of that, nothing will be touched and

you will be notified at once. I assume your protocol requires an immediate alert to the appropriate federal agency. It would be their decision as to what action would follow." Julie added, "I hope you haven't discussed this issue in any area of your facility that might have been compromised."

"We have already thought of that, Miss Campbell." The voice paused, followed by a hearty, "Thank you. You've been very helpful. You'll be hearing from us very soon."

Julie stared at the receiver in its cradle and wondered whether the man had been asking if Touchstone would participate in a cover-up. Then she dialed again, telling the operator at the Motor Vehicle Division that she wanted to speak with Anna Knox.

"Julie! It's been a while, and I'll bet I know what you want."

"I'll get a written request in the mail today, Anna. It's just that I'm in a hurry on this one." While it wasn't illegal for the clerk to give out information from public records over the telephone, it was probably against regulations to release it before the written request had been approved and appropriate fees paid. But Touchstone had an account with the MVD—and a few other government agencies that held public documents—and the office had marked the last two Christmases with small remembrances to Anna, among other public servants allowed to receive gifts under fifty dollars in value. Most important, Julie had never failed to follow up with a written request.

"License or owner?"

"License—Colorado 498 AVF."

"Just a moment." Then, "Here it is—a rental. Save-On Rent-A-Car. 15543 Smith Road."

"Thanks, Anna. The e-mail's on its way."

And it was; Julie pressed the shortcut to bring up the form and send it before she considered her next search in public records. The Touchstone Agency didn't have a good contact in the Denver Police Department other than Detective Wager— and even that one stretched the definition of good. So she would have to go through channels: the Information Division of the Colorado Bureau of Investigation. Like other government agencies, the CBI supplemented its budget by marketing to interested citizens and taxpayers all the information allowed by law, though "all" was something of an exaggeration—no state police agency revealed complete information on arrested suspects, nor were individual records always up to date. And since the Information Division's monthly subscription fee had been changed to a per-search fee, it would be cheaper for her to make the search in person rather than over the telephone.

She downloaded three copies of the Public Request for Arrest Information form, filled in the blanks, and headed west toward Kipling Street. The day was clear and the morning cool with that freshness of high altitude that comes in the early days of autumn. In the residential neighborhoods on each side of the twin strips of the Sixth Avenue Freeway, the native cottonwood and locust trees—aware of the suddenness of early snows—already showed patches of bright yellow. Midmorning traffic was light, the drive pleasant with its views of the mountains filling the western horizon, and Julie let her mind go over last evening as she tried to make sense of the rental car that had followed her home.

Her father found a big difference between merely staying in shape and getting in shape suitable for wrestling. The pull of recently stretched muscles made him wince as he sprinted up the three flights of iron stairs to Touchstone Agency's offices. But if that brief fling with Doctor Witch had shown him anything, it was that he needed to be in the best physical condition before getting into the ring with anybody. Not that he had any intention of going that far, but you never knew. And anyway, Raiford had lately been puffing pretty hard on these same stairs—more than he should have—so the workouts were called for. Too many beers had sneaked up on him and brought a feeling of mortality he didn't like.

Julie had laughed when he mentioned that feeling to her. She pretended to discover new wrinkles on his face and even another gray hair or two. And this morning, beside his telephone, was a translucent pill accompanied by a note: "Vitamin. Men your age can't be too careful."

The kid always did have a sassy lip. He bounced the capsule in his hand, then shrugged and washed it down with a paper cup of water. No sense wasting it.

Another note told him where she had gone and asked him to check out a license from Save-On Rent-A-Car. "Followed me home last night" was the terse explanation that stirred worry. The summary of her conversation with Mr. Stephens was puzzling, and he pondered its meaning while he waited for the mail. But all that came were bills. He stacked them carefully in the middle of Julie's desk—an unpleasant duty for the junior partner with the sassy lip—and headed for Smith Road.

Raiford parked beside a cinder-block office and eyed the young man behind the counter. He looked to be in the twenty-dollar range, and that's what Raiford showed between his fingers when he introduced himself and asked to look at the rental contract on 498 AVF. What he got in return was worth a lot less: a Tucson address that directory assistance told him wasn't in that town. He bet that the driver's license—an Arizona permit to a John Wilson—was a phony, too. The clerk hadn't been able to give him a description of Wilson because he wasn't on duty yesterday afternoon when the car went out. "That was Sarah. She'll be coming in around two if you want to talk to her."

By the time Raiford made it back to the office, his daughter was at her desk studying a Xerox sheet. Raiford told her what he had found out, including what Salazar said about American West.

"A new local promotion is starting up?"

Raiford nodded. "Sal said I could open on one of their cards in a couple of weeks."

Julie wrote a note. "Let's see what Bernie can find out through incorporation documents."

"I told him I wanted to go slow—get a little more experience before going public."

She slid a sheet of paper across her desk toward him. "Rap sheet. Paul Arnold Procopio."

"Sal says I should think about the WWE or WCW if I do OK locally—says I have a good chance to make the big show."

"What? Who?"

Raiford's shoulder bobbed. "My agent. Salazar."

"You have an agent?"

"That's what I've been trying to tell you: a signed contract. Even as we speak, he's developing my ring personality."

"Ring personality? Dad, you're not going into the ring!"

"Hey—my agent tells me I've got what it takes: good looks, good body, good sex appeal." Raiford shook his head. "Endorsements, fame, money . . ."

"Dad!"

"I could be a star. You could say you knew me when."

"Do you really want to do this?"

"The roar of the crowd—the thrill of combat . . ."

"A broken nose. Cauliflower ears."

"Women screaming for me."

"Their sixty-year-old husbands throwing bottles at you."

"And no more boring hours on surveillance."

"And no more clients like Technitron—now it's beginning to sound good."

"Sure is. What's this about someone following you home last night?"

She told him. "I called Ms. Morgan and told her about it—and that whoever it was seemed more interested in me than in her."

"If it happens again, call me. Whatever time, wherever you are, please call me and we can work out an evasion plan."

She hesitated. "If it seems serious, I will."

"Serious or not, Julie, call."

"All right, Dad. But I'm sure last night was just a scare tactic."

Which seemed to impact Raiford more than his daughter: when you were young, the line between ignorance and courage was pretty vague, but he knew better than to push that thought on her. He sighed and changed the subject. "What's that note from Stephens about?"

"I have the feeling he was after something—something he wanted to know before they make their decision."

"Such as?"

"Whether or not we would keep quiet if their security was compromised. But I'm not sure. We'll find out soon enough." She tapped a sheet of paper. "Take a look at these names from Caitlin Morgan. They're Chertok's latest visitors."

"The Honorable Roger A. Morrow? State representative from District Thirteen?"

"That's a maybe—all she had was the last name. But the Honorable Roger A. Morrow did personally order Detective Wager to cease and desist from harassing one Mr. Chertok."

"Oh?" Raiford murmured what he called the Three-C Rule: " 'Coincidence Causes Curiosity.' Isn't District Thirteen west of town? Up in the mountains?"

"I'm not sure. But most of the lower-numbered districts are in and around Denver."

"Who's Paul Arnold Procopio? Caitlin mentioned him to me."

"One of the other frequent visitors." She handed him another paper. "With a rap sheet."

Raiford glanced down the page. It held several juvenile entries, all misdemeanors, all guilty pleas: car theft (joyriding), second-degree criminal trespass, assault in the third degree. The latter two had most likely been plea-bargained down from felony charges. The adult record included another pair of misdemeanors and guilty pleas that also looked like deals made with an overworked prosecutor: criminal intimidation and sexual assault. A third misdemeanor Procopio didn't bother to bargain on—possession of a gambling device or record. And a felony conviction for manslaughter. He served two years of a four-year sentence on that one. "He's had nothing new in eight years," said Raiford. "You want to bet our boy got religion?"

"I'll bet he just got smarter in junior college," said Julie. "Or he's been out of town."

"My vote is for out of town. Twenty-five years of being dumb, he's never going to get smart." Raiford looked up. "But what's his business with Chertok? And Morrow?"

"That's the question, isn't it?"

"That's why I asked it. You're supposed to give me the answer."

"Right. I forget you're a dumb wrestler now." Actually, an answer was starting to form in her mind, but as yet she couldn't see any connection with Lidke. Julie once more dialed the Motor Vehicle Division and the extension of Anna Knox.

"Julie—suddenly two calls in one day! You must be working hard."

All work and no pay, but Anna wasn't interested in hearing about that. "Feast or famine—you know how it goes. I need a copy of a driver's license for one Paul Arnold Procopio." She spelled the last name and gave the woman the birth date from the police record.

Anna said, "Just a minute," but it was longer than that. Finally, her voice came back. "He's not licensed in Colorado. I don't have anything on that name and birth date."

Which supported the idea that he'd moved out of state and saved Touchstone copy fees. "Thanks anyway, Anna." Julie tried the offices of Mammoth Productions but found the line busy. A few minutes later the redial button was more successful. Caitlin answered.

"It's Julie. How are things going?"

In the instant of silence, she could imagine the woman glancing toward Chertok's door. "Nothing different," she said cheerfully. If overheard, it could have been the answer to any question.

"Good. Can you let me know as soon as Procopio or Morrow has another appointment? It's important or I wouldn't ask."

The voice dropped into rapid words. "Mr. Chertok's seeing Mr. Procopio for lunch today."

"Where?"

"I don't know."

"No problem. I'll check on you again after work."

The woman' voice rose. "That's fine. Thank you for calling."

Raiford lifted his eyebrows in query.

"Here's the plan," said Julie.

The plan was simple: tail Chertok from his office to Procopio, then follow Procopio wherever he went to learn whatever they could. Julie and Raiford picked up Chertok as he left his office building a few minutes after noon. He drove a BMW, metallic blue and easy to spot in the busy noon-hour traffic of Colorado Boulevard, the main north-south artery cutting through "the other downtown."

"Can you speed up a little, Dad?"

Raiford, driving the associates' second unobtrusive car—an old Toyota Corolla—glanced over. "Just keep your eye on him. We'll catch him at the next light."

"If he's not in Utah by then."

"He can't go any faster than the car in front of him, Julie. And the Gray Ghost can't go any faster anyway."

Both statements were true; she settled against the spongy seat back. Raiford pulled into the queue at the light, sliding into the BMW's blind spot on its right rear fender. Julie glanced at the vehicle's license plate and its frame bearing the importer's name in large red letters. "Why do all these people buy their Beemers from that dealer in Cherry Hills?"

"Prestige car, prestige dealer. That makes them prestige people. Besides, Chertok probably leases—gets a new one very year or two."

The BMW darted across two lanes to make a quick left in a gap of oncoming traffic. Raiford went past, angling for the next corner. The businesses on that side were in one of a seemingly endless string of mini-plazas, the single-story kind with glass and aluminum fronts and names that told what they offered: Ur Pet-Store, Best Liquors, Millie's Party and Game Supplies. Only a few cars were parked in the lots and there was a mild sense of hopelessness in the wind-blown litter at their doorways. Raiford weaved past overflowing trash cans in the narrow alley behind the plaza and pulled into traffic in time for Julie to spot Chertok turn right two blocks away. By the time they reached the corner, his car was parked in a lot behind a Greek restaurant. Raiford paused at the curb to let Julie out near the white building with its blue sign YIA XARA! then turned into the next cross street. He nosed out a parking place and walked back; Julie had checked out the restaurant and was waiting near the corner.

"He went inside by himself. Want some moussaka?"

"I'm hungry," he said. "But you'd better go in. Chertok knows what I look like. I'm parked just around the corner."

Raiford watched her go through the doors, then tried to get comfortable and ignore the slow pace of his watch's minute hand and the growls of his empty stomach.

At last Julie strode around the corner. Slipping into the rider's seat, she stifled a burp. "The spanikopita was good. You like spinach pie, don't you?"

"When I can get some."

"Boy, am I full—and I had to eat too fast." Another stifled noise.

"You have my sympathy."

"Thanks. Look for a Cadillac Allante, brown, light over dark, cloth top."

The vehicle pulled out of the restaurant's driveway and, after it turned out of sight in traffic, Raiford followed. "Procopio?"

"Has to be. Chertok met only one guy."

The Cadillac led them west on Cherry Creek Drive. The crowded lanes curved between narrow strips of green embankment and scattered trees where office workers sat eating sandwiches.

Raiford let the brown car slip across at University Boulevard, then caught up again on Speer where bumpy asphalt tunneled under the shady trees of the Denver Country Club neighborhood. At Logan Street, the car turned north into the abrupt glare of concrete and asphalt. Just beyond Tenth Avenue, it slowed and pulled into a parking lot that served several adjoining commercial buildings. A sign said RESERVED PARKING ONLY. ALL OTHERS TOWED. Raiford paused again while Julie jumped out. Then he swung around the block to find his own parking.

Julie waited at a corner bus stop. "He went in that building."

It was the tallest on the street, a narrow three-story brick with pale patches on one side to show where a neighboring building had been torn down to provide parking. Abutting its other side was a glittering row of new, two-story town houses.

Over the entry, chipped gilt lettering in a fanlight spelled THE BAKER BUILDING. The lobby was 1930s marble floor and granite walls, but its cramped size and weary feel worked against pretension. The musty smell didn't help either. An ornate gilded frame held a directory. Some of the plastic letters had fallen out to lie like rat droppings behind the glass.

"The elevator stopped at the third floor," said Julie.

That floor listed Jordan and Kahn, Attorneys; The Animal Rights Center; Acme Des top Publish ng Corp.; and Inter-Mountain EnterPrizes. The letters for the last name contrasted with the yellowed letters of the other names. "Let's double-check in the parking lot."

The Cadillac was nosed against the wall. On a smear of recent black paint a new stencil said INTERMOUNTAIN ENTERPRIZES PARKING ONLY.

"There you go: superior sleuthing in action."

"Sometimes, Dad, you surprise me."

"I'm going to surprise my stomach with some food. Then let's find out what surprises Bernie might have."

17

Raiford left Julie to deal with Bernie. For one thing, he didn't want to talk to his daughter any more about the rising cost of pro bono work in general and of Bernie's research fees in particular. As Lidke had complained, the ante to play the Game of Law was getting higher and higher. For another, he had a message from Salazar who said that his ring personality was ready for development.

But Raiford could not escape a discussion of finances. "First thing," said Salazar, "you need your medical insurance. Here's where you get it." With quick strides that bobbed his stubby ponytail, the stocky man dangled a printed form over his shoulder for Raiford to snatch. Salazar led the PI toward the side entrance of the Universal Fitness Center, a windowless cinder-block building in the old industrial section of North Denver. An unused loading dock and rusty railroad spur said it had once been a warehouse.

Raiford glanced at the corporate logo on the insurance application form—Universal Sports Medical Services. "You get a kickback on this?"

"Hey, what you think? I send the guy business, sure he's going to be grateful. By Jesus's left nut, he better be—he's my wife's cousin." Salazar looked back at Raiford. "You got a attitude about that?"

"Just wondered if there's anybody not making money off me."

"Anybody has anything to do with you makes money off you. That's why they do it. What, you one of these welfare types wants something for nothing? And one more thing—this health club. Today's free. You're my honored guest. Starting tomorrow, you pay. Here's the contract and list of club fees. You'll want to sign for the six-month daily rate. That bottom line there—you don't have to read all that shit, just sign."

"I thought they were supposed to pay me to work out here!"

"For what? Who the hell are you? Right now, you're nobody. When you're somebody, then you can negotiate." Salazar used one of the keys on his ring to unlock the metal fire door. It opened on a narrow passage that led between the building wall and a fiberboard partition to an empty locker room. "This is the professionals' dressing room. You're a professional now. That's what you signed up for, the professional rate."

"Don't tell me, let me guess: you get a headhunter's fee for new members."

Salazar was offended. "No—that's penny-ante crap! I'm one of the owners! Now sit down and listen up because here's your new life." The shorter man wagged a thumb to aim Raiford toward a wooden bench. It ran along the front of a row of metal lockers set against a partition. Raiford sat obediently; Salazar remained standing, lifting on his toes in order to look down at his new property. "I'll start you out as part of a babyface tag team. But you're a cherry, and that means your partner's got to carry you. He's one of the finest workers in my stable, and he'll teach you the game. You'll pay goddamn close attention to what he tells you and do everything he says with no lip. And you learn it fast. The faster you learn, the faster we get you in front of the public and the faster you start bringing in revenue."

"This is with that new outfit? American West?"

"It's with who I say it's with. That's not your worry. The story line's not your worry. Your worry is to learn moves from your partner and to sell moves to the audience."

"How much do I pay this guy?"

"Thirty percent of your take for any tag-team appearance—after you take my commission off the top."

Raiford figured Salazar took an additional ten percent of that thirty for services rendered. "Pretty soon I'll be paying to wrestle."

"You know what, hombre? That's what most people do! Go on, haul your ass to any of these wrestling schools, if you can find one in this neck of the woods. Go on: see how much that costs you! Five hundred initiation fee. Fifteen hundred for six months' training. And that's for the no-name programs, hombre! What I'm telling you is you got a good deal here: I'm getting you started right off in the ring—in the ring, man!—and you got a trained professional, a real worker, as well as me to tell you what to do. And for what you're paying, you can't do no better than that nowhere!"

"All right, all right. I signed the contract."

"Fuckin' A. And you don't live up to that contract, your ass is out and nobody's spilling milk over it. And don't think anybody's getting rich off your ass. What I'm making off you now is pin money, man. You're a investment of my very valuable time that right now adds up to a loss for me. Maybe even a gamble—you know what I mean?—because you won't be earning jack-shit for a long time!"

"Until you make you and me rich."

He nodded with exaggerated slowness. "That's what I'm telling you—we're in this together. And you can't get there without me. If you get there at all." He yanked open a door in the row of dented metal lockers that wobbled on bent legs. It reminded Raiford of his junior high dressing room, which had been in an alcove of the rural school's industrial training shop. "Now, here's a set of tights you can use for today. Get your own down at Tanks-A-Lot Sportswear. Tell them I sent you and you get a professional discount."

"Owned by another in-law?"

"What the hell difference that make? You want a discount

or not? You got a mouth on you, you know? By all the pricks of Saint Sebastian, you better learn to keep it shut until I tell you what comes out of it, you know?"

"OK—fine—what's the name of my tag-team partner."

"Colonel Crush. You heard of him, right? No? Well, a lot of people have—he's got a lot of exposure. And a following—I start you out with his following, which is a hell of a lot better than you could find anywhere else. East Coast, West Coast, wherever. Your team's called the Death Command. You're Major Mayhem. Colonel Crush and Major Mayhem—good, huh? I came up with it last night. A major's not as big as a colonel, right? So it gives us a story already: you do good, you're getting better, and after a while you want to be a colonel, too. So the story's already set up for a big grudge match between ex-partners, see? But you got to do good." He paused to dare Raiford to object. "All right. Get suited up. George— that's Colonel Crush, George Harmon—is already on the mat, warming up."

The mat was a double thickness of cotton padding on a low platform that filled the center of a large and ill-lit weight room. One wall of the room was lined with a long mirror that ran in height from knee to ceiling; below the mirror was an equally long shelf holding assorted dumbbells. At one end of the mirror, from a row of clothes hooks, hung wide leather stomach belts salt stained from layers of dried sweat. At the other end were a drinking fountain and a pay phone. A sign on the wall over the fountain warned of herpes and added that all athletes must wear wrestling shoes and full tights when working on the mat. The facing wall held tiers of barbells and iron discs of all sizes. Slant boards were propped at one end. Another sign said THIS IS NOT YOUR GYM—KEEP IT CLEAN OR KEEP OUT. Raiford could guess which of the owners had placed that one. In a corner of the ring, pulling against the elastic ropes, a hefty man in a sweat suit twisted and squatted through a stretching routine.

Salazar dragged a folding metal chair from a corner. "Hey, George—here's the cherry. Say hello to Jim Raiford, then teach him what he needs to know."

"Glad to meet you." Colonel Crush had mustaches over each corner of his upper lip and a shaved gap under his flattened nose. The mustaches drooped around his mouth to join two patches of cropped whiskers that framed a shaved and jutting chin. A red bandanna covered his head. "Mr. Salazar tell you about the money? What my percent is?"

"Thirty."

"Good. So let's see how you do."

It didn't take Bernie long to run a screening on Procopio, Inter-Mountain EnterPrizes, and American West. But she came up with nothing on the last one. "Are you certain American West is the full name, Julie? I have eleven companies with those words in their name, but none that seems to have anything to do with wrestling or sports promotion."

"Nothing at all?"

"You said it was a new company—it's possible they haven't yet gone through all the legal steps to get their charter. If that's the case, it won't be on file until they do."

Julie hadn't thought of that and made a note to dig a little more. "What about InterMountain EnterPrizes?

"It's a brand-new company, too. Private, licensed in Colorado about six months ago for the usual 'all legitimate business.' The principal officers are Ronald G. Hensleigh, president and chief executive officer; Kenneth R. Pfeifer, secretary; Daniel A. Chertok, treasurer. Unless a couple of those people are millionaires, they have to have some silent partners or heavy investors because they're starting out with capital assets listed at two-million-plus dollars."

"How much?"

Bernie repeated the figure. "I went ahead and checked out the names and they don't sound like millionaires to me. Hensleigh's an agent for various music groups—rock bands, country and western, even some individual artists. I didn't recognize any of his clients, but I'm not into the pop scene. I can access information if you want to know more about them, but you can probably find as much as you want on Google. Pfeifer's an attorney with his own practice and no partners. I couldn't determine what his specialty is, but he's not ranked among major firms. And Chertok you know."

Julie did. "Any idea of what kind of 'legitimate business' we have here?"

"I could scan public documents for title transfers and registrations. Something might come up." A shrug entered her voice. "Then again it might be a waste of money."

"Any possibility of finding what bank the corporation uses?"

"Always a possibility—never a guarantee, and something

like that would have added expenses." Bernie did not have to add what those expenses might be, nor would she over a telephone.

But from past queries, Julie knew that when the woman said "added expenses" she really meant it. "Let's hold off on that for now. Maybe I can find another way and save a little. How much will it cost to go through public documents?"

"Corporate name alone, or including the officers' names?"

"Corporate name."

"State, county, city, or comprehensive?"

"Comprehensive."

She gave a figure and Julie sighed. "OK, Bernie. The usual ASAP."

"You got it."

And Julie did. A few hours into the afternoon, the fax rang and its printout listed legally recorded transactions by InterMountain EnterPrizes. They were few but recent, and impressive: a plat of land in the township of Central City, Gilpin County, $950,000; application for liquor and gaming licenses with the state Liquor Enforcement Division and the Gaming Division in Central City; applications with other state and federal agencies to set up business as a corporate employer: tax number, employee retirement fund account number, employee medical insurance and provider; application to Gilpin County and Central City Township for permits to erect a multiuse commercial building with a cost estimate of $1,750,000—followed by a hand-scrawled note from Bernie, "if you want the filed real estate description and building blueprints, I can get them."

But Julie didn't need any more information right now. What Bernie told her confirmed the suspicion that had been building: the legitimate business that InterMountain Enter-Prizes was involved in was the legalized gambling that had brought a minor economic boom to the old mountain town of Central City and a major one to its neighboring mining town, Black Hawk. It explained why Procopio's name was nowhere to be found in the company documentation: he had a criminal history and was forbidden by state law to be associated with gaming or casinos. Julie guessed that the almost three million the investors had come up with probably had a criminal history of its own. That would explain why Chertok was so nervous about her dad nosing around. Bernie's information didn't need to explain why that much money would be invested in Central City—that was explained by the new municipal parkway that linked I-70 to the town and cut out Black Hawk, as well as the recent vote to change state gambling regulations to allow higher limits on poker stakes and to add more games such as roulette. Interesting, but none of it offered a reason for Chertok to attack Lidke. Still, one of Lidke's partners had—officially, anyway—committed suicide in Central City.

Making a few more notes, Julie faxed another request to Bernie asking her to check out Procopio's name in Chicago as well as any ties to Rudy Towers, and to see if there were any papers or liens indicating that the newly acquired Central City real estate was being used as collateral for a bank loan anywhere. After that, she telephoned the State Gaming Commission to find out when the hearing was to be held for InterMountain EnterPrizes's gambling license. A secretarial voice told her it was scheduled for 10 a.m. on October 15: two weeks away.

Then she called Lidke, identifying herself, since the office phone—for an additional fee—stated "Caller Unknown" on any caller ID.

"Gambling?" Faint in the background, Julie heard the now familiar crash of a heavy body slamming onto the suspended mat. "I put a little money in the football pool sometimes. Sometimes buy a lottery ticket, go out to lose some at the dog track. But that's it."

"And you've never heard of InterMountain EnterPrizes?"

"They a wrestling promotion?"

"Not that I know of."

"Then I ain't heard of them. What's going on, Miss Campbell?"

"We're still trying to find the link between you and Chertok."

"You know what the link is—he don't want my competition."

"But we have absolutely no evidence that Chertok has anything to do with Rocky Ringside or with you. Moreover, he has a lot of money invested in a gaming project up in Gilpin County. Enough to give him a big incentive to avoid trouble of any kind with you or with anyone else. The slightest whiff of criminal activity and any corporation he's involved in will have trouble getting its gaming permit."

"Well, I don't know anything I ever done that ties in with gambling. Not right off the top of my head."

"How about Rudy Towers? Did he have anything to do with Chertok or anyone in Gilpin County?"

"I don't think so. But I can't say for sure. Why?"

"His body was found in Central City."

"Oh—yeah. I didn't think of that." The line hummed slightly. "I don't know of any connection that way, but maybe there could be. Rudy didn't tell me everything he was doing." After a pause. "He had a lot of deals going all over the place." He added, "I guess that was a kind of gambling: he was always hustling some deal or other."

And he had been worried about money. Often, people who worried about lost money had dreams of winning it back at the tables. "What about a new wrestling promotion called American West? Ever hear of them?"

"American West . . . . What about them?"

"I understand they're local. Have you run across them?"

"I heard talk somebody wanted to start another local promotion. But that's about it. What've you heard?"

"That they're working on an affiliation with the FWO."

"Aw, shit!" Lidke's voice held the tumbling of high hopes. After a second or two, he said, "That's the link, then, ain't it? That's the reason Chertok's pulled all that crap. He don't want nobody staking out the local venues so he can make a sweetheart deal with this American whatever."

The possibility was there, and Julie had considered it enough to want to hear Lidke's opinion. But she still could not see Chertok endangering a major gambling project with possible charges of intimidation, arson, and homicide—not over a business as small as Lidke's. "Do you know anyone in American West?"

"I tell you what I do know: they're not going to push me out."

"Do you know their full corporate name? Or where their offices are?"

"Why you asking all that, Ms. Campbell? You know I ain't got the money to pay you any more!"

"Because of the Palombino murder." She added, "And we're doing it on our own."

"On your own? Then do it on your goddamn own, lady, and leave me alone!"

Blame the messenger. Julie hung up the receiver and let her hand rest a moment on its smooth plastic. Lidke would naturally be upset to hear about the new competitor, especially to learn it would be working with the FWO. One or two events by American West with big-name wrestlers visiting from the national circuit, and Lidke and any other unaffiliated promoters would be blown away. She stared at her notes and turned things over in her mind. Then she dialed again.

"This is Julie, Caitlin. May we talk for a few minutes this afternoon?"

"I can't. Mr. Chertok has a meeting and wants me with him."

"Do you have a moment or two now?"

"Yes. He's out of the office."

"Has he said anything about Rocky Ringside or our investigation?"

"No. I don't believe he's given any thought at all to you or that man you're working for. He hasn't mentioned a thing."

"That's good. But keep your guard up. When you gave me that list of his frequent visitors, didn't you say one of them staged the local FWO bouts?"

"Vic Schmanski. Mr. Chertok works with the arena managers on business details and scheduling, but Mr. Schmanski is the one who actually produces the show."

"May I have his address and phone number?"

"I have phone and fax. I don't have a mailing address for him. He does all his work by phone or comes over here."

Julie dialed the Schmanski number and when the man himself answered, she spoke quickly. "This is Mary Ellen Petrovski with the *Denver Post,* Mr. Schmanski. I'm doing a story on the wrestling scene in Denver and I hear you've been a major player in putting together a deal between the FWO and American West to promote local shows and talent. Can I ask you a few questions about it?"

"Jeez—news travels fast! But it's not much to talk about yet. We're still in the organizing stage, you know? Trying to iron out business arrangements, venues, appearances, schedules, them kinds of things."

"It really sounds exciting, and I know a lot of readers

would be interested to learn about the possibility of the sport expanding in the Denver area."

"Well, yeah, good. But, like I say, it's a little early to go for publicity. If the deal falls through or we have delays, we could get, you know, egg on our face."

"I can do an in-depth piece and hold it until you're ready to announce. My editor will go along with that, and the story can help you out when you're ready for publicity. Is American West the correct name of the local promotion you're dealing with?"

"American Sports and Entertainment."

"They're a new promotion?"

"Yeah. Brand-new. That's one of the reasons things are up in the air. They got no track record, and FWO doesn't want to affiliate with a loser. Affiliates got to be able to produce, you know?"

"A farm club? Is that what FWO is after?"

"Something like that, yeah. We think Denver's ripe for more professional wrestling venues, and with enough local talent and interest, we can develop live wrestling shows. But like I say, we're ironing out details and we're not ready to announce nothing yet."

"Who do you talk with at American West?"

"Their lawyer. Ellis Huggins." At Julie's insistence and her assurances that the story would not break prematurely, Schmanski gave her Huggins's telephone number. She thanked him.

"Hey, always a pleasure to help the fourth estate—just

remember when our press release comes out, I helped you, OK?"

"Believe me, I won't forget."

When she hung up, Julie used the online reverse directory that Touchstone subscribed to. The address listed for Huggins's number was in the 1100 block of Bannock. It wasn't one of the prestige locations for attorneys, but it was only a short drive away.

18

Salazar hung around for half an hour or so to watch Colonel Crush and Major Mayhem throw each other across the ring. Before he left, he reminded them that they had the potential to be the greatest tag team in the Western Hemisphere (and Japan, he said, where they could make a lot of money) if they listened to what he told them. The Colonel showed the Major the best way to land, not merely to avoid injury, but, more important, to get the biggest noise out of the ring's deck and the strings of metal washers underneath. "Most decks are plywood set a couple inches above a metal frame. That way, when you hit, you get some bounce and the washers make a lot of noise." The Colonel demonstrated the proper form for knee drops—"Take up the weight with your own heel, see? Like this"; the clothesline—"You don't do anything, just stick your arm out and let me run into it"; the forehead butt—"This one's kind of tricky. It's all in where you put your hands and thumbs, and you don't want to mess up unless you really want to hurt somebody." He coached Raiford through other moves, first slowly and alone, then faster, until finally he joined Raiford and they went through them like the intricate steps of a folk dance.

After a lesson on some of the more universal hand signals that told the opponent what throw to expect, they combined the gesture and its move. A series of routines varied the throws until Raiford had them reflexively memorized and both men were sweating heavily.

"Next time," the Colonel said, gasping for breath as they hung on the top rope, "we'll work on high spots—flying scissor kick off the top rope and such."

"I can't . . . wait."

"Hey, we're just getting started. We got finishing moves, too. Like the Power Bomb. You really got to sell finishing moves because they, you know, finish off your opponent. They really got to look good. And you'll want to wear a wristband—that's where you hide your razor. Some people use their belt or the top of their boot. But the place I like is in here along the back of my arm. I don't want it cutting any veins if my wrist gets bent down hard."

"A razor? You mean like in razor blade?"

"Yeah. For juice."

The Major, still panting, pushed himself off the rope. "Maybe you better explain that a little."

The Colonel ran his fingertip across the purple nicks on his forehead just below the hairline. "Blood. Fans go nuts when they see real blood. You set it up so the other guy gets the audience's attention, you know, he argues with the ref or screams at some fan. Then you juice a little like this." He put both hands up to his face as if reeling with pain. The Major watched two of the colonel's fingers slip under the wristband and then wipe quickly across his forehead. "That quick. It'll sting at first. You got to cut deep at first until you get some scar tissue built up. Then you hardly feel it and it bleeds easier, too."

"Juice."

"Yeah. Scalp cuts, they bleed like mad. After a while, a little nick and you got all the juice you need. But you don't want to do it too much. Just for the special treats, you know?"

"I'll remember that."

"We can work it into our routine after a while. But first we'll be doing mostly prelims. Developing the audience for the bigger matches later on. That's where the card builds up to the juice. Every thing on the card is timing for the story line." The Colonel grinned, teeth large and uneven beneath his mustaches. "No premature juicing, you know what I mean?" They climbed wearily out of the ring. Dark stains of sweat marking their tights. "But, hey, you learn real fast—you're a good athlete. It won't be long before we move down the card. You're going real good."

"Thanks, George." Raiford followed the man to the shower

and stood soaking in the hot water to steam soreness out of stretched, abraded, and twisted flesh. "You've been in the ring a long time?"

"Nah. Just four or five years. Some of these people been wrestling fifteen, twenty years. They develop a following, you know? Name recognition, endorsements. Even if they don't hit it as big as Hulk Hogan, they still make a good, steady living."

"So why are you starting all over with me?"

"I used to wrestle as Terrible Tony Titan. Ever hear of him?"

"No."

"That's why I'm starting over." He added, "Salazar said I'd do better as part of a tag team, and I don't have much to lose. I've invested enough time in the business, so I thought, what the hell, I'll give it a try."

"But why a new man? Why not get a partner who already knows the game?"

"Somebody who knows the game wouldn't pay me to teach them!" George laughed and then frowned as he scrubbed soap in an armpit. "Besides, I've had a hard time finding a partner."

"Why's that?"

"I'm gay. That's why."

Raiford stared through the thin veil of water at the figure an arm's length away. "Gay? As in . . . um . . . ."

"Homosexual. But you got nothing to worry about. I've been married to the same guy for fifteen years."

"Married?"

"In a church even. He's been very active in the movement to legalize domestic partners."

"Oh. That's nice." Raiford finished his shower and slowly wrapped his towel firmly about his waist. "So the other wrestlers know this and don't want to be your partner?"

"I don't go around bragging about it. But I'm not ashamed of it, either. A lot of people just can't handle it, is all. But, hey, I'm not the only gay wrestler in the game. In fact, my first manager had a casting couch in his office. Tried to get me on it." George spat something. "He was a real pig."

Raiford, his back to the man who was toweling himself dry, tucked his shirt into his pants and zipped up. "So why don't you have a partner of your—ah—persuasion?"

"The ones I know, I don't like. Besides"—George, too, was modestly dressing behind the open door of his locker—"there's HIV."

"AIDS?" Raiford thought about that. "What do you mean?"

"Suppose I had a tag partner who didn't practice safe sex? You work out with somebody every day, the risk goes up. I mean even in the ring, it's good to be careful, you know? That's why there's no spitting anymore." George finished buttoning his clothes and looked over the locker door. "They outlawed juicing for a while, but the Nielsen went down, so it's back. Just don't smear it on anybody else." He added, "You got to watch it with straights, anymore, too. Anybody can get AIDS. But if you got a tag partner active in the high-risk population, you're really asking for trouble."

On the way out the narrow passageway to the building's back door, George said, "And another thing, some of the story lines call for gay wrestlers now—men and women. Political correctness, I guess, but they mostly make them the scumbags. Capitalize on the audience's homophobia." He shook his head. "I don't want to contribute to that." They paused in the parking lot. "You're not too comfortable with this, right?"

Raiford shrugged. "Well, I have to admit—"

"No problem. But like I say, I'm married. Happily. And we've both been tested HIV negative and plan to stay that way."

"I'm glad to hear that." Raiford knew of gays in every walk of life, but he had never wrestled with one.

"This tag team is strictly business," said George. "Our private lives are strictly separate from what goes on in the ring. Not many people outside the game know I'm gay, but you want to take time to think it over, right?"

"I have to admit it surprised me."

"What I'm saying is, you don't have to sweat a lot of people thinking you're gay just because I am—wrestlers all got an image, and mostly it's nothing like what they are outside the ring."

"I won't quit for that reason, if it's worrying you."

"I'm relieved to hear that. The last guy Salazar tried couldn't take the idea and did quit." He stood by the open door of his Isuzu Trooper. "Salazar didn't want me to tell you, but if we're going to be a team, something that important shouldn't be hidden."

Raiford agreed. "I'd rather hear it from you now than from somebody else later. You take any heat from the other wrestlers?"

He shrugged. "It's happened. Mostly, it's from guys unsure of their own sexuality, you know? When I was the Terrible Titan, I used to wear a gladiator costume into the ring. One time this wrestler yelled out—and this was on television, man—'That ain't a glad-he-ate-her, it's a glad-he-ate-him!' " George shook his head.

"You pop the guy?"

"Broke his back. I didn't have any trouble after that." Another shrug. "But like I say, now they have scripts for gay wrestlers, even story lines with the babyface's girlfriend getting hit on by butch women wrestlers. Look, Jim, this is a big chance for me to get my career going, and I aim to give it my best shot. If we can work together on it, we both might make it. That's the only thing I'm interested in."

"Fair enough."

"Good. Maybe you can come over for dinner sometime. Anthony's a real good cook—makes great Italian food."

Raiford watched the square rear of the vehicle, listing slightly to the driver's side, disappear into the late evening glare.

The offices of W. Ellis Huggins, attorney at law, were on Bannock Street in an area that was zoned for business but still had a few residences scattered among the commercial activities. A small wooden sign with Old West lettering said LAW OFFICES, and beneath that, Huggins's name. The building was a residential cottage whose change to commercial use consisted of a coat of bright blue paint. The small houses on each side were still used for families, and their paint had been left by the landlord to thin down to the color of the wood beneath. The idea was to let the property depreciate in tax value while rents increased because there were fewer and fewer places near downtown for the families of those who worked in the service and janitorial jobs. It added up to a bigger profit margin. Apparently, Huggins paid enough rent to justify this cottage's new tax assessment. Which, Julie figured as she entered the living room with its stained and faded wallpaper and muslin drapes, probably had not gone up much.

"May I help you?" The very young woman who looked up from the computer screen pulled an earphone out of a spiral of brown hair and smiled.

Julie introduced herself. "Mr. Huggins said I could drop by."

"Oh, sure! I'll buzz him." She pushed a button on the corner of her desk. "He'll be right out. You want to sit down, you can." She turned back to the glowing screen and plugged the earphone back in before pressing the keys with labored care. A new high school class ring glittered on her hand.

"Miss Campbell. Come in, please." Huggins had blond hair that swept back in waves from a high forehead to curl at the top of his collar. He smiled under a pair of tinted wire-frame glasses and motioned toward his office. A new desk, a new leather swivel chair for clients. Two plain bookcases filled one wall where a dresser probably stood when the office had been a bedroom. Julie recognized the worn spines of the books as the *Colorado Revised Statutes,* and suspected that these same volumes had been in the offices of other fledgling attorneys before Huggins bought them. He settled behind his desk. "On the telephone, you mentioned something concerning American West Sports and Entertainment?"

Julie nodded. She had told Huggins that she wished to talk with him about the rumored tie between the FWO and the newly formed American West. "Mr. Schmanski told me there was a deal in the works."

"Yes, I am in negotiation with Mr. Schmanski on behalf of American West. But we haven't arrived at any definitive stage yet. May I ask what your interest is in possible dealings between FWO and American West?"

To call herself a casual observer or a reporter probably wouldn't make a friend of Mr. Huggins, Esquire. "I've been hired by a client active in the local wrestling scene. He'd like to speak with the principal officers of American West before they sign with FWO. He believes some mutual profit could develop from combining his established local promotion with their projected one."

"I am authorized to receive any and all communications directed toward the American West Corporation." Huggins leaned back into the swivel chair's springs. The man's fingers—pink, stubby, and deeply wrinkled at the knuckles—made a little tent under his nose. "Just what does your client want to offer that might be of interest to my client?"

"Years of experience in professional wrestling and a thorough knowledge of the Denver area, which would be vital to any newcomer to the region. He also has an established and highly successful wrestling school and gymnasium. More to the point, he has a number of promising young local wrestlers already under contract. They have a large following of local fans. If you could tell me who the company officers are, I'd be happy to put him in touch with them."

"American West is a private corporation made up of silent partners, Miss Campbell." Huggins's voice was patient. "They're silent because they want to protect their privacy. That's why I'm the authorized spokesman. Any deal your client wants to offer, he can discuss with me and I will present the matter to the corporate board." He paused, then, "Does your client have a name?"

"Otto Lidke. Owner of Rocky Ringside Wrestling."

"Oh?" Huggins stared at her for a long moment. Then he carefully made a note of the name. "And you've come here with his authorization?"

"I'm working on a case for him. I come here in conjunction with that."

"What kind of case?"

"Mr. Lidke has been threatened, his property attacked, and his partner murdered."

"Murdered? A man was murdered?"

"Joe Palombino." Julie watched Huggins's eyes behind his tinted lenses. "Mr. Lidke thinks someone is trying to prevent him from developing his wrestling promotion."

"That's not a very compelling argument for a partnership with American West, Miss Campbell."

"The potential profit could add up to a great deal of money, Mr. Huggins. Perhaps someone sees my client as a competitor for that profit. That same someone might perceive American West as a competitor, as well. But together, Rocky Ringside and American West might stand up to a corporation as big as, say, the FWO."

"Are you implying that the FWO—Mr. Schmanski and his people—are responsible for murder?"

"Not at all. I'm just using that organization as an example." Julie scooted away from that line of argument. "You must know that wrestling promotions require a license and that your principals' names will have to be divulged to get that license."

"Are you attempting to give me legal advice, Miss Campbell?"

"I'm attempting to discover why you won't further your clients' best interests by letting me present them with my client's proposal."

"Consider yourself to have presented it, Miss Campbell. I will inform them of your visit—I certainly will." The man stood. A gold Phi Beta Kappa key swung brightly across his dark vest. "Meanwhile, I have a busy schedule. If my client wishes to pursue relations with your client, I will be in touch. Good day."

Dead end. Julie sat in her car and tried to think of ways around Counselor Huggins. There was no obvious reason why the principals of American West should want anonymity. As a detective, Julie had learned that occasionally people did some weird things for no reason at all, but more often the reason was money. Always *cherche la money*. Yet there was nothing shameful in making money on a wrestling promotion. And unlike a gaming license, a ticket to promote sporting or entertainment events wasn't restricted nearly as much. If, for example, one of the principals had a history of ties to the underworld, it would make no difference as long as it wasn't a betting sport. So why the secrecy?

Huggins could be on the telephone right now talking to the principals. Julie eyed the robin's egg blue cottage with its old-fashioned sash windows and shrubbery lining the walk and foundation. It wouldn't be difficult to go in and plant a bug. Risky and illegal, but not difficult. It was something to consider.

Meanwhile, it was well after two. Julie swerved through light midafternoon traffic toward Smith Road and the office of Save-On Rent-A-Car. The woman who had checked out the car that had followed her home last night should be on duty by now.

Her name was Sarah and she frowned as she listened to Julie's request. "498 AVF?"

"Yes. To a man called 'John Wilson' of Tucson, Arizona. But the address is a phony, and I suspect the name is, too."

She turned to a computer, fingers dark against the rattling keys. "That vehicle came back this morning to our Convenient Check-In over at DIA. The customer had twenty-four hours left on his rental."

"Do you remember what he looked like?"

"Lady, do you know how many people I see in a day?"

"Anything at all about him—tall, short? Color of hair? Any facial hair or jewelry?"

She let out a long breath and stared somewhere at the ceiling. "498 AVF—well, let me see. . . . It was an afternoon rental, that I remember. He wasn't too tall." She chewed her lip. "I can't remember if he was bald—he wore one of these flat caps. You know the kind, have a little brim up here. Sean Connery wore one in that movie he was in . . ."

"Did he have a beard or mustache?"

"Not that I recall."

"Heavyset? Thin?"

"Suit he was wearing didn't fit well." She shook his head. "That's about all I do remember."

On her way back across town, Julie tried to fit the information into some kind of pattern. Despite Caitlin Morgan's belief that her boss didn't suspect anything, Julie had expected the clerk to describe Chertok. But that man would never wear ill-fitting clothes. He could have had someone else rent the car: used an accomplice, hired someone. That would also explain Chertok's apparent lack of knowledge about Julie's visit to Caitlin's house—the accomplice following Julie might not know where Chertok's secretary lived. But suppose he reported to Chertok the various places that Julie had visited? And included Caitlin's address? That thought made Julie feel the push of time at her back.

19

The morning *Denver Post* had the story on page two of the Local News section: "Attorney Slain. William Ellis Huggins, 32, was found shot to death beside his car in the 900 block of Yuma Street. A police spokesman speculated that robbery was the motive. . . ."

Julie found a parking place just down from the bright blue cottage with its Attorney's Office sign. The front door opened when she pushed it and she found the young woman behind her desk. This time she wasn't trying to type. In the silence of the cottage she seemed to be moving papers from one stack to another without really knowing why. She looked up as if Julie might provide an answer.

Her name was Jennifer and she needed to talk. "I read

about it in the paper this morning." Behind large glasses, her hazel eyes were damp and worried. "I didn't know what to do. I mean, should I come down and open the office or not! I mean, people—clients—might call, you know? But I don't know what I ought to tell them."

She had been hired six months ago when Mr. Huggins opened his practice. It was her first job and she got it while she was still a senior in high school and she really liked the work. Mr. Huggins was just getting started and he promised her that after a while if she did real good, she would get a raise and he would even pay for her to take night classes at a school for legal assistants. In time, she might even learn to manage the office for him if the business grew like he expected it to. No, there wasn't much business yet—mostly drunk driving cases and some wills and some business contracts. Mr. Huggins said it was tough for lawyers to get started on their own, but lately things seemed to be getting better. "At least Mr. Huggins seemed a lot happier, and yesterday after you were here, he even came out and joked a little bit about getting rich as a sports manager, and now he's . . ."

Julie watched the girl dab a wadded tissue at her eyes. "I'm sorry, Jennifer. It happened so suddenly, and it's left a hole in your life."

"Yeah!" She sniffed. "That's just how it feels. I mean, it's not like . . . but he was my boss and all and just yesterday . . ."

"When was the last time you saw him?"

"When I left work yesterday. He stayed late a lot and dictated stuff for me to type in the mornings—correspondence and legal forms to fill in. And he said . . . he said, 'See you tomorrow.' " A new tissue was yanked from the box on her desk. "And then this morning I read about him being shot and all."

"It's very difficult, Jennifer."

"I mean, do you think I did right to come down and open the office?"

"That was the right thing to do. Clients will be worried about their cases, and you'll need to bill them for any work Mr. Huggins did prior to—ah—this morning. In fact, I'm here about a case I was working on with Mr. Huggins: the American West company."

"You were working with Mr. Huggins on that?"

Julie nodded. "That's why I was here yesterday. There are a few loose ends to clear up before going ahead with the contract. The people involved will be very sorry to hear of his death, of course. Shocked and sorry for his family. But they will also need to have their work completed as soon as possible. Do you know who I might get in touch with to find out what they'd like done with their business?"

Jennifer welcomed something concrete to do. "American West Sports and Entertainment?" With another sniff and careful deliberation, she pressed keys on the computer and scanned a document. Julie moved so she could read over the young woman's shoulder.

"Here it is."

Julie was already writing down the single name on the file: Joanna Louise Gerwig. No address, telephone number, or e-mail line.

"May I see the complete file, Jennifer?"

"All the files are in Mr. Huggins's safe. This is just the billing program. And only Mr. Huggins has—had—the combination."

"Did he leave anything for you to type this morning?"

"No. The in-box was empty."

"Have the police been by to interview you?"

"No. You're the only one who's come so far. I just don't know what I should tell people when they do."

Julie patted the girl's shoulder. "It's possible the police will want to look through Mr. Huggins's files, so don't clean up his office or throw anything away. When clients call, tell them that Mr. Huggins is deceased and they should contact another lawyer and ask that lawyer to call you for their files. And be sure to tell them you will bill them for any pending charges." She added, "And keep close account of your own time, Jennifer—your salary will have to come from the estate when the office is liquidated."

She thought about that. "Do you think I'll get paid this week?"

"Do you know how much is in the office accounts?"

"No. Mr. Huggins takes—took—care of the finances."

"I'm sure there will be enough money in the corporate account and in office equipment to cover routine expenses such as your salary. But do keep a careful record of what you do and the days you work, just to be sure." She added, "And you might look to see if Mr. Huggins made out a will." Except a lot of lawyers never got around to making out their own wills.

"I don't have a letter of recommendation, either. I don't know what I'll do for another job."

"You have some experience now, Jennifer. That should help."

"I hope so." She looked around, more tears trembling in her eyes. "I liked working here. I hope I can get another job in a law office."

Julie hoped so, too. She handed the young woman a business card. "Here's my card if you have any more questions. Call any time, Jennifer. And if anyone asks about American West, please tell them to call me at this number."

Back at the office, Julie dialed Detective Wager who told her he wasn't the one who caught the Huggins homicide. "That was Ashcroft. He's off duty. Was the victim another one of your customers?"

"No."

"Well, now he fits the definition of a lawyer you can trust."

"That's almost funny, Officer Wager. I never realized you knew any jokes. But here's why I'm asking about him: he may have been involved with local wrestling promotions—just like Palombino."

"Oh?" Then, "Tell me more, Julie. In fact, tell me everything."

She explained about the negotiations between American

West and the FWO. "I haven't yet talked with Schmanski. I wanted to learn a little more about Huggins's murder first."

"Schmanski. One of Chertok's frequent visitors, right? On that list you gave me?"

"You're sharp today, Gabe."

"Our fair city's in safe hands. What's Schmanski's tie to Chertok?"

"They both work for the FWO. Have you come up with anything on the other names?"

"For some reason I just haven't gotten around to it, Julie. All those donut breaks . . ."

"I understand. And I know you will call the instant you do find something. But I just gave you a possible link to Palombino. Is there anything you can tell me about the Huggins case?" In the silence that followed her questions, Julie could imagine the homicide detective leaning back to gaze at the ceiling, lips pursed to ponder a decision.

"Huggins isn't my case, understand? So all I have is what's known around the office."

"That's more than I've got."

"Damn well should be. Anyway, the victim was found lying beside his car about eleven p.m. by a couple of transients cutting through the railroad yards. Shot twice in the chest, but you'll have to pump Ashcroft for the ballistics report. He thinks it was a robbery—victim's wallet empty, no watch or rings. The usual. Could be that, or the transients took what they could before reporting him. The time of death was probably between eight and ten p.m., but the autopsy's not in yet, and I don't have access to it—ask Ashcroft. No leads that I know of. Again, ask Ashcroft."

"Huggins's car was still there?"

"That's affirmative. Towed to the impound lot and forensics is working on it. Maybe finished by now. Ask Ashcroft."

"Any papers or other documents found with him?"

"I don't know and you know who to ask, right?" Then, "You looking for something specific?"

"More information on American West. I'm having trouble finding out who the principals are."

"Ashcroft will be back in tomorrow." Wager added, "And don't mention my name to him, OK? Let us not leap merrily to the assumption that the Huggins case is related to the Palombino case. I'll keep the possibility in mind, but right now they're separate and I want to keep it that way unless something definite comes up."

Her father had told Julie about the long history of animosity between Wager and Ashcroft. In fact, between Wager and almost everyone else in the PD. "My solemn word, Detective Wager."

"Your solemn silence is worth more—unless you're talking to me."

Julie could not find a Joanna Louise Gerwig or a J. L. Gerwig in the online telephone books or on other computer sources. If the woman lived outside the metro area, Julie would have to call Bernie. The paper hunter's telephone recorder took Julie's request for a search on that name. Then she telephoned Schmanski.

"I read about it. I don't know what the hell we're going to do now, Miss Campbell. Huggins was the only person I ever talked to on the deal."

"Did he ever mention a Joanna Louise Gerwig?"

" . . . No."

"Did he ever drop any other names connected with American West?"

"No. If he did, I wouldn't be so worried. I mean we're talking a big commitment here, and major promotions and venues. I'm all set to go with rental deposits, scheduling, advertising, printing—all that has to be set up—public relations stuff, advertising space. The whole schmear, and it takes time. Now I got to wait to hear from people I don't even know!"

"If you do hear from anyone, would you call me, please?" She gave the man her pager number. "Any time, day or night."

"What's so important about this for you?"

"My editor's excited about local wrestling and he wants to get the story before anyone else does. He's afraid Mr. Huggins's death might draw the attention of the competition to the subject." It was the best lie Julie could come up with on the spur of the moment.

But the idea of competition worked. "Oh. Yeah. I see. All right—anything I hear, I'll let you know. Your back and my back, they both itch, right?"

Julie allowed as that was true.

The message coming through the telephone speaker was for Raiford, and the voice was Salazar's. "George tells me you're ready for some exposure already. That's good—real good—you're doing what I tell you, and now you'll be pulling in some money. So I got you set up for a demo match. Get down to Tanks-A-Lot today—right now—and get your outfit. I already picked it out for you. All you got to do is give them your name and pay for it. Just tell them you're the one Mr. Salazar said was coming in today. Then be at the gym by three."

Julie glanced at the wall clock. "You're going to be pushed for time, Dad."

At lunch, they had discussed the Huggins murder and what it might mean. And though they hadn't come to any conclusions about its relevance, they did decide what to do next. Julie, while waiting to hear from Bernie, would keep digging into InterMountain EnterPrizes for any possible connections to Lidke. Raiford would again interview the wrestlers who had been at the gym on the day of Palombino's murder for anything they might have remembered since or forgotten to tell Julie.

He, too, glanced at the clock. "Shouldn't be any problem. I'll swing by Rocky Ringside on the way to Tanks-A-Lot."

"Does Touchstone get a percentage of your ring earnings?"

"What earnings? Everybody I talk with takes a percentage of me. I'm beginning to feel like a twelve-slice pizza."

"Your manager says you'll be making money, and your partner says you're ready for exposure."

Her father's expression was odd. "Yeah, well, exposure . . ."

"What's that mean?"

"Nothing. Just don't count on seeing me in the ring."

Julie stared in surprise as her father marched out and closed the door emphatically.

Among the routine correspondence and bills in the day's mail was the printout of Chertok's credit rating. It was brief—the sheet listed no credit cards, and the only borrowing was a home loan that had payments of almost $1,500 a month. No notices of delinquency. It was, Julie noted, the history of a man who paid most of his bills in cash and who didn't leave a paper trail for the IRS. She filed it in the manila folder bearing Chertok's name and turned to the yet-unopened envelopes in the morning mail. One of the things that never showed up in movies or detective stories was a hard-hitting, hard-drinking private eye filling out a questionnaire from her local professional organization about whether she preferred that the Yellow Pages list her business under "Detectives," "Investigators," or both. Julie marked "all of the above" and sealed that return envelope. The next was another bill: Bernie Riester's fee for a Data Report on Mammoth Productions, and four Criminal Conviction History searches in Denver and neighboring counties and in Colorado state records for Chertok. The total wasn't too bad—at least not more than Touchstone's current bank balance could cover.

She finished writing out the check and was logging the expenses when the telephone rang. The voice was Bernie's assistant to tell her that Paul Arnold Procopio had an arrest record with the Chicago and Cook County law enforcement agencies. Convictions included one count of receiving stolen goods and one as a repeating professional gambler. The last felony conviction (gambling) had been six years ago. He had also served time in Cook County Jail and in Joliet. He was on the habitual criminal list but was not on parole, having served his full three-year sentence before being released two years ago. "A full sentence means he probably got in trouble in prison, Miss Campbell. They're so overcrowded that they routinely give early release on nonviolent convictions." He added, "In fact, I'm surprised they even sent him up on gambling— that's not an offense against person or property. He must have crossed somebody important on a bet or something."

"That or they took his Colorado record into account. Did you find any connection to Rudy Towers, or to Palombino?"

"No, ma'am. And, apparently, the Central City property you were interested in is free and clear of any liens. There's no record of any bank or lending firm involved with the transaction, either. So the purchasers probably paid cash."

"That's a lot of cash."

"More than I've got in the bank."

More than most people had in the bank—and given banks lately, that was probably a good thing. It was also a possible way for somebody to launder that large amount of money. "Anything on Gerwig?"

"Not yet. We've checked credit listings, city directories, and vehicle, birth, and death records, county recorders, schools. It would help if you had a birth date or a last known address."

"If I had that, I could probably find her myself."

"We'll do our best."

The telephone chirped again as she was about to leave for the InterMountain EnterPrizes office armed with clipboard, questionnaire, and lapel badge identifying her as an agent for J & J Marketing and Advertising Research. It was her father.

"Julie—Lidke's closing his gym."

"Quitting?"

"One of the guys here said Lidke told him he was selling out. Said the new buyers would honor their gym subscriptions, and they'd be the ones promoting local matches. Guess who the buyer is."

"Not American West!"

"How'd you guess?"

20

Lidke didn't want to talk to Julie. "American West holds all the cards. A couple days ago they made me an offer I couldn't refuse. So I sold. That's all there is to it. That all right with you, Miss Campbell?"

"Who did you deal with?"

"Some lawyer. Huggins, Muggins, whatever. He sent the papers, I signed, the courier witnessed, and he took them back before the ink was dry."

"Did anyone threaten you, Mr. Lidke?"

"No."

"Are you satisfied with what they gave you?"

"What they gave me? What they gave me!" When he spoke again, his voice was calmer but still tense. "What they gave me was a chance to stay in the game. That's it: I'm still in wrestling. It's just not my promotion no more. All right? That's what they gave me. And seeing as it's my life, I'd like to get on with it."

The telephone went silent. Julie punched in Schmanski's number.

"That so? Bought him out?" Schmanski's voice showed mild interest. "I don't know that it makes any difference to me. Just means American West's got the region sewed up now. Means we picked the right local promotion to go with." He added, "If we ever hear from anybody."

"No one's been in touch with you yet?"

"Naw. I keep calling Huggins's office. His damn secretary keeps telling me I should get another lawyer and she'll turn the files over to him. I mean, I try to tell her our deal don't work that way, but I don't think she's got all the horsepower she needs to run her motor, you know?"

"Settling the office's accounts is a big responsibility—I'm sure she's afraid of making a mistake. Will you call me as soon as you hear from someone at American West?"

"Sure, sure. If I hear." He asked, "Say, who made the deal with Lidke?"

"Huggins."

"Yeah. Figures. No bad-mouthing the dead, and all, but I wish the dumb son of a bitch had left a note who to get in touch with in case of emergencies. And who to give the damn files to! The rest of us got lives to live, you know? I thought lawyers were paid to think of those things. You know, contingencies."

Julie said she knew. Then she headed across downtown on

Seventeenth for the offices of InterMountain EnterPrizes. It was on the third floor behind a door with an old-fashioned panel of frosted glass. The decor of the reception area featured a high ceiling, the odor of stale cigarette ashes, and a secretary with a very prominent chest that formed a rest for long curls of auburn hair. She looked startled as the door opened.

"Help you?" Her defensive tone belied the words, but Julie smiled and flashed a clipboard with an official-looking questionnaire.

"I'm with Information and Advertising Marketing and Research. The Greater Chamber of Commerce is doing a survey of new businesses in the area to see what they need by way of support. InterMountain EnterPrizes is a newly chartered corporation, isn't it?"

"I think so. I just started working here last month." She stuffed a magazine beneath the typing shelf of her desk. The computer slowly writhed with the bright geometric forms of a screen saver. An open door showed a second office with a desk that looked unused.

"Who may I speak with about your company's needs?"

"Nobody's here but me right now." She relaxed enough to smile back. "That's why you, like, scared me when you came in."

Julie smiled and nodded. "The Greater Chamber of Commerce is very eager to do what it can to help new businesses get off to a good start." She flourished a ballpoint pen over the clipboard. "I could come back later, but it would really be helpful if you could answer a few questions for me now." She went on without waiting for assent. "What's your employer's name, please?"

"Mr. Hensleigh." She spelled it.

"Thank you. First name?"

"Ron."

"And your name?"

"Malena Hays." She spelled that, too.

"An unusual name, Malena, and lovely, too. Any other people work in the office?"

"Just Ron, right now." Her voice dropped as if the empty room might hold listening ears. "I mean we haven't done much business since I been here. Ron says we're, like, in the development stage."

"Perhaps you can tell me about that."

As the secretary talked, Julie showed she was paying close attention by nodding often and making little *mmm* noises. Ron Hensleigh was only in the office a few hours each day, but he'd recently told Malena that things would be picking up very soon. As to what kind of business Hensleigh and InterMountain were in, it had something to do with finances and venture capital. But all she did was answer the telephone whenever it rang, which wasn't a lot, and it was always for Ron, anyway, and if he wasn't there, the caller just hung up— no messages. She did sometimes type a letter, but there wasn't much of that, either. In fact, working here was pretty boring so she brought along a lot of magazines and Ron didn't seem to mind. He paid regularly, which was the most important thing, wasn't it? And if she didn't have to work very hard to get paid, that was okay with her and seemed okay with him, too. But it was a little boring just the same. Time went faster when you had something to do and you, like, felt better about doing something, you know? But Ron said he wanted her here eight hours a day. Said clients could start visiting anytime, and besides he liked to see her when he came into the office. He was that way, always joking about how pretty she was, but she figured he was married, you know? And she wasn't about to get tangled up in anything like that, and Ron wasn't really pushy or anything, just, like, hinting, you know? Mr. Procopio? He's not a client, but he comes in sometimes—in fact, Ron said he could use his office. Sort of share it when he needed to, and she was supposed to help him with anything he needed, but he hadn't asked her to do any work yet. All he did was make some calls from Ron's phone. Mr. Pfeifer gave her a letter to type now and then, but he didn't come around much, either. He's the corporation secretary and legal expert. He has another office somewhere else, and Malena guessed most of what he did went on there. Mr. Chertok dropped by now and then, usually when Ron was here, and sometimes brought Mr. Morrow. Malena liked that because then they all went out to lunch and usually took her along. To some really nice places. One afternoon Mr. Chertok even brought his own secretary along and she and Ron and them went out for drinks, kind of like a double date, Ron said.

"You all had a good time?"

"Oh, sure! Mr. Chertok's a real kick—he knows funny stories about everybody!"

"And did you and Mr. Chertok's secretary get along?"

"What? Oh—sure. She's kind of quiet, is all. But real pretty."

"Is Mr. Morrow the state representative?"

"I don't know. He's really full of himself, I know that. And Ron wants me to be especially, like, nice to him, and we always go to good restaurants when he comes, so I guess I get paid for it." She made a little face.

"You don't like him?"

"Well, he's old! And you just know he's married. And you know what he wants, too."

"What does Ron say about that?"

"He just laughs and says to be friendly to him because it's important to the company. But that's all I'm going to be!"

"Do you ever have dealings with sports figures?"

"Sports figures? You mean like football players?"

"Or wrestlers. Or wrestling organizations."

"God, no. What would we do that for?"

It was a good question and one that Julie didn't see any answer to. She finished jotting something on the questionnaire and thanked Malena for her help. As Julie closed the door, the almost empty office seemed even colder.

Raiford hauled his wrestling tights up his waist and peeked through the tent flap at the small ring he and the others on the card had set up in the late-afternoon sunshine of the mall's parking lot. A bright banner stretched against the yellow bricks of a ComputerLand store said "Fairview Mall

Crazy Bargain Days" and another announced "The Mall Fall Show—Live Wrestling Demonstration 3 PM!" Behind him, in the trapped heat and oily smell of the closed canvas, the other five wrestlers also suited up. Their talk was a low mumble against the tootling music from a small kiddie carnival on the other side of the large and crowded parking area. The wrestlers were all from Salazar's stable, lesser lights still working on their image and audience appeal. But all were more experienced than Raiford and were scheduled to play two different names and costumes. Salazar said it would be too much of a gamble to give two shows to a cherry, and besides, this was a fixed-fee performance and there would be no double pay to somebody as new as Raiford. Other than George, the other wrestlers didn't have much to say to him except for a nod or a brief—and challengingly strong—handshake.

Raiford and George were scheduled for the grand finale where the Death Command would wrestle the Sicilian Brothers in the performance's only tag-team demonstration. They would have fifteen minutes in the ring, George told him. The script called for two pairs of matches each before the final free-for-all. In the first, Major Mayhem faced Don Leone for three minutes. The Major gets in trouble and tags out to Colonel Crush. Colonel Crush and Don Leone go through their three-minute routine. The Don gets in trouble and tags out to Capodicapi. Then Colonel Crush and Capodicapi start the third pairs match and after two minutes, the Colonel gets pulled into the corner by Don Leone. That's when Major Mayhem jumps in to rescue him while the referee argues with Don

Leone. The Major and Capodicapi have two minutes before Don Leone and the Colonel come in for the final free-for-all. When Capodicapi pins the Major, the match ends with the Colonel and the Major screaming for revenge in a rematch.

"Just take it easy and watch the signals. It won't be any different from what we been doing in the gym." A khaki uniform coat decorated with rows of campaign ribbons and gold epaulettes stretched across George's shirtless torso. He peeked through the tent flap at the crowd. "This ring's a lot smaller, so watch your flips and rolls. When we go in, make a few runs across to get the feel of it before the first routine." His voice dropped. "And keep an eye on Don Leone over there—he likes to pop cherries."

"Say what?"

"He likes to make new guys pay their dues." He tilted his head toward the hulking figure who squatted on a folding chair to lace up calf-high silver boots. The man's first appearance was as Chief Cocacoatle, the Aztec Warrior, and he was scripted to win because of the many Hispanics in the area. He glanced up to catch Raiford looking at him, and beneath the daggers of black and silver makeup marking his face, his eyes narrowed as he produced a smile that wasn't really a smile.

"Thinks he's tough?"

"He's tough enough. He's just a little psycho, is all. He believes his own hype."

"They're going to win anyway, aren't they?"

"Yeah, but that's not the point. Win, lose, that's in the script. Teaching humility to new guys, that's the point."

"What about Capodicapi? Is he a basket case, too?"

"Doug Trujillo. No, he's a nice guy. He plays a rule breaker and all-around bad dude, but he'll work with you to put on a good show."

The nice guy was stretching a black mask across his head and tugging the eyeholes straight with his thumbs. A long ponytail of black hair swung across his broad back.

"I hope I can remember the script."

"I'll remind you when we meet in the corner. Just concentrate on the hand signals. That's what you don't want to forget. You only got ten to remember. You got them down?"

"We went through them enough times."

"Well, don't get excited and forget—it happens. This is just a teaser show, and it's short. There's no juicing, no high spots, no big story lines to develop. Watch how we do it in the early matches. Look for our signs and pay attention to our timing. When you get in the ring, just think of it like being in the gym. All we're doing is building up an audience for the big shows coming."

"OK."

George was apparently worried that his partner would have stage fright. "It's only a small crowd—Salazar's drumming up local audiences and giving us some live practice. If today goes right, and no reason why it shouldn't, we could have a match with some people from that new promotion. A live audience is just what you need."

"American West? The one Rocky Ringside sold out to?"

"I don't know. Salazar just said something about dealing

with some local outfit. But you just keep your mind on today. Put on a good show, and let's see how the fans react to Major Mayhem."

By the time the tag teams entered the ring, there weren't many fans left. Thirty, maybe fifty people, mostly male and mostly young, stood with their backs to the lowering sun and squinted up as Colonel Crush and Major Mayhem climbed through the ropes.

After posing briefly, they stripped off their uniform coats with their medals, ribbons, and epaulettes and tossed them to the equipment manager waiting beside the ring. Then George nodded at Raiford. They began roaring and thudding at each other's shoulders and arms, then ran across the platform like enraged bulls. Raiford, counting the steps from side to side, flung himself against the ropes to test their resiliency and somersaulted on the canvas to get the size of the bouncing deck. He tried telling himself that it was no different from running onto a football field, except that the crowd was a lot smaller, there were only two on a team, and he was almost naked. He followed George's lead, flexing and strutting around the ring, bellowing noises at the uplifted faces gaping and grinning, and—in the back of his mind—he was glad he hadn't told Julie about this. Because if he had, he knew damned well whose face would be smiling up from ringside.

The announcer, voice rising to an amplified scream that drew more audience from the kiddie show, heralded the Sicilian Brothers. The two ran from the tent and scrambled hotly through the ropes screaming what sounded like Italian:

"Muerto al cabroni . . . pizzaroni onna capo! Bomba il vaticano!" The referee tried to hold them back until the bell rang, but Don Leone lunged across the canvas to drive his shoulder into the back of an unsuspecting Major Mayhem and send him whipping against the ropes. A stitch of ripped muscle stung along Raiford's ribs as he clung to the bouncing elastic.

George's voice hissed in his ear. "Sell it—sell the pain!" From the corner of his eye, Raiford saw Colonel Crush straight-arm Don Leone who staggered back across the ring and into his partner.

Raiford didn't have to do much acting. His breath grunted in shallow gasps, and he tried to twist the pain out of his back as he hung on the rope. Don Leone flung off his cape and lunged again across the small and crowded ring, eyes wide and staring at Raiford and mouth open in a snarl of hatred.

Raiford dropped to one knee and swept his other leg forward to tangle Leone's feet. The impetus twisted the man awkwardly as he tried to catch himself. Shoving off the canvas with both feet planted solidly, Raiford drove a sharp, solid punch that had his full weight behind it. His fist sank to the wrist in Leone's thick middle, and the man's eyes bulged and shot red. Then his mouth rounded with a sour puff of breath as he stared unseeing across the parking lot. Grunting short, futile attempts to suck air, he collapsed to his knees, arms wrapped around his middle, head bobbing as he gasped. Pushing the referee aside, Major Mayhem locked an arm around the man's thick neck and thudded his skull against the booming canvas deck. "You want to play games?" The rage in his voice was not pretense.

Capodicapi, diving off the ropes from his corner, wrapped his arms around Raiford's chest and heaved back. "Let him go," he grunted. "Take it easy."

Colonel Crush fell on Capodicapi as Raiford clung to Don Leone's neck.

Capodicapi whispered, "I'll drag you to the corner. Kick out when we're there."

A pale and sweating Don Leone still struggled to breathe as Capodicapi hauled on Major Mayhem. Roaring, Colonel Crush staggered back from an elbow by Capodicapi as Major Mayhem was dragged from a still grunting Don Leone. Capodicapi lifted a writhing Major Mayhem from the canvas and plunged him back down, his feet crashing against the deck. Swinging his torso away, Major Mayhem muttered, "You tell that asshole he pulls any more shit, I'll unscrew his head from the waist up." The Major twisted and kicked out. Capodicapi bellowed and stumbled as Major Mayhem butted Capodicapi's chest, staggering him backward to trip over the still woozy Leone who was trying to haul himself away from a growling Colonel Crush.

The referee stepped in to push the wrestlers to their corners so he could start the match. Raiford saw Capodicapi say something to his partner. Leone, ashen face slick with sweat, nodded. He didn't meet Raiford's glare. For the rest of the match, Don Leone remained at arm's length as they went through the falls. When the referee ended the free-for-all by lifting the Sicilian Brothers' hands, a voice carried through the spatter of applause and boos from the small crowd. "Aw man, what a bunch of fakes!"

In the tent, George toweled off as much sweat as he could before gingerly putting on his street clothes. "I detest gigs that don't have a shower!" Then he wagged his head. "You did all right, partner. For the first time, anyway. Work on the hand signs and especially the timing. Get into the throws faster. And learn to act hurt. You got to sell the pain, you know? That's what people come to see. But for your first time, it was real good."

Raiford winced at the torn muscle along his ribs that was beginning to stiffen as his body cooled. His shirt snagged on sweaty, scuffed patches of stinging skin, and he, too, wished for a hot shower. But he found himself absurdly pleased at George's words. Capodicapi looked across the dimly lit tent to give him a thumbs-up. Don Leone was busy wiping off greasepaint and did not look around.

Julie closed the office around seven without hearing from her father. In the last week, he had grown almost silent about his wrestling career. All he would say was that he was going to the gym to work out, or he was going to watch a practice match. It wasn't as if he were hiding information; rather, there simply seemed to be nothing to report. But there was none of the impatient grumbling he usually had for these slack and unprofitable times that came with most cases. Instead, he seemed preoccupied. And, Julie had to admit, that was better than having him restless and irritable.

Neither had she heard from Mr. Stephens of Technitron. By now, that company should have announced its choice of a security agency, and with Stephens she felt that no news was bad news. She had spent a lot of time calling together a team of agents and specialists who were holding open a few days in case the contract came through. Rob Haney said that he had other jobs pending that could be delayed, but only for a short time. And now that short time was nearing its end. Julie wouldn't blame Rob or any of them if they preferred a bird in the hand rather than waiting for one in the bush.

It was possible, of course, that Stephens was using the Touchstone Agency's proposal for lowering the Wampler bid. It wasn't ethical, but it wasn't illegal, either. And, Julie reminded herself as she drove down the alley toward her garage, they had no choice but to wait.

She paused while the garage door lifted, then eased forward over the lip of concrete that marked the garage floor. She was almost past the doorjamb when she heard the shot. It was the flat pop of a hand weapon with a short barrel, and it came from her right, from a part of the alley she'd just driven through. At the same instant that her ears and mind registered the sound, she also knew that the sniper had missed because she was still alive to hear the noise. She killed the engine, jerked open the door, and plunged headfirst toward the concrete. Pulling her legs from the narrow space under the dash, she dragged herself on elbows toward the rear wheel and the open garage door. As usual, she was unarmed. Denver was not an open-carry city, and licenses for concealed arms were hard to get even for PIs, so Julie rode with her weapon in the trunk of her vehicle. The challenge now, of course, was to get to it.

Sliding along the gritty coldness of the cement floor onto the gravel of the alley, she listened for the sound of another shot or, worse, footsteps running toward the garage. The only noises were the yap and howl of neighboring dogs startled into barking, and the voices of a television program behind one of the fences. Low against the curve of the rear fender, Julie reached up to blindly lift the hatchback's handle. The latch clicked and she shoved the door up slightly, hand groping into the wall recess for the pistol wrapped in its small towel. A crackling noise made her lower the door quickly to turn off the dome light and, one eye peeking past the rear bumper, she saw down the alley a lightless car slowly backing toward her. The silhouette of a hunched head and shoulder leaned out of the driver's window. It was too dark to glimpse more than the lumpy figure, and as Julie rolled back into her garage, the muzzle flash blinded her and she felt the hair on the side of her head lift suddenly and heard the thunk of a round tear through a board. It whined up into the night sky. The dogs' frenzied barking reached a higher pitch and from one of the back porches a bright light flashed across a lawn and a man's voice called, "What's going on out there!"

Julie blinked rapidly to clear the blossoming red and yellow glare from her eyes. But all she could see was a quick flash of brake lights and the shadowy car spinning its wheels to spit gravel in a frantic sprint down the alley. She ran a few steps after it, the still-wrapped pistol in her hand. But the vehicle was gone, rocking in a fast turn at the street. Its tires squealed on macadam as the engine rapped hotly and it disappeared.

"Hey—what's going on?"

In the dark, a man's shadowy head poked over his fence. "That you, Miss Julie? You OK?" The dog, somewhere at the bottom of the fence, barked excitedly.

A deep breath controlled most of the shakiness in her voice. "Some prankster, I think, Mr. Poletta."

"Sounded like shooting to me. You want I should call the police?" He spoke toward his feet. "Hush, Scooter. Hush now."

"No. It was just a car backfiring. It's gone now."

"Scared the heck out of Scooter."

"Me too—don't worry. And tell Mrs. Poletta there's nothing to worry about."

"You're sure, now?"

"Yes. Thank you."

"OK." The dog gave one last indignant bark. Mr. Poletta's silhouette turned back toward the lit porch.

And Julie, looking down the black alley to where the car had disappeared, ran a finger over her still tingling scalp and slowly became aware of the chill stiffness that had gathered along her spine.

21

"Did you get a look at him?"

"Not him, not his car." Julie drew a deep breath and let it out slowly so its nervous sound would not go over the telephone to her father. The bullets had missed. *You don't worry about the ones that missed—it's the next one coming you want to focus on.* When she had been a little girl, she'd heard her father's voice in the living room say that to some guest. The wry laughter of both male voices had been punctuated by the clink of ice in their glasses. "What about you, Dad? Anyone giving you trouble?"

Raiford tried to control his breathing, to let the shock of her news drain away and his pulse slow. "Nothing as exciting as your adventure. What about Chertok's secretary—have you checked on her?"

"I called just after it happened. She's fine." Julie had not told Caitlin the reason for her call. "I didn't file a police report. They'll never find the slugs, and it's not worth the time and paper. But if he's after me, he might come after you."

"He's after you, Julie. It has to be the same guy who followed you from Ms. Morgan's house, and this time it wasn't just a warning." He interpreted the telephone's silence as agreement. "Maybe you should back away from this—"

"Dad."

He knew that had been the wrong thing to say even as he spoke. "Please don't be stubborn, Julie. I'm very worried."

"It worries me, too, Dad. But it also warns me. I will be careful. But if I can't handle something like this, I shouldn't be in the business."

Raiford sighed. "We've been sticking our noses pretty deep into Chertok's business," he hinted.

Julie had been considering that fact. "Maybe it's time to dig a little deeper."

"Things are already stirred up enough!"

"What things? And why? We don't know, do we?"

"If you're thinking of calling the Gaming Commission, it probably won't do any good. They've had eight months to check out InterMountain for their license. If anything has been found, they would have rejected the application already."

She had been thinking about the state Gaming Commission—once again, her father's thoughts and hers ran parallel—but his angle of vision was not exactly hers. "I can do it quietly." It wasn't what but how she intended to do it quietly that would worry her father. So she said nothing about it.

Julie pursued it the next morning with a call to the news department of the *Denver Post*. "Gargan? It's Julie Campbell."

The reporter's voice took on a note of warmth. "The lovely Julie! Please tell me you're hungering for my body!"

"Sorry, Gargan. I'm on a low-fat diet."

"Ouch!"

"But I do have a story that might interest you."

"Everything you have interests me. Now tell me you've solved our fair city's latest homicide, much to the chagrin and embarrassment of our legal minions."

Julie had met Gargan when he was writing a series on the private security business. His slant had been that the phenomenal growth of the industry was due to ineptness and waste in police departments around the country, and particularly in Denver. Fortunately, Gargan was among the many people despised by Denver Homicide Detective Gabe Wager, so it had not taken too much effort to convince Wager that comments about any lack of ability among Denver's finest had been Gargan's and not hers. "How about organized crime moving into Black Hawk and Central City."

There was a short pause. "Tell me more."

"Ever hear of Sid Chertok?"

"Who hasn't?"

She told Gargan about the man's Chicago background and his shadowy financial ties to mob-run businesses.

"Any evidence that the mob's financing this project?"

"Only a hint or two. But it's worth a closer look." She added, "That's a lot of start-up cash to come up with on a fairly risky project."

The telephone was silent again. Then Gargan began talking more to himself than to Julie. "They just had a big merger up there. . . . Two of the biggest casinos were bought up by a third—some outfit from Texas . . . 'Arizona Bullion,' I think they're called." Then to Julie, "But Chertok himself seems clean, right?"

"Has to be, to get a license. But he does spend time with one Paul Procopio." She spelled the name and listed the extent of that man's experience with the legal system.

"Evidence?"

"Bernie Riester: public documents and news files."

Bernie's name stirred only Gargan's professional jealousy. "Well, that's something I can check out. But Chertok can always claim he didn't know anything about Procopio's record." He asked, "Does this Procopio have any official position with InterMountain?"

"Not on paper. But the office secretary says he comes in on a regular basis and uses the office telephone. My guess is he's the mob rep. Keeps an eye on the books."

"But Ron Hensleigh's never been connected in any way with organized crime."

"Neither has the Honorable Roger A. Morrow."

"The state senator? What's he have to do with this?"

"He's also a frequent visitor to InterMountain's offices."

"Has he ever been seen with Procopio?"

"I hear they all have lunch occasionally."

"Witnessed?"

"Not by me," Julie had to admit. "But if they go to a public place . . ."

"Yeah. But everybody's got to eat, even senators." Gargan spoke to himself again. "Central City, Black Hawk. Both towns have gone through half a dozen mayors. They keep getting involved in sweet real estate deals with casinos."

"They can't do that?"

"Not while they're in office—conflict of interest. But that's where the money is—and a lot of it." He added, "And both towns are in State District Thirteen."

"Morrow's district?"

"Yeah. But the prohibition applies only to city officials, so a state senator can make deals with whoever. And Morrow's on the Senate Transportation Committee." The line was quiet again. "All right—I smell smoke, but I don't see any fire yet. I'll dig around a little and see what I can find out."

That was all Julie wanted from the reporter who was not noted for his discretion. "If I run across anything else, I'll let you know."

"Thanks, Julie. I owe you dinner and drinks—how soon do you want to collect?"

"When you win the Pulitzer."

"That's a definite date!"

It certainly was: never. She hung up and gazed out the tall, arched window and thought. InterMountain was now threatened with publicity, and if Chertok was behind the shooting, the heat might make him call off the assailant. But even if it didn't work, it felt good to go on the offensive—against anyone. Which is what she told her father when he came into the office later in the morning.

The big man leaned against the wall near the window, holding his body stiff as if nursing a sore back or a pulled muscle somewhere. He wore a sweat suit and had a towel wrapped around his neck. Patches of dark told Julie that he had just done his five-mile run, but the exercise had not lessened his concern. "Suppose it doesn't work that way, Julie? Suppose Chertok's not behind the assaults on you? Suppose his feelings get hurt and he wants to get even?"

"Dad, he'll be too busy putting out that fire to worry about us. And speaking of being busy, what have you come up with?"

Raiford told her what he'd found out from George and the other wrestlers on last night's card. "In short, Salazar's working on a program to develop local names."

"Taking over Lidke's idea?"

"Taking over his wrestlers, too. And just like Lidke dreamed, it could turn into big bucks. But it will be the FWO circus, not the Greco-Roman wrestling Lidke wanted." Raiford slowly twisted his torso and winced. "You know, Julie, if it wasn't Chertok who sent somebody after you, maybe it was somebody in American West."

"Why?"

"Maybe there's something in the American West contract that Lidke might challenge." Raiford shook his head.

"There has to be some strong reason why someone would try to kill you—someone is really worried about what we're doing."

Julie leaned back in her swivel chair and stared at him for a long moment. Then she pushed one of the memory buttons on the telephone. Bernie Riester was out of town on another of her speaking engagements, but her assistant told Julie that they had not yet found anything on Joanna Louise Gerwig. "We can expand the search, if you want us to, Miss Campbell."

The cost of which would not be covered by any client's bill because there wasn't any client. "Keep digging, please." She hung up and rattled the computer keys for the telephone number of the Columbine Arena. John Hernandez answered and Julie identified herself. "Just one question, Mr. Hernandez—"

"Why the hell should I talk to you?"

"Because what you say might help clear up a couple of murders."

"What?"

"Murders. I'm very serious. Two people have been murdered. Now, you told me you received a call before I visited you. That person advised you not to rent to Rocky Ringside Wrestling, am I right?"

"Goddamn it, I already told you—"

"It's all right, Mr. Hernandez. I'm not working for Rocky Ringside anymore. Their business has been sold to American West. Was it someone who said they spoke for Mr. Chertok?"

"I ain't said anybody—"

"You said it was a woman. You said she told you that Rocky Ringside's insurance was not comprehensive. Did she at any time mention Mr. Chertok's name? My guess is she did not. Am I right?"

Julie thought the man's silence confirmed her guess.

"Chertok's a big name, Mr. Hernandez. He carries a lot of weight in the booking business. I can understand your reticence. But if his name was not mentioned, it will not harm him to say so. It can only help him, in fact." She waited, but the man remained silent. "Two murders, Mr. Hernandez. Two men leaving behind wives and children. Do you have any idea who did call you?"

"His secretary."

That wasn't what Julie expected to hear. "Chertok's secretary?"

"That's right, Miss Know-It-All. Said I shouldn't waste my time contracting with Rocky Ringside because their insurance was no good. Told me to hold off because there would be a new and better local promotion looking for an arena on an exclusive basis."

"His secretary? She said she was Chertok's secretary?"

"Yeah."

"Thank you, Mr. Hernandez." Julie slowly placed the receiver on the cradle and stared at her father.

It couldn't have been Caitlin Morgan. Julie didn't think it could have been the woman. But her father asked "Why not?" and Julie had no answer.

"Think about it, Julie. Chertok hears about some possible deal between the FWO and American West. He wants to protect the FWO's future interest in any local productions. Hey—suppose Chertok is American West! Suppose he put together American West when he heard that the FWO was looking for a local affiliate?"

"I just don't have the feeling she's been lying."

"This game is full of good liars, Julie."

That was true.

"Or maybe she told you only as much as Chertok wanted her to tell you. It's a good-paying job, right? She doesn't want to lose it."

"But why have her tell me anything at all?"

"So he can control what you know. And," Raiford added, "through his secretary, he finds out where you are with the Lidke case." He asked, "Does his secretary know that I'm with Salazar?"

"No."

"I haven't been shot at, have I?"

"But we come back to 'why,' Dad. If Chertok is with American West, then he already has the local wrestling scene sewn up. He has no need to kill Huggins or me."

"Think, Julie: the lawyer knew who the American West principals are, and you talked with him. Chertok can't know how much Huggins told you."

But the pieces still didn't fit together. "Even if Chertok is American West, it's no crime to outmaneuver your opposition or even buy it up. And Chertok needs a low profile because of his gambling venture. A casino can make as much in a week as his wrestling promotion makes in a month."

"But suppose he only gets five percent of the casino's profits versus a hundred percent of the profits from his wrestling promotion? And name me a crook who doesn't think every penny's worth grabbing. All Chertok had to do is ask a little help from Chicago. That way he doesn't know who the hit man is or even who hired him to go after you. He's clean."

"If that guy had been a professional, I wouldn't be here now."

They bickered a bit about whether a professional killer would have fired at Julie from so far away with a handgun, and whether or not he would have used a silencer. Raiford said there were dumb professional killers just like there were dumb everything else, and maybe Julie just had the bad luck to get hit on by a loser. But neither of them came up with an answer, and they both felt tired and frustrated. Like, Raiford sighed, they were trying to shovel sand uphill.

Raiford had a lunch meeting with Salazar—George called to say it was very important, and that he'd be there, too, but remember: with Salazar everything was Dutch treat. Julie struggled to focus on the routine paperwork that multiplied unaccountably. But, finally, she gave in to the thought that kept nagging at her concentration and called Chertok's office. Caitlin Morgan answered that Mr. Chertok was still out to lunch and she was free to talk.

"Has your business been good lately?"

"It's getting better. The worse the economy is, the more people seem to want entertainment." She added, "And September and October are big months on college campuses—musical acts, usually—and next spring's bookings look good, too. Why do you ask?"

"Have you dealt with the Columbine Arena?"

The line was silent a moment. "Is that the one on East Colfax?"

"Yes. Has Chertok done any business with them?"

"Not that I know of—not since I've been here. But it wouldn't surprise me if he has in the past. Sometimes he wants a smaller venue if an act might not draw well. Five hundred seats full looks better than a thousand half empty, he says."

"Have you talked with John Hernandez lately?"

"Who?"

"The manager of Columbine Arena. John Hernandez."

"No . . ."

"He says you called him recently."

"Well, perhaps at some time. But I don't remember his name."

"Caitlin, he says you advised him against renting space to Rocky Ringside Wrestling. That you told him their insurance was bad."

A long silence. "Is this an interrogation?"

"I'm only trying to find out what happened."

"If I have spoken with that man, it was very brief and unimportant. I have never advised him or anyone else about renting or not renting to anyone."

"He insists it was Chertok's secretary who called."

"I can't help what that man insists. I know what I did and did not do." She paused, then, "Thank you for your help and concern, Miss Campbell. But I don't think I wish to hear from you anymore."

It wasn't Caitlin Morgan. Julie could swear that the woman's voice held the injury of insult. Her conviction was sealed when she called Hernandez back to ask if he'd ever talked to Chertok's secretary at any other time.

"No. Why?"

"Could it have been some other woman?"

"She said she was Chertok's secretary. I didn't ask for her goddamn ID card."

"Did she leave you a number to call back?"

" . . . No. Not that I remember."

"Thank you, Mr. Hernandez." And Julie meant it.

Her next call was to Chertok's office. Caitlin answered the telephone, her tone cooling rapidly when she heard Julie's voice. "I want to apologize, Ms. Morgan. I spoke with Mr. Hernandez, and he said only that it was a woman who claimed she was Chertok's secretary. He's never spoken with you at any other time and did not recognize the caller's voice."

"I'm relieved that you believe me. Good day." The line clicked.

OK—everybody makes mistakes. And this line of business required duplicity, suspicion, distrust, a cynical probing for secret motives, and the disbelief of innocence. It was a great life if you didn't weaken. But at least Julie had tried to correct this mistake, and she felt a little better for that effort. Still, she had more than a little suspicion that in the future Ms. Morgan would be much less the cooperative operative.

Her next call was to Detective Wager.

"Hi, Julie. And before you ask, no, I haven't had time to investigate Chertok's friends, relatives, or business associates."

"That's not why I'm calling, Gabe. I just wondered if you've run a ballistics comparison on Palombino and Huggins."

"What?"

"To see if they were killed by the same weapon."

His reply gave Julie the answer. "Huggins is not my case. What do you know that you're not telling me, Julie?"

"It's not what I know; it's what I'm guessing."

"That the same weapon killed them both—I got that. But what makes you suspect the cases are linked?"

"I'm a detective, Gabe. I'm paid to suspect things."

"Don't play games, Julie. If you or your old man withhold evidence, you will have problems. Real problems. I will bring charges." The Spanish lilt came into his voice, betraying his frustration. "Now tell me what the hell is going on—everything."

"From my angle, the two killings seem connected, that's all. It's an idea based on a guess based on a feeling. You know how that is: it's a thought that might lead somewhere, but it's not strong enough for probable cause and it certainly won't hold up in court." She added, "But maybe you got the tip from a confidential informant."

After a brief pause, the detective said, "Yeah. I'll call you back."

The maître d' led Raiford to a corner table in the smoking section where George and the Cuban sat. Salazar, the level of his head somewhere below George's shoulder, looked up as they approached.

"Goddamn glad you could finally make it, Raiford!" His voice cut through the quiet conversations of neighboring tables. "It's not like I got all goddamn day to schmooze, you know what I mean?"

"Hey, be happy I'm here."

The smaller man's mouth sagged open. Raiford settled onto a chair and nodded pleasantly to George.

"Be happy! By the placenta of sweet baby Jesus! I get you one demo match and now you start telling me what to do? You are the one listens to me, Raiford! This is business—your future—the future of the Death Command, and more important, my future! By God if you—"

"Good afternoon, gentlemen. Would you care for something else to drink before ordering?" The waiter's smooth voice rode over Salazar's outburst. A startled face at the next table turned away quickly as Raiford winked at it.

"Another orange juice," said George.

"Draw me a beer," said Raiford and leaned over the shorter man. "See, Sal? I'm listening."

"By the Virgin's holy nipples . . ." He sucked a deep breath and glanced at the waiter. "Cuba libre. Double this time."

The waiter thanked them and took a long time to write the orders.

"OK." When the waiter finally left, Salazar's voice was calm. "We start all over. Forget being late, Raiford. Forget wasting my valuable time. And above all forget the wise-mouth crap. But remember this: I am the manager and if I think you're not serious about this project, you're through. Understand? Finished—finito—done for. You can be replaced tomorrow because there are a lot of people eager to be where you are!"

"Sal, believe me, I'm serious. Nobody's more serious than I am. Ask my friends—ask my mother! I gave her gray hairs because I never laughed. Raiford the Reticent, that's me. What project?"

George spoke before Salazar could explode again. "He wants to get us on this new local circuit with the American West people. That's the new outfit used to be . . . ?" He looked to Salazar for help.

"What used to be Rocky Ringside Wrestling. That is, if it's not too much bother for you, Raiford. If it doesn't interfere with your career as a comedian!"

"Tag-team matches, Jim. Pueblo, Colorado Springs, Fort Collins, Cheyenne, Casper, Rock Springs. It's a tank circuit, but it's with the FWO and it's a good start."

"Goddamn right it's a good start!"

George sipped at his orange juice, his tongue playing with

a bit of pulp hanging on his lip. "We can get a lot of ring time in front of different audiences. Open up new venues in the region and develop our product at the same time. It could be a good deal."

"Goddamn right it's a good deal! I set it up. The FWO brings in national names to headline the main event, and American West provides local talent—that's you people—to fill out the cards."

"Who'd you talk with at American West?"

"What the hell difference does that make?"

"I read in the paper where their lawyer was killed. Maybe they're not in business anymore."

Salazar's dark eyes blinked once. "I got a contract. A signed contract with American West. That's what contracts are for, in case one of the parties drops dead or changes his mind or something."

Raiford shrugged. "That's good. But who signed it? The dead lawyer?"

"Goddamn it, you think I don't know my business?" The cigar jabbed across the table. "Vic Schmanski and me, we put the deal through. We been working on it for months, wiseass. We drew up the contract and Schmanski got the signatures three weeks ago. It's signed by the principals of FWO and American West, and the American West Corporation's still alive regardless whether that lawyer's dead. You think I waste my time on spec?" Salazar leaned back in his chair. "I don't think you know what the hell I do, Raiford. And tell you the truth, I don't think you could find your own ass with both hands, either."

"The contract between American West and the FWO was drawn up three weeks ago?"

"The ink was dry three weeks ago. Now if you are totally and completely satisfied that I, Raoul Salazar, know my own goddamn business, and that this is serious enough for your consideration, I'd like to start discussing the future of the Death Command. Is that all right with you, Raiford? You know, just a few little things like your routines, product packaging, slot on the card, public relations gigs, story development. And tonight's practice with the new wrestlers so they don't break your fucking neck when you get in the ring. Nothing important, you understand, just your whole, entire, complete goddamn future!"

"Sal, my life is in your hands."

"You better goddamn believe it!"

22

Julie's father came into the office around three. She told him about Caitlin Morgan.

He considered that. "And you believe her?"

"It was the way she reacted, Dad. I really think she's telling the truth."

"It would be nice if you were right. . . . OK—let's consider that assumption. If she wasn't the one who called Hernandez, who else could it have been?"

"That's the problem, isn't it?"

"Yeah." Then, "Here's a quid pro quo: Salazar says that American West and the FWO signed a contract for local promotions three weeks ago. Which, of course, is before American West bought out Lidke."

"And before Palombino was killed!"

"Yep. If the deal was already made, why should anybody worry about Rocky Ringside? And why would anybody kill Palombino unless it really was a botched robbery?"

Julie thought about that. Her father was right: Where was the money in an outfit that was already squeezed out of the picture? No matter how much Lidke might squeal, FWO and American West could simply roll over him and Rocky Ringside. Which gave credence to Chertok's denials. But even if Chertok had been telling the truth about not viewing Lidke as viable competition, why had the promoter been so defensive? Who called the arenas to shut Lidke out? And who torched Lidke's car? "I've been looking at it from another angle, Dad." Julie told him her idea about the two murders.

"The same weapon? That's what you think?"

"Just a guess. Gabe's supposed to call when he gets the ballistics comparison back." She added, "I think some pieces are finally starting to fit together."

Raiford planted a large shoe on the window rail to gaze at the distant mountains. He whistled a faint tune through his teeth. "Yeah . . . yeah, they are. But why would he do it?"

"He wanted it all."

He whistled again. "It could mean a lot of money, all right. But with American West signed to FWO, there was nothing to get."

"Did he know that?"

"Maybe not. But there has to be a tie-in somewhere."

"It's us. For his cover."

Whistle. "But even if the bullets match, Julie, it's only circumstantial. Without a clear motive, without the weapon and a chain of possession, it's still circumstantial."

The telephone rang before Julie could address that complication. A woman responded, "This is the secretary for Edwin M. Welch, regional representative of the Wampler Agency. May I have Mr. Raiford, please?"

She could, and Julie turned on the speakerphone so the secretary could have her, too.

The line was silent for a few seconds, and then Edward M. Welch himself said how delighted he was to find Mr. Raiford in. "I know you have a busy schedule, Mr. Raiford, so I'll be brief. The Wampler Agency have been awarded the Technitron bid, and Mr. Stephens has asked me to—um—notify you. Apparently, Technitron elected experience and resources rather than mere price."

"That's their choice."

"Yes. Of course. And we believe it was a wise choice."

"We differ on that. What can I do for you, Mr. Welch?"

"Yes," the man said again. "I called to say how impressed we at Wampler have been with the thoroughness of your security survey—the discovery of the—um—minor security issue."

"It wasn't minor. Whoever set up the initial program— your agency, I believe?—made a royal screwup."

"Yes, well, that's of course your opinion. Be that as it may, I have been asked by Mr. Stephens to ascertain that the information concerning that particular issue will remain—um—

proprietary. I assured him that, as a professional with primary loyalty to a client, your discretion in the matter would be a given. However, he wishes to be reassured that such is in fact the case."

"You're asking if we intend to alert the FBI to the unsecured ducts?"

"In a word, yes. I'm authorized to assure you that any future project that may be—suitable—to your agency will, in due course, be forwarded to you from Technitron." He paused. "Conversely, should you see fit not to honor your—um—professional ethic of confidentiality, Technitron—and Wampler Agency, of course—would be forced to take such action as we deem necessary to protect our good names."

"Does that mean you people with good names found bugs in the ducts?"

"It does not."

"Right. Well, we made our report, Mr. Welch. We made it to the person who paid for it and it's his to do with what he wants. As far as we know, no laws were broken, so we have no obligation to inform the authorities."

"I'm pleased we can do business in such a professional manner, Mr. Raiford."

"We're not doing business, Mr. Welch. Our business was with Technitron, and we prefer not to do business with them any time in the future."

"Then I'm relieved we could arrive at this—um—understanding."

"I don't think you understand a damn—" But the connection was broken. Raiford dropped the receiver on its cradle and glared at Julie. "You're going to tell me I should have taken the bone Technitron tossed us?"

"Not at all."

What really grated on Raiford was the smugness in Welch's voice. In his mind's eye, he saw Stephens and Welch agreeing solemnly that, thanks to their skill and diplomacy, a potential brush fire had been averted. "You think we should make a report to the Feds?"

Julie wagged her head. "They won't find any bugs."

"You'll take Welch's word for that?"

"Any bugs Wampler might have found are gone by now. That's why they left us hanging for so long—to have time to sanitize the ducts."

His daughter was right. Welch's call had been to tie up a loose end: if Touchstone agreed to the dangled carrot, fine; if not, Technitron might lose some time hosting government inspectors and filling out papers, but there would be no evidence to support a charge of breached security. Raiford drew a long breath. "Well, we wouldn't want dirty money anyway, would we? How could I tell your grandmother I was associated with an outfit that put profit above principle? And I know my daughter wouldn't do that unless she really had to. So I'm happy with how things worked out."

"Of course you are—that's why your blood pressure's so low. Don't you have a wrestling match to go to?" Julie smiled. "You can exercise your happiness there."

Raiford explained to Julie that it was not a mere practice

but also a very important meeting between Salazar's wrestlers and the American West stable. "Salazar wants us to start working with one another. All one big happy family."

"Lidke will be there?"

"I don't know. I heard he came in as one of American West's new trainers." In the doorway, he added, "But it was pretty dark when we met in the gym's parking lot—I don't think he'll recognize me. And besides, Salazar wants to introduce a new tag team called the Death Command." Closing door behind him, he said, "People who know say they're pretty good."

Julie, in her own way, wrestled with an idea; and if Lidke was away from home, she could pursue it.

In the glow of the porch light, Mrs. Lidke stared up at her in surprised silence. Her arm held the door half open, but her thick body hid behind it. "Otto's not here."

"It's you I wish to speak with."

"Me?"

"Yes. About the burning of your car and a few other things."

"I . . . Well, Otto's not here. . . ."

"I'm sure he won't mind. He hired us, remember? May I come in?"

"I . . ."

Julie slid past the shorter woman's arm. "Thank you. Are your children home?" She smiled. "That's Patty and John, isn't it?"

"Yes." She wore a polyester pants suit that bulged at the

waist and emphasized her curved shoulders. Julie wondered if it was the onset of osteoporosis. Her legs carried her only as far as the first chair, a wingback placed at a precise angle to a coffee table that, in turn, was centered across from a love seat. Both chairs were covered with bright flower patterns that tried to make a cheery statement against the rigid silence of a blank television set and the rest of the house. Julie glimpsed the collection of her husband's photographs and trophies in the family room. But even this smaller room, which seemed to be Mrs. Lidke's space, held a few framed photographs. One featured a football player, number 51, making a jarring tackle. Among the other photographs were framed school pictures of Patty and John. Mrs. Lidke's photograph was not on display.

"I can't tell you anything. I think you should talk to Otto. I don't know why you want to talk to me."

"I tried to call him," Julie lied. "I couldn't reach him."

"Oh." Then, "Well, he's at a gym. A new one over on Colorado Boulevard." She added, "He's a trainer now—he has a new job."

"But I came to talk with you, Mrs. Lidke." Julie sat on the well-used couch and smiled at the woman. She did not smile back. Her eyes were wide with tension, and she kept rolling her lips between her teeth as if she wanted to bite them shut.

"How are Patty and John? Are they settled back in school now?"

She nodded. "They're not here. Patty's doing her homework over at a friend's house. John's at a movie."

"Good—I'm relieved that the incidents haven't disrupted their lives too much." Julie smiled again. "Your husband's a very ambitious man, isn't he?" She gestured at the photographs in the neighboring room.

"I . . . I suppose so."

"And he believed very strongly in Rocky Ringside Wrestling."

"Yes."

"And you did, too, didn't you?"

"Yes. I suppose."

"Mrs. Lidke, can you tell me where your husband was on the night of August 13?"

"When?"

Julie nodded. "I know it's hard to remember that far back. It was the night Rudy Towers committed suicide up in Central City. Was your husband at home all that evening?"

The loose skin under her chin quivered. In the street outside, a car drove past slowly. Its motor made a dull throb and its tires over the fallen leaves crackled like a small, hot fire. "He . . . I . . . Yes. Yes, he was home. All night."

Julie nodded again and smiled as if she believed the woman. "I'm glad to hear that. Have you two been married a long time?"

"Eighteen years. Going on nineteen."

"And you help Otto with his business?"

"I used to. Not much now. Just sometimes."

"You do the bookkeeping? Tax returns? Perhaps make an occasional phone call, that sort of thing?"

"He don't have time to do everything. It takes—it took—a lot of time to run the gym."

"I imagine so! Where were you two married?"

"Where?" The shift in questions surprised her. "L.A. We met out there. I was in high school and he was in the service."

"Oh? What branch?"

"Navy. He was stationed at Long Beach. We met at a rock concert. I went with some girlfriends and I met him."

"Sat next to you? Came up and introduced himself?"

She shook her head, relieved to move from questions about her husband's business, relieved to move into a past that was safe—a time when things were fixed and unthreatening. "He was in the Shore Patrol on duty. A lot of sailors went to the concerts there and the navy sent people to help keep things quiet."

"This is before he tried out for professional football?"

"Before he went to college, even. We got married and then he got discharged. He used his G.I. bill and he had a scholarship, too. For football and wrestling. San Diego State." Her eyes touched on the football photograph and Julie recognized the Aztec logo on the player's helmet. Another photograph showed a pyramid of wrestlers kneeling on one another's backs. Over them, a banner proclaimed "San Diego State University." Lidke grinned from the bottom tier with the other heavyweights. "He tried pro ball for a while after he graduated, but he wasn't big enough." She added, "They want real tall people, you know."

"Yes. You went to college with him?"

"I was a business major, but I didn't graduate. Patty came along. And then John." A shake of her head. "There wasn't time for schoolwork and family."

Julie nodded understandingly. "Did you advise your husband to sell out to American West?"

The caution and fear rushed back to make her face a stiff mask. "You got to talk to him about all that."

"Can you tell me where Otto was last Thursday night?"

"Thursday?"

"That was when the lawyer for American West was killed. Ellis Huggins."

She blinked, face pale. "I don't know what you're talking about. Maybe you better go now." Standing quickly, she jerked a commanding hand at Julie. "You better go!" She strode stiffly to the door and yanked it open. "Please!"

Julie smiled. "Have a nice evening, Mrs. Lidke."

Halfway down the block, Julie pulled to the curb to telephone Bernie's office. Her assistant answered and Julie told him to check the California Bureau of Vital Statistics for a marriage license on Otto Lidke. "It'll be eighteen or nineteen years ago. Los Angeles County, probably—Long Beach residences, most likely. Age of parties at the time probably late teens for the woman, mid-twenties for the man. I want to know the woman's maiden name. As soon as possible."

"We'll have it for you shortly."

Raiford ignored the sour odor of stale sweat rising from his unwashed wrestling tights. He hovered at the rear of the group of hefty men gathering around the practice ring and moved to stay out of Otto Lidke's sight. In the glare of the ring light, he could see changes in the man that had been invisible when they met each other in the darkness of the parking lot where Palombino was found. Lines were etched deeply around Otto's eyes and at the corners of his mouth, and he prowled uneasily as Salazar climbed through the ropes and began to talk. But with his large head and a short torso that bulged under his tights, he was, Raiford had to admit, still like his name: round at both ends.

Salazar opened the session with a long speech about how glad he was to have the opportunity to meet with the wrestlers who had been members of Rocky Ringside and were now with American West, and how glad he was that the talented and respected Otto Lidke had joined the American West promotion as a trainer, and how glad he was that everybody was now, through his—Raoul Salazar's—contacts associated with one of America's major wrestling promotions, the FWO. He pointed out how modern the Universal Fitness Center was and that promotion members would get reduced rates. Its quality was guaranteed, he said, because it was another Salazar endeavor, and Salazar could do a lot of good for the local wrestling community provided the local wrestlers paid attention to what he, Salazar, told them. Then he introduced two world-famous wrestlers from the FWO who needed no introduction and who would now put on a short demonstration of holds and falls by way of warm-up for tonight's practice: the Terrible Titan and the Beast Slayer.

The audience watched closely as the two, without their stage makeup and costumes, went through a series of throws. The men stopped often to explain the hand signals, the points, the choreography of certain throws that would ensure proper leverage. "One-two, three-four—like that, see?" The Beast Slayer glared at the intent faces outside the ropes. "You got that? Short-long, short-long, and you hit down here. You don't do the right steps on an aerial, you're going to hit up here. You hit up here, somebody's going to get hurt."

At the end of the demonstration and following a round of applause, Salazar announced American West's plans for regional wrestling and the intense schooling that was coming as preparation for careers in the FWO. "Now you people don't worry—unless you're no good, then you better worry. We're gonna have cards to fill a dozen regional venues. If you're good enough, you'll be slotted in. But we got to know if you're good enough to wrestle for us locally and maybe make it to the FWO. We got to know that our valuable time won't be wasted on pansies who can't take the program or don't want to make it to the big show. We want this promotion to start hot and get hotter, you know what I mean? So we got room for new wrestlers, all right, but we're only going to take the best." Then he announced that four talented wrestlers already chosen for the first tag teams would put on a demonstration at the end of the evening: Chief Cocacoatle and Handsome Johnny Sands, and Colonel Crush and Major Mayhem. "Right now," Salazar said, "I have a very important planning meeting to attend that will affect all our futures, so I'm turning the session over to my close friend Otto Lidke who will take each one of you into the ring and show you what kind of wrestlers American West is looking for. Let's see if you trainees got the guts to make it."

Another round of applause and the human cannonball climbed through the ropes and gestured the first trainee into the ring. "What's your name?"

The redheaded mound of beef answered, "Ray."

Lidke, almost half the younger man's size and twice his age, said, "OK, Ray, look out for yourself." He moved with blurry speed to grapple the unsuspecting man's arm and lever him into a body slam that made the watching wrestlers gasp.

"First thing you got to learn is to land right. Ray don't know that yet. Some of you others been with me, you know what it's all about. Herm"—Lidke called up another young man while Ray, his breath making little whining sounds, brokenly pulled himself out of the ring—"come up and show us how it's done."

Otto circled Herm who crouched warily and pivoted to keep facing the man.

"What we want to do is make sure you people know what the hell you're doing when you get in the ring. Understand?" Round head on round torso, Lidke talked as he moved sideways, his hands circling each other. "You get in the ring and don't know what you and your opponent's doing, somebody's career might be over. Hell, somebody's life might be over." The watching faces nodded and Lidke dropped into a quick scissors, the mat jangling with the crash of his body. Herm howled as the thick legs trapped him and he flung himself backward with a louder crash. Then they both stood.

"How'd he know what move I was going to do?" Lidke asked the surrounding faces.

A tentative voice said, "Hand signals?"

"What hand signal? What'd you see?"

No reply.

"Herm—what hand signal'd I give you?"

"Scissor kick—two hand rolls and a flat palm." He demonstrated.

"All right. You get hurt?"

Herm grinned and shook his head.

"Me neither. But it sounded good and it looked better. That's the way it should work." He gestured to another man. "OK—you: come up. Let's go through the same fall. Watch my hands for the signal, and sell the fall when you make it."

Raiford edged around the outside of the crowd and past the redhead who was still grunting and pulling his torso from one side to another to stretch out the pain. A worried friend asked, "You all right, Ray?"

"He slammed the shit out of me, man." He twisted again and winced. "Son of a bitch is short but, damn, he's fast and strong."

Raiford stood behind them to tap Herm on the arm. "You were working out at Rocky Ringside the night Joe Palombino was killed, right?"

Surprise lifted the man's eyebrows as he looked around. "How'd you know?"

"I saw your name in the newspaper as a witness."

"Oh. Well, yeah. But I left before the shooting."

"Was that before or after Otto went to get the pizza?"

"I don't know. Before, I guess. He was still there when I left. Why?"

"I know Joe's wife. She's a sweet kid. Really torn up over it. Loved the big lug, you know?"

"Oh. Yeah." He added politely, "He was a nice guy, Joe was."

Raiford nodded. Up in the ring, another pair of thick bowed legs flew in an arc against the glare of the ring light and smashed heavily. Behind the clashing sound of the canvas deck, the bell of the wall telephone jangled loudly and one of the trainees answered it. He held it high toward the ring. "It's for you, Otto. Says it's real important."

"Crap. OK, you two—go through the routine. Hand signal, timing, takedown. I'll be right back."

The short man, agile despite his appearance, hopped down from the ring apron and tucked his head into the phone's hood. Raiford asked Herm, "Did Joe or Otto act in any way strange that night?"

"Strange?" The square jaw moved a bit in thought. "I don't know about strange. Otto had a lot on his mind, I guess. He can get pretty intense, you know? Yells a lot and makes us go through the holds and escapes until we get it right. And if we don't get it right, he'll bust our balls until we do. Sometimes he gets a bit crazy about it but that's good, you know? That's what you want from a good trainer."

Another thought. "But he did seem kind of anxious to get finished. Like he was in a hurry."

"How about Joe?"

"Same old Joe, as far as I could see. You know, walking around saying, 'That's good—a little more noise. Make the pain work for you.' " Herm added, "Otto's the one who really wants us to learn to wrestle. Joe was OK, and he knew some good stuff. But he didn't push like Otto." Another thought. "Joe was more interested in the . . . the presentation side of it. You know, the showbiz."

"Otto was in a hurry to finish up that night?"

The question surprised Herm. "Yeah! Didn't even have us finish the cleanup. Just told us to go on home and he'd take care of the rest."

From the corner of his eye, Raiford saw Otto slowly hang up the receiver and stare for a long moment at the blank wall. Then the squat, heavy man turned slowly, like—Raiford thought—the gun turret of a tank. He searched the group watching the two wrestlers grunting against each other. Then he saw Raiford.

"Well, by God!"

He walked slowly toward Raiford, torso swaying with each muscular stride, to stare up into the taller man's face.

"By God, it is you!" A wide grin clenched his cheeks and made him look like a Halloween pumpkin. "You know, I thought I knew you. But you were over there where the light's dim and I wasn't sure. 'Naw,' I said to myself. 'What would old Jim Raiford be doing here with a bunch of meatheads. A smart guy like old Jim Raiford.' " He held out a hand to grip Raiford's fingers and hold them tightly. "That daughter of yours, she told me you guys dropped the case. I'm not paying anymore, you know. So what are you doing here? And wrestling as Major Mayhem!"

"We're still on the case, Otto. Pro bono."

"Yeah? Pro bono? And now you're a pro wrestler? That makes you pro-pro bono, right?" Lidke tightened his grip on Raiford's hand. "Maybe you're better as a pro wrestler than you were as a pro shyster, right?" His voice rose to turn the audience's faces from the ring toward the back of the room. "Hey, gentlemen. Here's half the Death Squad tag team, Major Mayhem." The man's weight pulled Raiford's arm. "He's going to demonstrate some special moves—show us amateurs what real professional wrestling's all about! Let's have a hand for my old buddy Major Mayhem!"

"Thanks, Otto, but I'll be working with Captain Crush later." Raiford tried to slip his fingers out of the man's grip, but the thick fist held even tighter. "Let's get together after the demonstration."

Otto yanked again. "Sure. But first these guys got to see a real pro like you in action." His eyes squeezed almost closed in the clenched flesh of his grinning cheeks. "Let's do it, Jim. Let's give a real professional demonstration."

"No, Otto."

"What do you guys think? The Major don't want to go a

few falls with his buddy Otto. Too good to wrestle with old Otto—afraid he might hurt me."

Good-natured jeers and catcalls.

"OK, people, look up. This is something real professional wrestlers like Major Mayhem here got to watch out for!" He spun low, full weight behind his shoulder and, yanking Raiford's arm toward him, drove his elbow like a spear into the man's unguarded ribs.

An explosion of pain and air driven from his lungs, Raiford doubled over. Before he could cover up, something solid and numbing and red smashed into his face. He tried to punch at the arm still holding his hand as his legs stumbled backward into some chairs. But all he could hear and even taste was the metallic twang of another hard hit ringing in his skull. Something metal—a folding chair?—slammed across his back and skull and half bounded him forward; he tried to shake his eyes and mind clear, but another solid force thudded him again. Somehow he was no longer able to feel the floor beneath his feet, and in his head the roaring of his own blood mixed with another loud, hoarse sound, an insane voice screaming in his ear, a raging scream and arms that tightened around his chest like a vise so he couldn't breathe and just as he recognized Otto's voice, he felt himself in the air and tilting over to plummet headfirst toward the floor. He tried to tuck, tried to roll, the reflex of his training, but he landed on the point of his shoulder and a fiery, tearing wrench cut through the numb chaos to tell him that something had gone badly wrong with part of his body. He tried to pull away from the ripping fire in his shoulder, rolling to find some angle that would lessen the pain. Against the hazy glare of light, a wide black shadow lurched over him and he had a flash of a red face twisted with screaming hatred and then the shadow plummeted toward him and, in a convulsion of impact and shock, of thudding pain and a spray of orange and red flares, Raiford's mind turned off.

23

Julie felt tired but comfortably loose. The hard workout followed by a long soak in the gym's whirlpool relaxed her flesh and soothed her spirit. It wasn't quite as good as sex, but had a lot fewer complications. Reaching her apartment and pouring herself a glass of wine from the bottle chilled in the refrigerator, she checked her telephone for messages—none—and dialed the office answering service. The electronic voice began with the date and time of the first incoming call. It was a man's voice. "Miss Campbell, this is Sid Chertok. I've had a reporter all over my ass about InterMountain EnterPrizes, and he tells me you're the one who sicced him on to me. Now here's a news tip for you: there's only one place you could find out what you found out, and I want you to know I just fired her saucy butt. That make you happy?" The line went dead.

Julie sighed deeply and saved that message. She no longer felt so relaxed. The next item was a woman's voice, "Continental Electronics would like to invite the principals of the Touchstone Agency to a demonstration of their latest surveillance equipment on October 21 at the Merchandise Mart in Denver. If you plan to attend, please RSVP—" Julie pressed the erase button and went to the next message: B. R. Research Associates had information for Miss Campbell. Please call at earliest convenience. Julie saved that and moved to the next. "Julie, it's Gabe Wager. Both bullets came from the same .38. Call me as soon as you get this." The machine's voice chirped, "End of messages."

Bernie Riester once told Julie that she kept her office open around the clock because she sought information from all over the world; if it was midnight in Denver it was noon in Mumbai. Julie punched the speed dial for Bernie Riester's twenty-four-hour line.

"That maiden name you wanted, Miss Campbell—the one in Los Angeles?" Bernie's assistant sounded happy to provide the information. "Joanna Louise Gerwig was married in Los Angeles County to Otto Lidke. Both residents of Long Beach, California."

"Can you send documentation?"

"It was too late in the day when the information came through. I'll fax it to you as soon as we receive it tomorrow."

"Great!"

"We'll include our bill with it."

Not so great, but she lied and said she would be happy to

get it. Then she called Detective Wager's cell-phone number. He seemed to work twenty-four hours a day, too. He asked where she was, said he would call back on a secure landline, and a few seconds later her telephone rang.

"Yeah. The same gun killed Palombino and Huggins. You tell me what made you suspect that. You tell me what names you have. You tell me all the information you have."

"Otto Lidke. I think he killed his other partner, too: Rudy Towers."

"Whoa—who's that? Spell that name."

She did and told Wager about Towers's alleged suicide and gave him the Central City Police case number. "It's the only thing that fits, Gabe." She explained about the FWO contract with American West. "Lidke saw a lot of money coming. I guess you could say he wanted to make a killing."

Wager did not laugh. "Why kill Huggins?"

"Huggins knew that the principal in American West was Lidke's wife. My belief is that after I interviewed him, he figured out that Lidke had gotten rid of his partners so his wife would be sole owner of American West." She went on, "Blackmail—Huggins tried to cut himself in."

"Evidence?"

"His secretary—Huggins hinted to her that he might be a sports manager soon and make a lot of money. According to her, the only sports business he was handling was American West. My guess is Lidke wasn't going to be blackmailed."

"And used the same weapon on Huggins that he used on

Palombino. Frugal bastard." Wager asked for the name of Huggins's secretary.

Julie told him. "Have you found the gun yet?"

"No. But my confidential informant just gave me probable cause for a home-and-office search warrant." He paused. "This means Chertok's clean. Chertok and the Honorable Roger A. Morrow."

"You sound disappointed."

"Yeah," he admitted, "I am. A little relieved and a lot disappointed."

"But something's going on there, Gabe."

"If it ain't homicide, it ain't mine." He paused. "What's going on?"

"Some kind of arrangement between Morrow and Chertok and a casino." She added, "Gargan, the *Post* reporter, is looking at it."

"Gargan!" Wager made the name sound like a wad of spit. "Well, even pond scum can have some use—good luck to him. Any idea where Lidke is now?"

"At a gym, but not his old one. I don't know the address but I can page my dad—he's there with him." She added, "I interviewed Lidke's wife tonight."

"You what?"

"She's the public owner of American West. She's also her husband's bookkeeper. And I knew Lidke wouldn't be home. She acted very, very nervous talking about the business."

"She's going to be nervouser." Finally, he said, "You didn't do too bad—for a civilian. But it's time for you to back off, Julie. You and your old man. Don't do anything a defense attorney might call witness tampering."

"I hear you, Gabe. Good luck." Julie did not bother to mention that the detective now owed Touchstone. They would both remember that when the time came.

She dialed Caitlin Morgan's number, but the ring went unanswered. This late, both the woman and her children should be at home, but the rupture in Caitlin's life must have caused a rupture in her routine. She would try again later. There was no answer from Julie's dad's cell phone, either, nor from his pager. She gave it fifteen minutes and tried both again. No answer. Perhaps he was prancing around the ring in his wrestling tights—a scene she would have to see one of these days. Another quarter hour, no response other than the message center, and an increasing uneasiness. Julie swirled her wine and, draining the glass, punched in another number. Mrs. Lidke would know the name or address of the new gym. But it wasn't the woman who answered. Instead, a gentle male voice said pleasantly, "Hello?"

"Mrs. Lidke, please."

"She's busy right now. Can I say who's calling?"

It hadn't taken Wager long. "Are you with the Denver Police?"

The voice lost its welcoming note. "Who are you and what do you want with Mrs. Lidke?"

Julie identified herself. "Is Detective Wager there, please?"

Finally, a hurried Wager came on. "What?"

"The address of the gym where Lidke is. Do you have it?"

"Why?"

"I can't reach my dad. Not on the cell phone or the pager. It's not like him."

There was a silence. "You didn't hear?"

"Hear what, Gabe?"

"The people I sent to pick up Lidke said the guy had gone completely nuts. Beat your father up with a metal chair and disappeared. Happened too fast for anybody to stop it. He's in the emergency room at Denver Health."

He had been moved to the ICU by the time Julie arrived. His left arm was bound tightly across his chest as if he were trying to scratch his right shoulder. His head was held rigid by a neck brace so that his closed eyes faced the ceiling. The nurse Julie questioned told her that her father had a dislocated shoulder, concussion, and possible neck injury. They were waiting for the radiologist to finish reading the CAT scan and X-rays.

"Can he talk?"

The nurse's dry-looking face said she didn't like the idea. "He's under sedation."

"The person who attacked him is wanted for murder."

"Please keep it brief."

She bent over her father's chest that rose and fell in long, regular breaths. Despite his size, he looked fragile, and for the first time in years, she realized that he was not the man who often seemed like an older brother. He was her father and he would be fifty in another five years, and the face she thought of as ageless was now gray and lined and showed every one of his past years. A tangled surge of feelings clutched in her breast and made her eyes wet. "Dad? Dad! It's Julie—can you hear me?"

A hazy moan answered.

"I'm here, Dad. It's Julie. I'm here."

This time the moan was clearer.

"You're going to be all right, Dad. It's Julie—you're going to be all right."

"Suckered me. . . ." The dry rasp was hard to understand, but that's what it sounded like: "Suckered me."

"Dad, do you know where Lidke went? Where did Lidke go, Dad?"

The bandaged head moved slightly, followed by a grunt of pain. His eyes opened enough to show the lower part of their irises in his effort to speak. "Don't know . . . sucker . . ."

"You'll be fine, Dad. Go back to sleep—I'll be back soon. You're going to be fine." Julie kissed his clammy forehead and prayed that her words were more fact than hope. He settled back into steady, long breaths as the intensive care nurse returned to gesture her away.

"Can you tell me who his physician is?"

"Doctor Davidson. If you will go to the waiting room, I'll tell him you're here."

"Thanks." The waiting room was around a corner of the corridor. Three or four others sat in the padded chairs and watched the silent television or read magazines or slouched wearily with their eyes shut. Julie waited and glanced at the slowly moving clock hands. After many long minutes, she felt the electric buzz of her cell phone. Its dimly lit window illuminated Caitlin Morgan's number. She went into the hallway to answer the call.

"Miss Campbell?"

"Yes, Caitlin. I heard from Mr. Chertok what happened. I'm very sorry."

"Yes."

Pushing aside thoughts of her father, Julie tried to focus on Caitlin's situation. "Don't let it get you down—there are plenty of jobs waiting for a good executive secretary."

"Miss Campbell—" The voice hesitated. "Can you come over?"

Julie hesitated. She was doing no good merely sitting in the hospital waiting room, but it felt right to stay close to her father.

Caitlin's voice, taut and nervous, broke the silence, "I really need to speak with you. I wouldn't ask but it's extremely important."

She knew what her father would say: *Sitting and worrying is a waste of time, Julie. Get busy and do something useful for our client.* Her dad would say that. *The case comes first,* he would say, and no one could tell her how much longer the doctor would be busy. "All right. I'll be there in twenty minutes." She left her cell-phone number at the nurses' station and hurried to the parking lot.

*   *   *

Julie parked in front of the condo. The lights over the recreation area on the other side of the commons showed a few ardent tennis players. They wore shorts but were bundled in sweatshirts against the evening's high-altitude chill. The thock of their rackets sounded faintly as Julie knocked and waited. Caitlin opened the door a few cautious inches to see who it was.

Julie studied the woman's wide eyes and pale, almost bloodless face. "What did Chertok say to you, Caitlin?"

Silently, she stepped back to let Julie in.

"Chertok belongs under a rock, but he's not as dangerous as he thinks he is." Julie started to add something when a wide shape stepped from the dining area and she understood the woman's terror. The revolver dwarfed in Lidke's fist looked tiny, almost toylike. But it wasn't a toy. Julie recognized it as a Colt Agent, an efficient .38 with a two-inch barrel. And she would bet it had been used before.

"Shut the door, Miss Julie. Both of you, sit over there."

Unconsciously, she pressed Caitlin behind her for shelter. "What do you want here, Mr. Lidke? There's nothing here for you."

"Move!" The pistol jerked, and the man waited until they slowly seated themselves on the sofa. "You're here, that's one thing. The cunt who just couldn't let well enough alone. Just couldn't quit poking your fucking nose into things, could you?"

"All right—you have me. You don't need Ms. Morgan anymore. Let her go."

The man's grin squeezed his eyes into narrow slits. "I need her. I got plans for her, Miss Julie. But you know who I don't need? You're the one I don't need." The grin went away. "Goddamn I don't need you! A sweet deal: for once I could've had it all. One fucking time in my life, I could've made it! And this time it's not Raiford who fucks me out of it but his goddamn daughter!" The hiccough of a giggle, oddly thin and high for such heavy flesh. "I should have known, right? I should've known a Raiford would screw things up again, right?"

"You hired us as cover for you, is that it?"

"Smarter than your old man, but you still screwed things up." The rage came back into his voice. "And now I got nothing—nothing!"

"What do you mean you have plans for Ms. Morgan, Otto?"

He blinked, coming back from his vision of lost opportunity. "Cops got my wife, right?"

"I don't know."

The pistol jerked up. "You know! Goddamn you, you know—you went over there—talked to her. You sent them after her—you know!"

"All right, I know. I know they were going to search your home. I don't know if they arrested her."

Outside, a few blocks away, a siren wailed and they listened intently. It came closer, punctuated by a flat honking as an emergency vehicle warned an intersection. Keeping the pistol pointed at Julie, Otto went to the window. His large body moved swiftly, its muscle-heavy awkwardness gone. He peered out through the curtains.

Caitlin, pale and tense, held herself tightly calm. "I'm sorry I called you—he said he would shoot . . ."

Julie waved away the obvious. "Where are the girls?" she whispered.

The woman's shoulders relaxed a fraction as she whispered back, "With the sitter, thank God. When I came home, I was so upset. . . . I asked Beth to take them out. . . ." The tension returned in full. "They'll be home soon. . . . Bedtime. . . ."

"Shut up!" Otto listened to the urgent, pulsing wail die away in the distance, then he stepped away from the window curtain. "They got Joanna. And they're going to offer her a deal to testify against me, you can bet on that." The pistol wagged back and forth slightly as if Lidke were trying to make up his mind.

"They can't make her testify against you."

"Goddamn it, I didn't say they'd make her. I said they'd offer her a deal!"

"Why do you want Ms. Morgan, Otto?"

"Trade. Her for Joanna. And a trip out of here."

"They won't go for it, Otto. Best if you give yourself up. Best for you and for Joanna, both."

"Bullshit! Don't try to tell me what to do, goddamn you!" After a rigid moment, the broad face relaxed. "I followed you over here a couple of times."

"You tried to shoot me. In the alley, you shot at me."

"I don't know how I missed. But you bet your ass I won't miss again."

There wasn't much else left Julie had to bet with. "Let her go, Otto. I'm as good a hostage as she is."

"No. You ain't. Cops'll worry more about a woman with kids. Besides, if I need to show them I'm not bullshitting, I'll send you out first. Feet first. And love it!"

"I know the cop in charge of the investigation. He'll listen to me. I can get through to tell him what you want. I can convince him you're serious." Julie saw the man's slight frown. "Think about it, Otto. What are you going to do, call up the nearest police station? Call up the DPD administration building this time of night? Ask to speak to the chief? He's gone home by now. Are we even in the city and county of Denver? You're going to waste a lot of time, Otto. Think: when you finally do get through to somebody who knows what you're talking about, they'll have a signed confession out of Joanna. You know she can't take pressure, Otto—she couldn't take pressure from you, she can't take it from them. You know that. Think!"

"Shut up!"

"Think, Otto. Her confession signed, witnessed, notarized—then it won't make any difference whether she's in custody or not. You know she can't stand up to—"

"Shut up, damn you!" Lidke took an angry step toward the sofa. Beside her, Julie felt Caitlin press back against the cushions. "Just keep quiet!" With his free hand, Lidke tugged at his lower lip, eyes on Julie's face but not seeing her. "What's the cop's name—the one you claim to know?"

"Let Ms. Morgan go."

"I'll blow her fucking head off if you don't tell me. I mean it!"

"Wager. Detective Wager."

The pistol sank back. "All right. Here's what we do. You call him. Tell him I got you and her. Tell him I want my wife and anything she's signed and I want them now. Then say you'll call back and hang up. Do it fast—I don't want no traces on the line. You got that? You don't talk no more than one minute, you got that?"

The home had two telephones that Julie could see. One, behind Lidke, was on the kitchen wall near the stove; the other was on an end table near the tiny brick fireplace. Julie went to that one. Lidke watched while she dialed, the stubby pistol barrel moving with the man's gaze. Caitlin, still seated on the couch, clasped her hands over her arms as if she were icy cold.

The duty clerk answered and Julie asked for Detective Wager.

"He's unavailable right now. Can I take a message?"

"This is Julie Campbell. It is an emergency. Tell him Otto Lidke has me and—"

Lidke said, "Hang up now!"

She did. "Otto, it takes as least five minutes to trace a call. You have to give me time to get the message to Wager." Julie didn't know how long it took for a trace, but she hoped the duty clerk's telephone had a caller ID.

"We'll wait five minutes and call back. Sit down."

Julie and Caitlin sat in silence. Otto, standing, kept glancing at his watch.

"All right."

She dialed Wager's number again. This time he answered and spoke quickly before Julie could. "Julie, if that's you, don't say anything. If you're in trouble, pretend the phone's still ringing."

Julie looked at Lidke. "It's still ringing."

Wager spoke rapidly. "Is Lidke armed?"

"Yes," she said. "We're waiting for Detective Wager."

" 'We'? Is that more than you and Lidke?"

"That's right. Detective Wager, please."

Otto shifted restlessly and looked at his watch.

"Can you say where you are?"

"No. I have to talk with him personally. Yes, it is an emergency. No, I can't give you my number." She shrugged at Lidke as if to say *what can you do with dumb bureaucrats?*

"Hang up," said Lidke.

Julie did. "He still wasn't in. But they expect him right away."

"Another five minutes."

They waited. Julie didn't sit this time. Instead, she drummed her fingers on the telephone and stepped nervously back and forth.

"What's the matter, bladder troubles?"

"You should just give yourself up, Otto."

"Shut up."

Finally, "Try again."

Julie, anxiously moving back and forth, dialed one more time. Each step took her nearer the fireplace with its rack of fire tools. When Wager answered this time, she played it straight. Lidke listened intently as she slowly gave him the message.

"Jesus H. Christ! Let me talk to the guy!"

"Lidke wants to talk with you." She held the phone away from her ear.

The round man took a step closer, staring at the receiver.

Julie wagged it at him. "How much time do we have?"

Lidke glanced at his wristwatch and, as he did, Julie threw the receiver at the man. He reflexively reached for it, the pistol muzzle lifting momentarily toward the ceiling. Julie whirled to grab the poker and swing hard at the man's thick wrist.

"Caitlin—run! Now! Run!"

From the corner of her eye, Julie saw Caitlin dash for the front door, fumbling with the dead bolt as the poker glanced off Lidke's knuckles and Julie swiveled it to jab viciously at Otto's face. The man lifted both hands to guard his eyes, and Julie swung again, snapping her wrists to make the iron bar whistle. It thudded hard on Lidke's forearm. The man's wide hand slacked with shock and numbness and the pistol dangled as he grunted with pain and lunged for her. Julie did not have time for another full swing, just a quick parry, a nudge, a desperate jab with the poker at the loosely held weapon to send it flying over the skewed couch and clatter against the wall. Lidke grabbed the poker with his left hand and ripped it out of Julie's grasp and, roaring now, lowered his head and lunged like a bull to crush her. She slapped a palm under Lidke's elbow and canted the charging man aside just enough to slip past, but Otto's large arm grappled back at Julie's waist and he turned quickly, expertly, to try and tangle her throat in a hammerlock.

She caught the point of Lidke's elbow in the crook of her arm and dropped to one knee, using his momentum and her back as a fulcrum to throw the heavy man. Otto, ominously silent, whipped through the air to crash on the rug and jar the entire house. Julie heard glass break somewhere, but Otto bounced up almost before she could stand and he charged again.

He was a wrestler. Now he wasn't opening himself up to counterpunches by swinging wildly or using his fists. Instead, he used his fingers and hands to grab for a controlling hold, to find a joint to bend backward until it broke. Julie rolled out of one of the man's grips by ripping the arm off her jacket, but it only gave her a second or two. Lidke, pale eyes stretched and blind with rage, lowered his forehead and came at her once more.

Julie dropped to scissor Otto's legs with her own, the wide body crashing on one of the chairs and splintering it. But the man was quick; Julie could not tangle the short, thick legs that pulled away, and Lidke was up again, a little more careful this time, a little more calculating.

"You know a little something about wrestling, don't you, Miss Julie. You could go on the dyke circuit."

Julie did not bother to reply. She sucked air and kept her eyes on Lidke's legs. They would tell her what he would do next.

"I love this." A grin stretched his lips wide. "This is what makes my dick hard: a genuine death match!" He feinted another high charge and then dropped low to go for Julie's legs. It was the classic move of a shorter man and Julie saw it coming. She braced off Lidke's heavy shoulders and kicked her legs back out of his reach. Knocking away the flailing arms that tried to tangle her own, Julie slid over the man's shoulders and snaked an arm around his thick neck to squeeze it in the bend of her elbow. The short man flailed, lifting Julie off the floor, then tried to run backward to smash her into the wall as Julie squeezed tighter and, somewhere in the back of her jolting mind, she wondered if the move had been a mistake: Lidke didn't seem to have a neck.

Julie dug her fingers deeper into the back of her own neck, feeling a slickness that could have been sweat or blood, but it made no difference. Either way, it threatened to break her grip, to slide her fingers off her flesh and let the jolting, heavy man wriggle away. She clenched her teeth and buried her head closer into Lidke's thick shoulder and squeezed even tighter. Fending off the stabbing fingers that frantically dug for an eye or ear or mouth, she hauled back to keep her arm across the man's windpipe and to press shut the arteries that fed his brain. Lidke's breath was shorter and louder now, a steady series of brief grunts that matched the convulsive heaves of his body and the flailing of his hands. She heard her blouse rip somewhere but felt only slightly the burning scrape of the carpet on her flesh. She squeezed tighter, the effort beginning to cramp her bicep as she wondered how much longer either of them could hold out. Clinging even closer to the shelter of the man's shuddering and hot back, Julie finally forced her mind to stop thinking about the stabbing pain of her elbow, the aching knot in her bicep, the numbness of her fingers and straining neck. She had to hold on. That was all there was to it: she had to hold on.

After a while, Lidke stopped heaving. Julie felt the body lose its rigidity and sag more heavily. But she did not ease up. Instead, as Lidke's neck and shoulder muscles began to soften, Julie worked her arm even tighter, sweating and quivering from the effort to keep the clamp against Lidke's windpipe. Her arm wanted to quit. Now it was an effort of will more than of flesh to keep the grip. She closed her eyes and tried to push her mind somewhere else, somewhere that did not hurt. Finally, in the growing silence, she became aware of the tiny voice coming from the telephone and she concentrated on it to keep from thinking about her melting arm: "Julie—anybody—hang on. We're on our way. . . ."

She did not know how long it was. Eventually, she slowly lifted numb fingers from her nape. Alert to any move he might make, she gingerly unpeeled her arm from the sticky flesh of Lidke's neck. But he remained limp. Her own neck was stiff and hot and could find no position that did not ache. Facedown, Lidke lay like a beached whale, mouth agape and face a mix of purple and pallid flesh. Julie, gasping on hands and knees with her head hanging, stared.

"Julie?"

She winced as her neck lifted her head.

Caitlin, crouched behind the overturned couch, held the .38 leveled at the prone man. "Are you all right?"

"I thought—" Her voice was squeaky from strain and dryness. She wearily cleared her throat the tried again. "I thought I told you . . . to run."

"I couldn't. He made me call you here. I couldn't just leave you. Are you all right?"

"Yeah. Fine. You?"

"Yes." The pistol sagged and she leaned against the couch and closed her eyes for a long moment. Then Caitlin picked up the receiver and began talking into it.

24

Julie was embarrassed to have Detective Wager find her wrapped in a blanket and not much else. You don't hear about detectives having their blouses ripped off while rescuing people, and Caitlin, giggling with near hysteria, had nothing large enough to fit Julie. No one giggled when the bills came in for repairing Caitlin's living room and replacing the broken furniture and television. The Denver Police said they had not destroyed the property—Lidke was peacefully unconscious when they arrested him, so they bore no responsibility. Caitlin's insurance company argued that they were not responsible either. They said Miss Campbell should have waited for the police to arrive and make the arrest, so it was reasonably avoidable damage. Which, her father said, could be the definition of life, too. So Touchstone did the right thing and covered the damage. Caitlin said she would repay them a little at a time, but neither Julie nor her father accepted that.

Mrs. Lidke got an even better deal. She turned state's evidence against her husband in exchange for custody of the children and the prosecution dropping any and all charges for abetting two homicides. Moreover, Salazar, saying it was out of sympathy for Lidke's unfortunate wife, hurried to buy American West from her. He got it at a steep discount.

When Julie and Raiford were both out of the hospital and limping around the office shuffling papers and answering telephones, Wager called to see how they were doing. He was happy to draw Julie's attention to an item in that morning's paper. "You see the *Post*? Gargan's big story?" It raised the question of collusion between Sidney Chertok, a local businessman who had a hidden interest in a new Central City casino despite vague ties with organized crime, and Senator Roger A. Morrow who was the chair of the state's Senate Transportation Committee. The alleged collusion involved the alleged illegal use of state funds to build the new parkway that linked Central City with I-70 and bypassed the rival town of Black Hawk. The problem was that parkway was supposed to be paid for entirely by private funds from Central City casinos and boosters. Moreover, the Honorable Mr. Morrow turned out to be another silent partner in Mr. Chertok's new casino. "The people in Black Hawk are pretty stirred up about it. They're talking a grand jury investigation."

Wager sounded almost as happy to learn that the X-rays had shown no spinal injury for Raiford, and that both he and

Julie were well on the way to recuperation. "And something else, Julie: I got a letter of commendation for our work on the two homicides. It's nice when things work out for a change."

Julie allowed that was the case.

Colonel Crush called to say he was sorry he and Raiford wouldn't be a tag team anymore, but he wished his ex-partner good luck and offered to bring over some home-cooked lasagna.

Salazar called to say he would be happy if Raiford had both a concussion and a broken spine, since he'd wasted a hell of a lot of his, Raoul Salazar's, very important time and money. And by the grill of Saint Lawrence, he, Raoul Salazar, would burn in hell before he gave another chance to a guy who was too damn chicken to get back into the ring just because he got a little bit hurt.

As Raiford hung up on that call, he said to Julie, "When American West gets our bill, Salazar will squawk even louder."

"Bill for what? Lidke's in jail!"

"We weren't hired by Lidke, remember? You wrote the contract with Rocky Ringside Wrestling. It was bought by American West for one dollar. Otto's wife sold it to Salazar who now owns its assets and its liabilities." He grinned. "And one of the liabilities is a bill for our services, including Ms. Morgan's new furniture."

A day or so later, Uncle Angus dropped by the office to thank Julie for her suggestion about hiring an office manager. Caitlin was, Julie's uncle said, honest, capable, efficient, and bright. As well as, he added with a glance at Raiford, a very attractive divorcée with two great kids.

EBOOKS BY REX BURNS

FROM MYSTERIOUSPRESS.COM
AND OPEN ROAD MEDIA

Available wherever ebooks are sold

MYSTERIOUSPRESS.COM

MYSTERIOUSPRESS.COM

Otto Penzler, owner of the Mysterious Bookshop in Manhattan, founded the Mysterious Press in 1975. Penzler quickly became known for his outstanding selection of mystery, crime, and suspense books, both from his imprint and in his store. The imprint was devoted to printing the best books in these genres, using fine paper and top dust-jacket artists, as well as offering many limited, signed editions.

Now the Mysterious Press has gone digital, publishing ebooks through **MysteriousPress.com**.

MysteriousPress.com offers readers essential noir and suspense fiction, hard-boiled crime novels, and the latest thrillers from both debut authors and mystery masters. Discover classics and new voices, all from one legendary source.